1915 Fokker Scourge

Book 2 in the

British Ace Series

By

Griff Hosker

Published by Sword Books Ltd 2014

Copyright © Griff Hosker First Edition

A CIP catalogue record for this title is available from the British Library.

Dedication

The Hero

'Jack fell as he'd have wished,' the Mother said,
And folded up the letter that she'd read.
'The Colonel writes so nicely.' Something broke
In the tired voice that quavered to a choke.
She half looked up. 'We mothers are so proud
Of our dead soldiers.' Then her face was bowed.

Quietly the Brother Officer went out.
He'd told the poor old dear some gallant lies
That she would nourish all her days, no doubt.
For while he coughed and mumbled, her weak eyes
Had shone with gentle triumph, brimmed with joy,
Because he'd been so brave, her glorious boy.

He thought how 'Jack', cold-footed, useless swine,
Had panicked down the trench that night the mine
Went up at Wicked Corner; how he'd tried
To get sent home, and how, at last, he died,
Blown to small bits. And no one seemed to care
Except that lonely woman with white hair.

Siegfried Sassoon

Chapter 1

May 1915 England

The chugging, steaming, steel leviathan which took me south seemed appropriate somehow. It was like a metaphor for the war. We were a metal machine and we were cutting a swathe through the green and pleasant land which was England. The steel rails cut an ugly scar through the land and reminded me of the ugly scars we had left in France and Belgium. The difference was that there they had a green and pleasant land no longer. They had a muddy morass criss-crossed by barbed wire and littered with unburied bodies. The war had destroyed the land. And soon I would be returning to the war that could not be won. At least I did not think that it could be won. We were still in the same parts of Belgium and France that we had been ten months ago when I had been a young cavalryman eager to go to war. I had become more of a realist in those ten months.

I had grown up in the country on the estate of Lord Burscough. My mother and father still worked and lived on the state as did my younger brother and one of my sisters. Machines were few and far between especially in the stables where I had worked. How ironic that I now flew one of the new-fangled aeroplanes over the fields of France. I had grown up with my feet on the ground but now my head was in the air.

My war had started in the cavalry but the slaughter of men and horses had persuaded me that I could not bear to see such fine animals killed for no good reason and so I had joined the Royal Flying Corps. For some reason, I found that not only was it easy, I was quite good at it. I had started life as a gunner in an F.E.2 and soon become a pilot. I was now Flight Lieutenant Bill Harsker with a handful of downed German aeroplanes to my name.

I thought back to the leave I had just enjoyed. We had been sent home from France following the Second battle of Ypres when some of the flying crews had suffered from the effect of the German gas. I had been pleased to come home to the bosom of my family. That they were delighted to see me was never in question but this time, as opposed to my first leave before Christmas 1914, was different. It was not my family who had changed but everyone else.

Most families knew someone who had died or had been wounded and the euphoria of September 1914 when we were going to show the Hun who was boss had evaporated leaving an empty and hollow atmosphere all around. When I went to the pub with my dad I still received the smiles and the banter but they were less sincere. It was as though I was to blame for somehow being whole. Even Dad noticed it and he was less than happy. I told him to let it go. The last thing I wanted, while I was at the front, was for Dad and his friends to be at loggerheads. The war would last too long for that.

I had flown over the battlefields and I knew that this war would not be over soon. The poor infantry were fighting over a few hundred yards of mud and wire. It was a brutal and ugly war. New weapons like the machine gun meant that casualties were no longer in the tens or twenties, not even the hundreds as they had in the Crimean War but in their thousands. I knew that I was lucky to be a pilot. If anything happened to me it would be final; a crashing aeroplane left no survivors. That was preferable to the living death I had seen on the boat and the train coming home from France. The men with no legs, half a face or some hidden wound which wracked them with pain, was the norm in this new, modern war. And then there were the ones whose blank dead faces told of demons and horrors hidden behind the mask they had adopted. They were the ones who terrified me the most.

I thought back to those days when I had had to tell my comrades' widowed mother that both her sons had been killed. I saw the devastation on her face when she anticipated the terrifying and lonely prospect of a life without husband, sons, and grandchildren. It was the very definition of infinity. It would seem to last forever no matter how short the actual duration. It had made me tell my family that I cared for them. It was not a family trait but I did not want to go to meet my maker without telling all of my family how important they were to me.

I shook myself out of my morbid and depressing thoughts. I took out and read, again, the orders which had come a week ago. Rather than returning to France I had been summoned to an airfield in Kent where my squadron was now based. They had been withdrawn, temporarily, from the front. I was relieved that I would not be in France for a while. Although I did not enjoy the war I did enjoy the camaraderie of the squadron. My two best friends, Ted and Gordy, had helped me settle into the squadron and shown me how to become a pilot. We had all saved each other, before now, when things went awry. My gunner and mechanic, Sergeant Sharp, was also more of a friend than a subordinate. We were a team in the sky. Air combat did that for you. Up in the sky you had to rely upon others as well as yourself. They became almost part of you. You had to think as one person. Charlie Sharp was my gunner and he sat less than four feet in front of me. We flew at the enemy with fabric and wood protecting us. If we did not think and act as one then the likelihood would be that we would die.

I knew that I was lucky in my commanding officer and my superiors. I had seen poor officers before; especially when I had been in the cavalry. My first troop commander had been a disaster and men had died because of his incompetence. He had been protected because he came from the officer class and the public school system. They were not all like that but the ones that were made me nervous. They were more of a liability than the enemy. Colonel Pemberton Smythe and Major Brack might be from the upper classes but they were down to earth officers. They understood flying and they understood war. Life with anything less would have been intolerable.

When we had stopped in Crewe Station a well-dressed man in his thirties entered the carriage clutching a newspaper. His well-fed features and his clothes told me that this was someone who neither used his hands nor went to war. He spied my uniform and proceeded to tell me how to defeat the damned Boche. He spat the word out as though he had had personal dealings with them. It was newspaper talk. He just saw the brown and did not recognise the branch of my service. To him I was just another soldier. I nodded seriously at all his suggestions. I had learned that arguing just upset the civilians. It was the same with the men in the pub in the village. They would never understand the realities of modern war. Their views came from the rags and tabloids. It came from journalists writing reports from Fleet Street and War office briefings. I could see that all had potential as writers of novels. They had the ability to take the truth and twist it into a completely new shape.

"The trouble is we need our soldiers to be more resolute. I know that, when we attack, we lose men but we keep retreating and losing more. If our chaps just persevered a little longer then the Boche would break." He was being very serious and I suppressed a smile at the use of the word 'we'.

He had no idea of what it was like to face machine guns; lines and lines of deadly machine guns. Guns which were set to a precise height and would mow men down much as a farmer would harvest wheat. In comparison, we had it easy in the air. We had, normally, one machine gun being fired at us from an unstable aeroplane which was moving quickly through the air. We also had a little protection from our own guns and an engine. An infantry man had nowhere to hide. The Germans knew where they would be going and the machine gun had been ranged to rake and harvest a precise piece of land. The poor Tommy had to trudge through that blood-soaked piece of earth to get at the machine gun. And before he could do that he had to clamber over barbed wire and finally fight, hand to hand to evict the German soldiers. It was a brutal and soul-destroying way to fight.

The man held up the paper waving it before me, almost in triumph. "Look at this. The damned Germans have started attacking civilians. They have sunk the Lusitania! They are not human! They are savages! They are not content with killing nurses and bayoneting babies in Belgium, now they attack unarmed passenger ships carrying civilians. That is why you chaps have to finish this sooner rather than later!"

It was on the tip of my tongue to ask him what he did and why he was not in uniform but it was better not to ask. The answer would only upset me. I allowed myself to believe that he was doing something useful; perhaps he was a doctor.

"Yes sir, we will try."

He smiled as though his words had converted another soldier from a quaking coward to a fearless warrior. He shook his paper resolutely as though it was his defence against the Germans. "Good! Jolly good! The British Tommy will show these Hun that they are braver men and that God is on our side!"

I closed my eyes and pretended to sleep. I did not think that God was on anyone's side. I had seen little evidence of the hand of God on the battlefield. As I sat in the peaceful dark of my mind I wondered why the squadron had been moved to England. I knew that we had suffered casualties during the last attack but I also knew that our squadron had been one of the more successful ones. Then I remembered when Major Burscough had been promoted. He had had to return to England to begin training men in the new Bristol fighter. Perhaps that was our fate. I involuntarily frowned. The Bristol was a single seater scout. I was not certain I would like to go to war in such an aeroplane. I was used to having Charlie Sharp as my gunner. The Gunbus was a steady, stable platform. It had its limitations; there was a nasty blind spot just below the rear of the aeroplane. The Germans could exploit that. Otherwise the aircraft was as good an aeroplane as we had. I was a conservative pilot. Change was not always good.

I was disappointed that Gordy had not joined my train at Crewe. I suppose that there were so many trains heading to London that the odds on us being on the same one was remote. Gordy and Ted had been the flight sergeants who had helped me through those first weeks when I had joined the Corps. Gordy and I had become pilots and lieutenants. Ted could have done so but he appeared happy to remain a gunner for the moment. Perhaps having young officers in charge of his aeroplane would change his opinion.

When I changed trains at London, I had to make my way from Euston to Victoria. I could have taken the underground which the locals seemed to enjoy but the thought of disappearing down a rabbit hole did not appeal to a country boy like me and I stepped out to walk across London. After the long train journey, it was good to stretch my legs.

The first thing I noticed was the huge crowds which filled the streets. They were like a river of humanity. Liverpool and Manchester were like villages compared with this metropolis. The second thing I spotted was the huge number of uniforms. It was not only men sporting uniforms from the army and the navy but there seemed to be many women too. Perhaps this was the future. Mother would have been shocked. In her world, you worked until you married and then it was your duty to bring up children. She would never understand women being involved in the war. I had also read of women in the large cities being used to make munitions. Mum would be shocked at the very idea.

When I reached Victoria, I was delighted to see Gordy smoking a cigarette and reading a newspaper as he waited for our train. His smile told me that he was pleased to see me too.

"Bill! Good leave?"

"Any leave at home is a good leave. And you? I thought I might have seen you on the train down."

He looked sheepish. "Ah, well I came down a couple of days ago like. Stayed in the smoke."

"You paid for a hotel in London? Have you come into money or something?"

"Well no, not exactly and I stayed with a friend."

This was becoming more intriguing by the minute. "A friend?"

He took my arm and led me away from the others waiting for our train. "Listen, you nosey bugger, it was a woman, right. I stayed with a woman."

"I didn't know you knew any women."

He burst out laughing, "Of course I know women."

"No, what I mean is, women friends with houses."

"Ah. Well she is a friend of my sister, Margaret. Her husband bought it in the first battle of Ypres and she is a widow. She was staying with our kid to help her get over her loss and I met her and…well she is a nice lady."

I smiled. "You don't have to convince me Gordy. If you like her then she must be nice."

He grinned and we returned to our seats. "Aye she is. Mary is her name. Her husband was an officer and he had a little bit of money. She has a little house in Tottenham. Not big but neat and tidy. She is going to have to get a job now to make ends meet."

"You sound as though you are sweet on her."

He looked shocked. "You don't stay in a widow woman's house if you are not serious."

"Are you going to marry her then?" It seemed a little hasty to me but I could not say that to my friend who was obviously smitten.

"Not while there is a war on. I mean I could go as quickly as her husband and it wouldn't do to make her a widow twice over. We have an understanding and I'll be sending her a little of my pay. Just until she gets on her feet you understand. Nothing improper."

I smiled. We were all that way. The upper classes might have their mistresses and affairs but our class knew how to behave. At least that is what my dad would have said.

Our train was announced and we joined the scrum to get seats. Our officer's uniforms and second-class travel warrants helped to secure us two seats by the window. As the train pulled out I ventured, "You have fallen remarkably quickly Gordy." I held up my hand as I saw his reaction. "I am just saying."

He smiled, as he lit another cigarette. "I know but as soon as I met her I knew. She is lovely and she is such a kind person. When I found that she was a widow and lonely I took her dancing down the Empire in Piccadilly. I did it to be polite at first but we chatted like we had known each other forever. I took her out every night for a week and we had walks in the park during the day. So, you see we packed a lot into a week. There is a war on and I didn't know when I would get to see her again."

I knew what he meant. The normal routine of courtship involved walks once a week then walks holding hands; meeting the family then, possibly, an evening assignation. Gordy and his Mary had packed almost two months courting into a week. I understood now. And I understood his reticence about commitment. My two elder brothers had died in the same battle as Mary's husband. They had left fiancées behind. At the same time, I was aware that I wanted children too. They were a legacy you left behind when you had gone. For the rest of the journey I speculated about my future. When would I meet a woman; let alone a woman I wanted to marry?

When we got off the train we asked directions for the airfield and found that it was only four miles away. It was gone six o'clock but the nights were becoming longer and we decided to walk. We set off at a good pace and hoped to cover the distance in less than an hour. As luck would have it we only had a mile to walk. A lorry came behind us and honked his horn. We turned and saw Quartermaster Doyle and one of his flight sergeants. He grinned. "Hop aboard, sirs. We might get you back in time for a bit of supper!"

We jammed ourselves in the back of the lorry and peered through the little curtain.

"Well Quartermaster. Why are we back in Blighty?"

He laughed, "I might have known they wouldn't tell you. Typical. Refitting, sirs. We have new F.E. 2 aeroplanes, sir. They look the same but they have a Rolls Royce Eagle engine. They are a nice little motor according to Senior Sergeant Lowery."

I was relieved and disappointed at the same time. I had thought we might have been given a new type of aircraft. Still a better engine might improve our chances of survival but that still left the blind spot behind the engine.

"Any other changes?"

He tapped his nose but his face had lost its humour, "You'll have to wait and see won't you, sir? Anyway, here we are."

The aerodrome was a field. There were tents as accommodation and I saw five huge marquees that were obviously the mess tents and the headquarters. This would only be temporary. As we pulled through the barrier I could see the sea some five miles away. That explained the position of the airfield. We could be at the battlefields in just over an hour.

We jumped from the lorry. Quartermaster Doyle waved his hand towards a group of twelve tents isolated from the rest. "Those are the officers' quarters. There are a few empty ones. Just grab one." He swept his arm around to a large marquee. "And that is the officer's mess. I'd dump your bags and see if there is still food on the go."

We looked in four tents before we found two empty ones. As neither of us had eaten since the morning we were ready for food, of any description. When we entered the mess tent there was a roar from the six officers there. To our amazement Ted was seated with them, resplendent in the uniform of a Second Lieutenant. He grinned as we walked up to him. "I only did it so as I wouldn't have to salute you two!

We both slapped him heartily on the back. The three of us were back together. It had felt odd to be separated at meal time and to have him 'sirring' us the whole time.

He nodded to the cooks who were clearing away, "Grab some food and I'll fill you in."

The cooks moaned in a good-natured way and then filled our plates up with bully beef stew. We grabbed some bread and a mug of tea. It was plain fare but it would fill us. Of that I had no doubt.

While we ate Ted talked. The younger officers, having finished, all left. "Yeah the Colonel asked me to try out as a pilot. I passed and he made me an officer straight away. He told me he needed pilots like us who had experience and were reliable." He looked around to see that we were not being observed or overheard, "The bad news is that we have a new senior officer." We both paused, mid mouthful, "Major Brack has been given his own squadron. He took a couple of the pilots with him." He must have seen the look of surprise on our faces as he added hurriedly, "Your flights have been left un-touched. Now the new Major is a Major St. John Hamilton-Grant." He made a face. "You will not like him. He is a toff but not like Major Burscough. His Lordship didn't talk down to you; this one speaks to you as though he has stepped into something unpleasant."

"Where has he come from?"

"According to the griff he was in command of a training squadron in England."

"He has no combat experience then?"

Ted stubbed his cigarette out and shook his head, "Not as far as we can find out. He likes to do things by the book. He thinks we should set an example for the sergeants. We have to wear a tie at all times."

I looked at Gordy who shook his head, "But this is stupid. When we are flying we are all wrapped up anyway."

"That's another thing he has changed, he wants regulation greatcoats to be worn when flying."

"But they are bloody useless in the wet."

"Ah he reckons we shouldn't have to fly when it is wet so there won't be a problem." He stood and stretched, "And lastly our new major doesn't like the idea of flight sergeants being promoted. He thinks every pilot should go through a flying school. I am glad you two are back because it means all the shitty jobs will now be shared out." He grinned. "It won't just be Joe Muggins here!"

"What does the colonel think about all this?"

"That's the problem, Gordy, the colonel's son was wounded and gassed at Ypres. The Colonel spends more time away from the squadron than with it. His son is critically ill and the Colonel is by his bedside.

You can't really blame him. If it was my son I would want to do the same."

"Blimey, a hell of a lot can happen in three weeks!"

"Tell me about it. Come on I'll help you get sorted. Reveille is at five thirty."

"Five thirty!"

"I told you, regulations and by the book."

Much later that night, as I lay down to sleep I reflected that it couldn't make all that much of a difference. Regulations were regulations and once we were in the air then it would be the same as it always was. This wasn't like the cavalry with its spit and polish and horse furniture to be burnished. We just flew our aeroplanes. It would soon go back to the way it was. I was wrong.

Chapter 2

We were told to be on parade and we waited in line. I was surprised when I saw him. The new major was a precise little man. He had a precisely trimmed moustache and his hair always looked as though it had just been trimmed. He had razor sharp creases in his uniform and starched shirts. As soon as he walked along the parade I felt dirty and I had my cleanest and best uniform on! He did not find anything to criticise us for but I knew that Ted was correct. The looks he gave to the three of us were looks of contempt.

He addressed us all in his shrill, piping voice. "The colonel is still indisposed and I will remain in charge for the foreseeable future. We are still awaiting three new pilots and so the order of business until they arrive is for you all to familiarise yourselves with the new aircraft. The new FE 2 has a more powerful Rolls Royce Eagle engine. Those pilots who have flown the earlier version will find a difference. Until we are issued with a more up to date fighter we will have to get by with these out dated Gunbuses. You will all spend at least two hours a day flying. I expect a written report each day on the route you took and any problems you encountered with the aircraft. We need to be as efficient as we can be before we return to France. That is all gentlemen. You are dismissed."

We saluted and turned to go, "Er Lieutenant Hewitt and Lieutenant Harsker stay behind for a moment, would you?" We turned. "Do sit down." As we sat down I realised the reason was because otherwise we would have towered over him. He closed his eyes and put his finger tips together. I suddenly worried that he was a Holy Joe and he was going to pray. However, he opened his eyes and then stood.

"Gentlemen, I am a plain-speaking man and I will come directly to the point. I do not like self-taught pilots promoted from the ranks. It is unnatural and sloppy. I prefer those officers who have been trained to fly and fight properly." We remained silent. There appeared little point, at least to me, in saying anything until he had finished.

"In addition, I think that the idea of three aircraft flying as a unit is counterproductive and a waste of resources. When we are fully equipped we will have twelve aircraft. I intend to use them to cover as wide an area as possible."

Gordy could not keep his mouth shut. "But, sir, the Colonel likes the idea of flights of three aircraft."

He smiled a mirthless smile. "The colonel is not here and so I will run the squadron as I see fit until he does return." He then glared at both of us, almost daring us to question him again. Then he smiled, "Ah, I see now; you two were paid extra as leaders. Yes, of course, being sergeants and from that class money is more important than rank." He shrugged, "I have no objection to you being paid more. The colonel, for whatever reason, saw fit to promote you to First Lieutenant. Officers of your class obviously need the higher pay more than the other officers."

I felt Gordy begin to rise and I clamped my hand around his wrist. I smiled, "Sir, may I ask a question?"

"Of course, it is Lieutenant Harsker I believe."

"Yes sir."

"You are the lucky pilot who has four enemy kills to his name."

I chose to ignore the fact that he had the numbers wrong and the fact that he said 'lucky'; it did not matter to me. "Well that is the point I was going to make sir. How many of the squadron have combat experience? I understand that Major Brack took many of the experienced pilots with him. So apart from us two and Lieutenant Thomas, how many of the squadron have experience combat against the Germans?"

He coloured and I wondered if I had gone too far even though I had kept my voice as reasonable as I could. "There are four of you for I believe that Lieutenant Campbell has also flown in combat. What is your point?"

"The reason the colonel introduced his system was to protect new pilots by placing them under the wing, so to speak of a more experienced pilot. We cut down the losses as a result."

"Do not worry about that Lieutenant. The new pilots are much better trained." He smiled, "After all I trained them. In addition, I will be drawing up standing orders which will make the possibility of losses almost impossible."

He sat down again, "Anyway I just wanted you to know where you stood. Of course, any advice you can give the new pilots about shooing down the Germans would be appreciated. However, if an untrained sergeant can shoot down four then it cannot be that difficult now, can it? Dismissed."

I kept hold of Gordy's arm as we walked back to our tent to pick up our flying gear. As soon as we reached our tent and were out of ear shot he exploded. "What an arrogant little jumped up so and so! Who the hell does he think he is to come in here and talk to us like that?"

"Our new acting commander I think. Listen, Gordy, the colonel will not be away for too long and when he comes back he will reverse these decisions."

"I hope you are right. At least we get to fly again and that is one thing at any rate."

As we walked to the aircraft I noticed some new flight sergeants and warrant officers. Obviously Major Brack had not just taken experienced pilots. There were a couple, in crisply pressed uniforms, who looked out of place. They stared at me as I approached Sharp.

Sergeant Sharp was waiting at the aircraft. He looked to have recovered from the dose of gas he had received over Ypres. "Well, Charlie, what is the new bus like?"

"She hasn't been up yet but she sounds more powerful. Did you have a good leave sir?"

"I did. Well let me have a look at the new bus and then we'll get her up. The new major wants a detailed report about the performance."

I saw the look on Sharp's face. It was a picture and told me that he had had a run in with the major too. I was now an officer and I had to keep my feelings to myself. The major would have to have my support even if I did not like what he was doing. I made sure that I went over every inch of the aircraft and then we took off.

I was disappointed at first. It was a more powerful engine and the take-off time was marginally shorter but our speed through the air didn't seem any faster than the earlier model. Sharp had not fixed the improvised speaking tubes we used as yet and so I tapped him on the head and pointed up. As soon as we climbed and levelled out I saw that we were moving faster. I gauged that by Ted's aircraft which was still at a low altitude. I began to leave him behind. That would be useful if we came up against faster German aeroplanes. We flew for the prescribed time and then landed.

I helped Charlie examine the engine and then left him while I went to write my report. I knew that I would be judged on this first report and I was the first pilot to report to the major. Captain Marshall was still the adjutant and he grinned when he saw me. "Why, you are keen, Bill."

"Yes sir, new commanding officer and all that. I do not want to upset him too soon."

His face darkened, "Temporary." He lowered his voice, "The Colonel will return." We both heard a cough from the major's tent and Captain Marshall said, "You had better get in then."

I handed in my report and as I turned to leave he said, "Just wait a moment Lieutenant Harsker." He read through the report and nodded, "A sound report, good." I breathed a sigh of relief. "However, it has come to my attention that you have been guilty of some lapses of military protocol." I wondered what he was talking about. "You addressed your Flight Sergeant by his first name. That will not do. It breeds a familiarity of which I disapprove and secondly, I noticed that you were working on the engine. I can understand a sergeant doing so but you are an officer. Please behave like one. You have been elevated from the ranks of manual labourers. Please conduct yourself appropriately. I do not expect to see you doing that in the future."

I left feeling more depressed than I had for a long time. Even when I tried my best and gained a little approval I was still criticised. I began to regret my decision not to follow Major Burscough to his new squadron. Perhaps I could apply for a transfer. I have always had this ability to argue with myself in my head. By the time I had reached my tent I had talked myself out of it. I did not want to leave my friends and that included Charlie. In addition, it would please the major if I did so and I was not willing to indulge that man. If he wanted to play by the regulations then I would oblige him. Sergeant Armstrong in the Yeomanry had taught me how to use regulations to help you."

Charlie gave me a strange look the next day when I formally addressed him as Sergeant Sharp and deigned to inspect the engine. "Have you set up the speaking tubes yet, Sergeant Sharp?"

"Er, yes, Lieutenant."

"Good then let us be about our business."

Once we were aloft I said, "Sorry about that, Charlie. I was reprimanded by the new major yesterday for being informal. There are a couple of new sergeants who were watching us and I think that one of them must report to the major."

I could hear the relief in his voice, "I thought I had upset you sir. I think I know the one you mean; Flight Sergeant Shield. He transferred here with the new major. None of the lads like him. He walks around as though he has a broom stuffed up his arse."

I laughed, "And I am afraid that I won't be able to get my hands dirty with you. Much as I would like to. However, there is nothing to stop me from watching you closely so that I keep my eye in. Right let's get on with this test. We will try a climb and see what the rate is and then I will try a few spins at altitude. The new bus is faster the higher we get and that might make for better turns."

We both knew that if you could turn inside an enemy then, with the flexibility of a moveable machine gun you had a chance to cause some damage. Now that we had the speaking tube attached it was much easier and I could warn Sharp about any sudden moves I might make.

It took until the middle of June for all of the new officers to arrive. Major St. John Hamilton-Grant gathered us all together a couple of days after the last of the new pilots had arrived.

"Gentlemen, we are leaving for France. Today the spares for the aircraft, the fuel and the ground crew will leave by lorry. There will be a separate convoy with our new tents. You will need to pack your bags for the Quartermaster Sergeant to take to the new base. The aircraft will leave tomorrow morning at six o'clock. We will be flying directly to our new base which is between Ypres and Loos. I believe some of the pilots know that area. It is clearly marked on the maps which Captain Marshall will issue as you leave."

He strode to the map on the wall and pointed to the red dot which would mark our new home. "The sector is quiet at the moment but there is likely to be an increase in ground activity soon which is why we are being sent there now. We should have at least a week to familiarise ourselves with the field and the dispositions of the troops. Any questions?"

Gordy stood and asked, "Sir, any news on the colonel?"

I saw the major's face darken and watched Captain Marshall shake his head slightly. Although a reasonable question it highlighted the fact that the major's power was only temporary. He coughed and looked down to shuffle some papers on his desk. "I believe there is no change in the condition of the colonel's son and so I do not expect him to join us in the foreseeable future."

When Gordy sat down I could see the anger on his face. Ted joined us as we walked back to our tents. We had to pack our bags. "I feel sorry for the colonel and all that but he owes us something. He was the one who promoted us. If the three of us were still sergeant gunners this wouldn't be a problem."

"Gordy, the genie is out of the bottle. You can't put it back in. All three of us were pleased to be promoted. And don't tell me you would happily go back to being the gunner for one of these new wet behind the ears Beer Boys."

Ted chuckled, "He's right Gordy. We have to make the best of it."

"By bloody hell, I never thought I would see the day when you would be the optimist and I would be the pessimist."

The three of us laughed and I put my arm around Gordy. "I think, my friend, that your new relationship with Mary might have something to do with that."

He looked at me as though I had slapped his face and then he slowly nodded, "You could be right. Well if you pair can live with this bastard then I will have to make the best of it too."

It did not take long to pack the bags and Sergeant Sharp carried his and mine to the lorries. It would not have done for an officer to carry his own bags. We kept enough clothes for the following day. There was enough storage space in the Gunbus to carry quite a lot of equipment. I had made sure that the Lee Enfield, the Luger and the ammunition were stored in the aeroplane. Both had saved us when we had had problems with the Lewis. Of course, we made sure that neither the major nor his spy, the odious Flight Sergeant Shield, saw them. They would definitely be viewed as a breach of King's Regulations.

As we had expected, when we did take off the three of us were the tail end Charlies. If the major thought it would be a humiliation he was wrong. I, for one, enjoyed watching the erratic flying of the line of aircraft in front of us. With the exception of the major and Lieutenant Campbell the others were rising and falling with alarming regularity. Of course, the major could not see what was happening behind him. Had I been in command I would have chosen the place we now occupied. I could tell which pilots would struggle once we were in combat situations.

I almost laughed out loud when the major could not find the airfield. It was obvious we were lost when we began to circle some thirty miles from Ypres. I wondered if our fuel would run out as we continued to hunt for our new home. Eventually I saw Gordy take matters into his own hands. He flew to the side of the major and waggled his wings; the sign for follow me. He then flew off towards Ypres. We knew where the town was and Gordy and I had looked at the map the previous day. We had a rough idea where the field would be. Finally, before Gordy became a dot in the distance the major followed. Within fifteen minutes we were landing on our new field.

If Gordy thought that his initiative would garner a reward in the form of a better attitude from the major he was wrong. He was dressed down before the whole squadron for having broken formation. He was punished by being restricted to his tent for a week when not on duty. Ted and I ensured that he did not spend time alone but the punishment was seen as unfair and increased the rift between Gordy and the major.

"The man is bloody incompetent Bill! You do not get lost going to your new base! Even a raw Second Lieutenant knows that! God help us when we get to fly combat."

The new field was adequate but a little short for my liking. The old Gunbus would have struggled to get off with a fuel load of fuel and bombs. In addition, none of us were happy about living in tents. When we approached the major about building wooden accommodation he became irate. "Gentlemen this is not a holiday. We are soldiers. The men in the trenches would love to have the comfort of a tent and so will we. There is nothing wrong with the tents.

Of course, once it rained and the ground became churned up with mud he changed his mind but that would be a month away and so we endured the unnecessarily hard life of a canvas camp. The new standing orders were displayed for all to see. They were depressing. We were each allocated a sector, an altitude, a specific route and a time when we would patrol. We were forbidden to leave our sector even if one of our colleagues was in trouble. When we saw the regulations even Billy Campbell joined our discontented trio. As one of the younger pilots he had accepted all that the major had said until the orders were pinned up. He had flown in Belgium and knew the folly of such a strait jacket.

"This is madness. If we fly the same height, the same place and the same time then the Hun will know. It will not take him long to have something waiting for us when we get over there."

I had thought this too but I had a half solution. "The thing is, lads, that we might all take off at the same time but we can vary our speed to reach the allocated sector at a different time each day. We can also vary the route we take over the sector and, unless we are unlucky enough to be next to the major, then we can vary the altitude."

Ted was back to being grumpy again, "What if we are attacked?"

Gordy snorted, "I, for one, am not leaving any of you in the shit! I will help anyone who is attacked."

I shook my head, "This one will court martial you Gordy. He is itching to find an excuse. You know that."

He shrugged, "I think a court martial might be just the thing. Do you think that people like General Henderson would approve of his tactics and his orders?"

We had met the General who we knew approved of the colonel's methods. "You may be right but you need to be careful Gordy. This is war time. They use the death penalty."

With that sobering thought we prepared our aeroplanes for our first flight over the battlefield.

Chapter 3

Even though it was summer there was little sign of green growth. From the air, the battlefield looked brown and was riddled with the black scars of trenches lined with faded sandbags and the sparkling savage teeth of the barbed wire. Once the autumn rains began it would become brown and rusted but for now it still looked like new metal. As we flew over the British trenches we saw the arms waving. I think we brought relief from the monotony of trench life. Once we had crossed No-Man's Land the air cracked and crackled with gunfire as they tried to shoot us down. Despite our standing orders I took the Gunbus up a couple of hundred feet. It made the chance of us being hit less.

"They are a bit keen eh sir?"

"They certainly are Charlie. I think we will come in higher tomorrow."

"Isn't that against orders sir?"

"Oh yes!"

We reached the end of our outward leg and we headed south. I would vary this for, if we flew north to south each day, there would be German aircraft waiting to pounce. I dropped to the correct altitude briefly. "Sharp, keep your eye out for signs of artillery and roads."

The railways had been shelled and bombed so much that the roads, this close to the front, were the only viable means of bringing up men and supplies. As we neared the trenches again I lifted the nose and began to climb. If you flew in a straight line at the same height then the gunners had more chance of hitting you. I went up and down as I flew the western leg of our patrol.

When we landed I was relieved. Leaving Sharp to check on the aeroplane with the mechanics I walked down the line of aeroplanes. There were just three without any damage; mine, Gordy's and Ted's. The others all had holes somewhere on the aeroplanes. When I came to Lieutenant Cole's I saw that he had a hole in his wing the size of a football. "You were lucky to get down, Lieutenant Cole."

"I know. Is the fire always this bad?"

I nodded. "And now that they know we are in the sector I would expect some German aeroplanes too."

As I passed the major's aircraft which had bullet holes along the wing he looked up from his inspection. "It looks as though you were lucky Lieutenant Harsker."

Keeping a straight face, I said, "Yes sir. It must be that rabbit's foot I carry."

When I handed my report to Captain Marshall he said, quietly, "Watch yourself, Bill. He has his eye on you."

"Thank you, sir. I will."

He smiled, "Us old ones are fewer in number, we have to stick together."

At breakfast, the next day, you could sense the nervousness amongst the young pilots in the officer's mess. One or two of them ate a little of their breakfast and then raced outside to bring it back up. The major's orders had put the young pilots in danger. The altitude was too low to be safe from ground fire. Hundreds of German rifles firing in the air had a good chance of hitting something. The anti-aircraft guns, too, would be able to have more chance of striking if the aeroplanes flew at the same height.

"I am going to see the Major."

Gordy snorted, "He won't listen to you Bill. He has fixed ideas. Someone will have to die first."

I shrugged, "I have to try. He can only say no."

And of course, he did say no. "I will not change my orders just because of a few bullet holes in the wings of our aircraft. The young pilots will learn to deal with it." He smirked, "If you could manage that then I am sure that these well trained young men who went to the finest schools in England will have no problem. Breeding and education will prove superior."

I had no argument to such an outdated and illogical argument. Gordy was right, someone would have to die before this stubborn man would change his mind.

Soon after we took off I began to veer to the south. I would fly a different outward leg. I had Gordy on one side of me and Ted on the other. I knew that I was safe from anyone reporting me. When Ted saw me getting closer I saw him wave and he, too, began to head south. I also began to climb. I climbed until I was beyond the effective range of a German rifle. As I passed the German trenches I could see the flashes of the small arms and hear the crump of their artillery. Clouds of smoke pockmarked the sky below me and I dipped the aircraft into a shallow dive to take us to our allotted altitude. The manoeuvre confused the gunners who had changed their fuses. The shells now exploded above us. A few pieces of shrapnel pierced the fabric of the upper wing but our stability was maintained. As I headed north I noticed a column of German vehicles moving up the road.

"Charlie, let's attack that column. Get ready on your machine gun. I shall fly along the column from west to east and then turn when the magazine is empty."

"Righto sir."

We both knew that it was a safe manoeuvre for any guns in the vehicles would be pointing east. The chances of us being hit were slim. I dropped down to fifty feet from the ground. To the German drivers it must have looked as though we were flying into their cabs. One of them veered to the side before Sharp had even fired and I saw the lorry overturn into the drainage ditch. When Sharp did begin to fire he was able to hit the cab and then stitch a line of bullets into the interior. I had no idea what they were carrying. It could have been men or supplies. One of them, however, had to have been carrying ammunition for I heard the explosion behind me.

"That's it sir. Out of ammo."

I began to climb and turn north once again. Our attack meant that we were the last to land and there was a reception committee awaiting me. The major stood tapping his leg with his swagger stick. Ted, Gordy and Billy Campbell were standing nearby as though examining Gordy's aircraft.

As soon as I was out he strode over to me. "Well Lieutenant Harsker, have you an explanation?"

I gave him my most innocent look. "What do you mean sir?"

He pointed to my aircraft, "You are late back and you have fired your weapons! Explain!"

"Oh that, we saw a column of German vehicles and we attacked them."

"That is not in my standing orders!" There was a triumphant note in his voice.

"With respect sir, you do not mention that in your standing orders. There is no reference to using our guns, attacking or defending ourselves. As there were no standing orders covering that eventuality I used the previous standing orders of Colonel Pemberton-Smythe." I gave him a puzzled look, "Did I do wrong, sir?"

He reddened, "I will amend my orders immediately. There will be no attacks without my permission." He turned to storm away.

"Sir, suppose we are attacked? Do we fire back or not?"

"Of course, but you were not attacked by an aircraft."

"Does ground fire not count as an attack?"

"Do not be pedantic. I will have a new set of standing orders within the hour!"

The others crowded around me once he had gone. "Well done, Bill!"

I shook my head. "I am not so certain but it had to be done. Are we observers or airmen?"

The orders we saw pinned to the notice board were quite clear; unless so ordered there was to be no attacking of ground targets. We were allowed to return fire at aeroplanes but no mention was made of barrage balloons. However, to make sure the Major had a briefing with us the next day to make doubly sure that we understood.

"Gentlemen, yesterday Lieutenant Harsker attacked a German convoy. I realise that I did not make myself clear and I have remedied the situation. We will patrol our sectors and report back what we see. Is that clear?"

The young pilots shouted, "Yes sir."

Gordy put up his hand, "What if they put up balloons sir?"

The major sighed, "We leave them alone."

"But sir, they are used to direct the fire of their batteries. If we do not attack them then our infantry may well suffer."

"Lieutenant Hewitt, are you incapable of listening to and obeying orders? We leave them alone!"

He was wrong and the four experienced pilots all knew that. However, we could do nothing about it. We had an uneventful patrol and we saw nothing. When we returned Gordy and I went to see Captain Marshall to have a quiet word. The adjutant was not a flier but he understood what we did.

"Sir, can you not reason with the major? This is an intolerable situation. Someone is going to die because of these rules."

"Keep your voices down. He may not be here but he has eyes and ears everywhere. I have tried but he argues that the pilots need more air time before they can engage in combat of any kind."

"Captain Marshall, when will the colonel be back?"

"I have no idea, Bill. But if you wish I will write to him and tell him that we are all missing him. If he is able to read between the lines then he could well return but he is very close to his son. You all know that."

We nodded. He was right. His son came first. The captain's hands were tied for he could not put more in the letter without it coming to the attention of the major. As commanding officer, he had to randomly check the vetted letters. He would be sure to look at one addressed to the colonel.

The Germans had put balloons up. As we flew towards them they winched them to the ground but the extra machine guns they had packed around their bases made it a hot area. Sergeant Sharp and I still varied our route and our height. I would rather be punished than risk our lives for an order which made no sense at all. It was lucky that we did; three Aviatik aeroplanes were waiting for Gordy as he flew over the German lines. They only had a rear gun but three of them could have caused us trouble. Luckily Charlie and I had just gained height and were above them. They were in Gordy's blind spot and he could not see them. They attacked in line astern.

"Sharp, get ready with the Lewis."

Because we had the height, when I began to dive we picked up speed. I knew that we would not reach Gordy before he was attacked but I also knew that he was a clever pilot. I had to hope that he would be able to out fox them until I could come to his aid. I saw the first Aviatik open fire. Gordy looked around and he began to climb. I saw his gunner grab the rear Lewis and stand on the cockpit. The German knew of the Gunbus' weakness and he was attacking from below. The climb aided Gordy but also allowed the other two enemy aeroplanes to bring their guns to bear on his engine and rear.

None of them saw me. "Charlie, wait until we are just forty yards from them before you fire. Short bursts!"

"Yes sir!"

I cocked the Lewis in front of me. If I got the chance I would add the fire of our second machine gun to that of Sharp. I saw smoke coming from Gordy's engine. He had been hit. The Gunbus is a solid aeroplane and the new engine was a good one. That said he could not last long with three machine guns firing at him.

When Charlie opened fire, the bullets stitched a line along the fuselage of the first aeroplane. I actually saw one of the cables severed. It sprang out of the fuselage and the rear Aviatik turned back to his own lines. The second Aviatik saw us and took evasive action to move away from Charlie's gun. "Sharp, keep firing at the one on Gordy's tail."

As the second German tried to loop to come on to our rear I gave a short burst from my Lewis. I was lucky, I must have hit his propeller for the aeroplane juddered and then began to turn away. When Charlie opened fire on the last German he realised the hopelessness of his situation. He had fire from front and rear; he turned for home. Undamaged but chastened.

I flew next to Gordy who waved his hand. He held up his thumb to show that he was safe to fly and he waved me back to my allotted patrol. We had a safe journey back. When we landed I saw that three of the aeroplanes had suffered damage of some kind. Gordy's did not show the damage but I knew he would not be flying the next day.

Leaving Sharp to see to our bus I ran to Gordy's craft. Ted joined me. "Thanks Bill!"

Even as he said it, I saw Ted give him a slight shake of the head as a warning.

"Thank him for what Lieutenant?"

It was the major. I had been rehearsing my answer from the moment we had begun our attack. "Sir, three Aviatik attacked us. Two attacked Lieutenant Hewitt and one attacked me. I drove off mine and when I flew close to the other two they flew away."

"You disobeyed my orders then?"

"No sir. Your standing orders were that we were allowed to fire at someone attacking us."

"I also said that no one was to go to the aid of a fellow pilot."

Gordy said, "Sir, aren't those orders contradictory? Lieutenant Harsker was only obeying the order to return fire. The fact that he was able to help me was incidental."

He came much closer to us and lowered his voice. "Proper little barrack room lawyers, aren't you? Typical of your class. Well you will not defeat me. I will reallocate the sectors. You will not be flying next to each other tomorrow."

None of us felt elated. A gunner had died in one of the other aeroplanes and a second one had been wounded. The Germans had attacked four of our aeroplanes. We were just lucky that they had not managed to destroy any of our aeroplanes. If they had had a decent fighter then we would have been decimated. We would be three aeroplanes short on our next patrol and I would be flying next to green pilots.

Ted was more upset than anyone for he had not been able to help his friend. "I'm telling you this; no matter what the orders say if I see a pilot being attacked then I will go to help him. Anything else, well it's cowardly!"

"I think that tomorrow the Germans will be waiting for us. There will be more balloons and more guns. Once they realise that we are not attacking them on the ground they will have free rein."

Gordy stubbed out his cigarette, "And you will only have nine aeroplanes. It will be like fleas on a dog! Make sure you have spare ammunition."

The good news about being moved was that I was no longer flying over the same sector. I had been limited in my routes out and back. With a new sector, I could fly on a new pathway that Lieutenant Holt, who had been hit by enemy fire and was grounded, had not flown. However, I was flying between Lieutenant Davies and Lieutenant Foster. One of them would notice if my altitude was vastly different from theirs. I also knew that we would be bound to run into Germans for they had attacked Holt the previous day. Both Charlie and I were alert and on edge. As we headed east I was grateful that we could not be attacked from behind but on the homeward leg Charlie would have to stand and face the rear all the way home. Travelling alone brought a whole host of problems.

I managed to fly fifty feet higher than we had been ordered. It was not much but I hoped it would put off the gunners who began to pepper the skies with hopeful shells as we flew over the German lines. My senses were all attuned and I listened to the air whistling through the struts. I also listened to the powerful throb of the Rolls Royce Eagle. I liked the new engine; it purred powerfully as we went deeper into enemy territory. It was reassuring to know that we had such a reliable engine. It was one less thing to worry about.

As I peered over the side I saw that there were fewer roads in this sector and they were smaller than the ones I had passed before. There was no chance of attacking ground targets here. I smiled to myself. I would have to obey orders as there was no chance of breaking them.

When I came to the end of the leg and turned I noticed that I was flying towards Lieutenant Davies. As he was slightly below me he did not see me and I took the opportunity of gaining a few more feet in height. As we turned to head west I said, "Right Charlie, on your feet. This is where the buggers will be."

"Right sir." He confidently stood and braced himself against the sides of the cockpit and cocked the Lewis that was in front of me. His eyes would now be peering behind us. He would be watching for the pouncing Germans. I did not have the best of views ahead but by straddling the cockpit the way he did Sergeant Sharp gave me a reasonable view in front of me. His face suddenly appeared before mine. "Sir, two Aviatiks and one of those new Eindeckers. They are on Mr Davies' tail."

"Get back on your Lewis. We'll try to help him."

"But sir, the major's orders!"

"Sod the orders besides we will just distract them. We will still be flying our allotted patrol. I'll just go down a little."

As we were behind and above Lieutenant Davies it meant that we had the advantage of speed over the three Germans. The Aviatiks were known to us. They had a machine gun fired by an observer and they had to be alongside or in front of their target to score a hit but the Eindecker looked to have a machine gun over the wing and the pilot could fire it. That was the machine we had to hurt. I was delighted to see that we were faster than all three German aeroplanes. The Aviatik was a slow beast. Even so the Germans fired first and the Fokker's steel tipped bullets struck the rear of Lieutenant Davies' Gunbus. The German ground fire had stopped. They were reluctant to risk hitting one of their own aeroplanes and I took the opportunity to close with the three of them.

"Fire when you can, Charlie! We are not after a kill. We just need them to leave Lieutenant Davies alone."

He opened fire at the Fokker first. It was at our maximum range and he emptied half a drum. Although only one or two of the bullets hit the German it caused him to pull the nose up a little and begin to bank left. He had no idea we were behind him. Davies' gunner took the opportunity to fire at their tormentor and bullets struck the undercarriage.

Sergeant Sharp emptied the rest of the drum at the Aviatiks which fired back at us. Their bullets hit the tail. As Charlie changed magazines I climbed a little. I saw the Fokker trailing smoke as it headed east. The two Aviatiks were dropping behind. They both opened fire again but they were too far away and when the British guns below us began to open fire they turned and they too headed east.

We resumed our flight and, as we drew close to Davies, he waved his hand in acknowledgement. I hoped he would be discreet when he made his report or, once again, I would be in trouble. I knew the day had not gone well as we taxied along the grass. There were just seven aircraft and all had damage of some description.

Lieutenant Davies ran over to me. "Thanks awfully, Harsker old boy! That was a little sticky back there."

"I was lucky that they were between you and I or I would have been too far away to help."

He had a puzzled look but my stare suddenly made him understand and he nodded vigorously, "Of course, they were between us. We were lucky!"

As I made my way to my tent Gordy and Ted joined me. "Two of the new lads were shot down. They were close to the sector we flew yesterday. There were four Aviatik waiting for them."

"What happened to them?"

Ted shook his head, "They came from below and hit them in their blind spot. They flew in tandem so that they were on either side of the Gunbus. If there had been just one other with them then the result would have been different. I saw one crash and burn and the way the other was falling I don't think they had any chance."

"What a mess. We are down to half a squadron because he insists on using the wrong tactics. He will only be happy when we are all grounded."

Gordy smiled, "Or he gets shot down!" It was a terrible thing to say but I think Ted and I agreed. The major was a disaster and a bigger danger to us than the Germans.

"And we met one of those Fokkers today. They are a lot more dangerous than the biplanes the Hun is using."

"That's all we need; better German aeroplanes and a commander who ties our hands."

In the event, we were all grounded. The major, although he did not admit that he was wrong knew that we could not fly with damaged aeroplanes and so we spent the next day repairing our aeroplanes. The major's young acolytes were beginning to see that the theory of aerial combat as taught by the major and the practical nature of it were two entirely different beasts. They began to talk more to Ted, Billy Campbell and Gordy. Their sergeants all sought out our gunners. Their experience would be even more invaluable and they could give practical tips on aerial gunnery. Of course, the major and his gunner did not need advice from anyone and they both assiduously avoided all contact with the four of us.

That evening in the officers' mess we told the young pilots of the way we had operated before. Lieutenant Campbell spoke the most for he was the only one of the younger pilots left from those who had flown in our flights. I could see that his words registered with them. I think that they had been taught that the airman was an individual who could fly his way out of trouble. That might have been true in the pre-war days but we now knew different. The Gunbus was the only allied aircraft which could hold its own. I dreaded the day the Germans improved their fighters. The Eindecker was a good aeroplane but, fortunately the pilot had to fire the gun over the propeller and that made aiming and flying more difficult. However, it meant that if he could get on your tail and below you he was in a perfect position to hit your engine.

With the aeroplanes repaired we went to bed early ready for an early patrol over the German lines.

Chapter 4

We were breakfasting when we heard the noise of aeroplane engines. They had a different sound to the Rolls Royce Eagle. "They are Germans!" Ted had an ear for engines and, at his words, we raced from the tent. We could see, less than half a mile away six twin engine German biplanes.

"They are bombers!"

Someone should have given an order to move our aeroplanes but all appeared frozen and were staring at the skies. Gordy took charge and just shouted, "Get your buses up in the air as quickly as you can!"

Ted and I ran to our aeroplanes closely followed by Billy Campbell. I saw Charlie running from the sergeants' mess. I had no flying gear but that didn't matter. We just had to move the aircraft before they were strafed, or even worse, bombed.

Charlie had the propeller spinning even as I clambered aboard. He ripped the chocks away and she started to move. He dived headfirst into the front cockpit and I began to taxi. We would be defenceless until we got in the air and I just prayed that we would get up quickly. I saw that Gordy was already lifting off. I eased back on the stick as we reached our take off speed and breathed a sigh of relief as we lifted. I heard the crump from behind and then the concussion of the first bomb blast made us rise alarmingly. A pair of bombs had hit the field where we had been moments earlier. We had no flying helmets and no speaking tube but Sergeant Sharp had the Lewis cocked and was ready to fire as we continued to climb. We knew what we both had to do. As I banked I saw that only four aeroplanes had made it into the air. I glanced below me and saw that at least three aeroplanes had been hit as well as a couple of the tents. There were fires burning. The aeroplanes had been fuelled and ready to go. They were like readymade bombs lying helplessly on the ground.

The bombers were turning for home. They would have to fly through us to reach it. I cocked the Lewis in front of me. I saw that they were a twin engine aeroplane; we later discovered they were the AEG G1. Like us they had a gunner in the front and another in the rear of the aircraft. We would be evenly matched. I picked one and flew directly at him. Sharp began to pour bullets into it and I heard the enemy's bullets striking our aeroplane. I half stood and began firing the second Lewis. I saw the gunner slump dead in his cockpit; I don't know which of us hit him and then the bomber began to bank. We had played a game of dare and he had blinked first. Before his rear gun could be brought into action our two Lewis guns began to do some damage. His starboard engine began to smoke and then caught fire. The effect was to swing the aeroplane around even more and the last of our bullets shredded his tail. With only one engine and no tail the bomber spiralled towards the ground. When it struck the explosion told us that there would be no survivors.

I glanced over my shoulder and saw four bombers heading east. One of them was smoking. I saw a fifth on the ground close to the airfield and armed men from the squadron's defence force were racing towards it.

We landed and, as we did so I saw the devastation caused by the attack. We had two aeroplanes totally destroyed and another three which were badly damaged. There were shredded tents and bodies littering the whole of the base. I saw Doc Brennan and the medical staff dealing with casualties for the bomb had struck the mechanics' mess. The effect of the bomb striking the cookers and ovens through a tent had been horrific and the flying metal which resulted had scythed through men like canister. The damage to the aeroplanes was bad but machines could be repaired. The dead men were harder to replace.

Ted came over to me. "Well done, Bill. That was a good hit."

"Who got the other one?"

"Billy Campbell. Gordy and I went for the same aeroplane and it is damaged but she'll get home."

The major stormed over to us. "Who gave you permission to take off?"

I was stunned, "No-one sir." I pointed at the destroyed and damaged aeroplanes. "I didn't want my bus to end up like that."

"Next time, wait for the command."

I know that I should have bit back my retort but I was angry. "And when will that come sir? In time to save us or in time to bury us?"

"That is insubordination! I could have you put on a charge for that!"

I had had enough of this martinet. He seemed hidebound by rules and regulations regardless of the result. I stared down at him. "Then do so, sir, or better still have me court martialed. I would love to give my account of the events to a court martial board and see what they say. The last time I spoke with General Henderson he seemed quite keen for us to shoot down German aeroplanes."

I really thought I had gone too far. His faced reddened and he glared at me. Then he turned smartly on his heel and strode off.

Ted shook his head as Gordy joined us. "That was a mistake, Bill. He will make you pay for that."

"What just happened?"

Ted explained to Gordy who shook his head. "If the old man doesn't get back here soon he will not have a command to return to."

The death toll was too high. We had lost ten valuable mechanics and cooks as well as fifteen others who had been wounded.

The major began to, belatedly, organise defences for us. Machine guns were dotted around the airfield and we were told to park our aeroplanes so that they were further apart. It was a little like shutting the stable door after the horse had bolted. We would now be down to eight aeroplanes and that was dependent upon our depleted mechanics being able to repair the two most badly damaged of them.

Ted was correct. I was about to pay for my outburst. The next morning, as we gathered for our daily briefing the major had an oddly self-satisfied expression upon his face. "We will not be patrolling our sector today gentlemen. The attack the other day has rendered us temporarily ineffective. We will patrol the sector from here to the front in case the Germans try a second attack. However, I wish to discover where the German bombers came from. Lieutenant Harsker has shown himself capable of shooting down enemy aircraft and so as our most successful combat pilot he can have the honour of finding the German bombers' airfield." He looked at me with a superior look on his face. He thought he had beaten me. "Even as we speak the bombs are being fitted to your aeroplane in case you do find it. Any questions?" No-one answered and he added, "Very well good luck everyone."

Gordy and Ted looked at me and shook their heads. "Bastard! This is a suicide mission Bill. Just fly over their lines and then come back here. One aeroplane behind enemy lines stands no chance."

"No Gordy. I will do the mission as ordered. If I refuse I play into his hands for I will look like a coward and I will not give him that satisfaction. It is my own fault for talking back to him. I will pay the price of telling the truth. He will keep on at me until he succeeds anyway so I might as well bite the bullet and get it over with."

As I went to my tent to get my flying gear I began to work out where the airfield might be. The odds were that it would be further from the front than the fighter airfields. It meant I had further to go and further to return. Even if I avoided the Germans on the way over they would be waiting for me on the way back. Perhaps Gordy was right and it was a suicide mission.

Sergeant Sharp was already at the aeroplane looking with some interest at the four bombs being fitted to the outside of the front of the aeroplane. "What's this all about sir?"

"It seems the major has great faith in us, Sergeant Sharp. He is sending us to find the German bombers who did so much damage to our own field."

His jaw actually dropped. "We are going alone? That is madness."

"I don't know. One aeroplane has a slightly better chance of getting through than a whole squadron. Besides, we do not have a whole squadron. We will just have to do the best that we can. But," I added cheekily, "keep a German phrase book handy eh? Just in case."

He laughed, "We are a pair of mad buggers sir."

"Bring a spare can of petrol. We may need it. And you will need to plot our course on the map so that we can tell the major where the airfield is when we get back."

The heavier engine, extra fuel and the bombs made the take off a little longer than usual but we eventually rumbled into the air. I told Sharp my plan as we climbed to ten thousand feet. I wanted to be well above any enemy fire from the guns on the ground. "Those bombers have a long range and I think they will be well behind enemy lines. That is why we have the extra fuel in case we run out. When we chased them from our field they were heading in this direction and I think they will have taken the shortest route to get back to their field. We are looking for a green patch of land with half a dozen twin engine aeroplanes. There will be a windsock such as the type we use." I chuckled, "And probably a

German flag too. Put that together and it should be easy to spot from up here so keep your eyes peeled."

Flying at the higher altitude meant that we were faster than the rest of the squadron and we overtook them before we reached our lines. They looked to be a pathetically small handful of aeroplanes. I hoped that they would not run into Germans. They were all flying with a large interval between them. They were, literally, sitting ducks.

The front line was even clearer from this height and stretched to the horizon in both directions. When we were over the German lines I saw an aeroplane below us. It looked to be the Fokker Eindecker. I wondered if it was patrolling or hunting my comrades. So long as the rest of the squadron was close we had nothing to fear from this small aeroplane which was less well armed and slower than our Gunbus.

I kept my eye on the fuel gauge. I had the engine trimmed so that we were getting the most out of the limited fuel we had. When the land became greener I began to descend. There were no guns firing at us here. There were no balloons to avoid. The gentle glide down slowed down the rate at which we were using fuel. I began to hope that we could get back without having to land.

Suddenly Sharp's voice was in my ears. "Sir, have a look up ahead. Is than an airfield?"

He was right, it was an airfield. I saw the windsock, the tents and the straight runway lined with the bombers. I dived down to four hundred feet to identify the aeroplanes. "Charlie, mark the airfield on the map."

"Done it already sir." There was a pause. "There look to be three of those twin-engine aeroplanes down there sir. It looks like there are men around one of them."

"Right get ready. Take two bombs and throw them when I say. I will turn around and you can drop the other two."

"Right sir."

There was no science to this, you dropped the bomb and let gravity do the rest. We had learned to throw before we reached the target and then we had more chance of a direct hit. The arc seemed to be important. We had not done it enough to be totally accurate. All that we could hope for was some damage. The craters we would create would be a good result. All I was attempting to do was get the bombs as close to the three aircraft as I could.

The machine guns opening fire told us that we had been seen. We were travelling too fast for them to hit but it was frightening. "Now!" I pulled back on the stick and kicked the rudder, we climbed and banked to the right. I immediately threw it the left and began to dive. "Ready!"

"Ready sir."

I could not see what damage we had done for there was a great deal of smoke. I took our bus further to the right. "Now!"

The two explosions lifted us slightly. I had brought the aeroplane lower than I had intended. With bullets trying to catch our tail I headed west. When I looked at the fuel gauge I saw that my climb and dive had used up more fuel than I had wanted. I had two choices: climb and risk running out of fuel or keep at this altitude and risk the gun fire from the ground. Neither was the favoured option. I climbed; the spare fuel meant that we could land and refuel. I also changed our course to take us further north. I did not want to run out of fuel over No-Man's Land. I needed a flat obstacle free field with no furrows. It was like wishing for a gourmet dinner in the mess.

I estimated that we were thirty miles behind the German lines and I also knew that were would be other German airfields closer to the front. Sergeant Sharp scanned the horizon for enemy aeroplanes. I was using the altitude to give some protection from enemy aeroplanes. The German had slower machines than we did and the long slow climb would take them a long time to reach us.

Sharp was standing and looking behind me. He attracted my attention and pointed down; there were two Aviatiks and two Fokkers spiralling up to reach us. The spiral rise was easier on the engine and yet kept us in constant view. Sergeant Sharp cocked both Lewis guns and waited.

"Try the Lee Enfield." I mouthed.

He nodded and took out the rifle. He leaned on the cockpit, his face close to my hands and he aimed at the aircraft climbing. It would be a lucky shot if he managed to hit them but, if he fired, slowly and methodically, it might unnerve them. We just had to buy some time. Time was as precious as the fuel which was rapidly running out. The FE 2 was not a good glider but, if I picked the right angle of descent we might be able to get down and refuel safely but we had to shake off our pursuers. If we had had more fuel then I would have used the Gunbus' superior speed to escape. More speed would just make us run out quicker.

The crack from the rifle made me jump. I saw Sharp work the bolt as he fired again. I was curious to see the results but I had to concentrate on the fuel. The engine gave a little cough.

"I am going down, Charlie, brace yourself."

As I pushed the stick forward I realised that we would, briefly be at the mercy of the Germans. I hoped that Lady Luck was still with us. I risked a glance over my shoulder and saw that there was just one Fokker and one Aviatik remaining. The other two were disappearing east. Either Sharp had discouraged them or they did not think we could be caught before we reached our lines. We began to pick up speed and the Germans dropped back slightly. I saw a patch of green ahead. It was behind the German lines but it looked flat enough to land.

Sergeant Sharp suddenly stood up and the Lewis began to chatter. At the same time, I felt the thump as steel jacketed bullets struck the tail. I could see that the field was young wheat. It would not be as smooth as an airfield but it would have to do. I watched the ground. Sharp resumed his seat clutching the empty magazine. I wondered why the firing from behind had stopped. I hoped that they had run out of ammunition rather than the alternative that he was waiting for us to land and hit us when we would be a sitting duck.

The nose wheel touched and I gave the slightest of movements with my fingers. The other wheels caught. We had no power, the fuel had run out some time earlier and we soon came to a halt. I grabbed the Lewis and fitted a fresh magazine. Charlie leapt out with the can of petrol and raced to the rear of the aeroplane. The two Germans swooped down towards us. The Fokker had a difficult job to hit us for his gun was above his propeller and he had to risk putting his nose into the ground to hit us. The Aviatik would have to fire when it had passed. It all meant that we had some time.

I pulled the trigger and gave the monoplane a short burst. I hit the side of the cockpit and he banked away. I fired a second burst at the biplane. Although I missed he, too, jinked away. As he rose the gunner sent a hail of lead towards us. The end of the wing showed where he had hit us. I heard Sharp shout, "Contact!"

I sat down and pushed the starter. The propeller spun, the engine coughed and then fired. With no chocks to hold us we began to move and Charlie leapt into the cockpit like a jack rabbit. It was now that we were at the mercy of the two Germans. They had turned and were flying towards us. I began to pull back on the stick. They were heading for us. The Fokker was firing while the brave pilot in the Aviatik was trying to get his gunner a shot. He had to get ahead of us to do so and that would mean it brought him into Sergeant Sharp's sights. Charlie's Lewis gun sprayed both of the Germans and a momentary movement to the side allowed us to slip between them. The rear gunner sprayed us with bullets and I heard the thud as they struck home. The engine began to falter.

We had been hit and we were not yet home. I turned west, towards the setting sun. We did not have the luxury of being able to climb and so I headed across the German lines hoping that our low altitude would confuse them. We zipped over the trenches no more than forty feet above them. We could see the German faces as they stared at the apparition which raced for home. Their bullets buzzed like angry bees but, mercifully, none struck. When I saw brown uniformed arms waving I knew that we were over the British lines and I began to look for the airfield. It struck me that I had never landed in the dark and there would be no lights on the field.

"Sharp. Get the flare gun out. When we are close to the field, fire three flares. We will see if we can use them to land."

To be honest I did not expect a landing we would walk away from. I just hoped I could get us down in one piece. There was still a glow in the west when I sighted the airfield in the distance. I began to lose altitude. Sharp fired the first flare and I saw the field illuminated as it slowly descended. As he fired the second one I saw a series of fires erupt along two lines. They were giving me lights to guide me. Although it was not the smoothest of landings I was just pleased to be down.

As soon as the engine stopped I closed my eyes and leaned forward.

I heard Gordy shout, "Are you all right, Bill? Are you wounded?"

I opened my eyes and smiled, "No Gordy but I am a little tired and I could eat a horse with the skin on."

My two friends helped me down. Ted chuckled, "Don't worry, the cooks have kept the mess open for you." They clapped me on the back. "Did you do it then?"

"Find the airfield?" He nodded. "Aye and we dropped the bombs on a couple of their planes."

Before I could say any more the major strode up to me. I wondered if I would get a well done or some praise. I should have known better. "I will expect your report in the next hour Lieutenant."

"But sir he hasn't eaten!"

He gave a grim smile, "This is war, Lieutenant Hewitt. He can eat when he has written the report."

I stared at him. He had hoped I would have died on the raid. I changed the stare to a smile. "I will really enjoy this food Gordy. Lead on!" I gave the barest of salutes and walked into the mess tent.

The major just spluttered. "In an hour Lieutenant. An hour!" He was almost squealing and I began to laugh.

As I picked up the plate of food Ted said, in all seriousness, "He means it! He's mad as a fish that one. He will court martial you."

"He can do. I am not worried any more. Besides we have the map and the report will be brief and to the point. It will take me no more than ten minutes to write it."

Gordy handed me a bottle of beer. "We thought you might like this too!"

"You beauty!" I drank the beer first. It went down in one and was probably the best beer I had ever drunk. The food was wolfed down in less time than it took to collect it. "Here give us some paper. Ted, go to the bus you'll find the map in Sharp's cockpit."

I had the report already in my head and I wrote it simply but I made sure it was well organised. By the time Ted had returned it was finished. "Here Gordy," I gave him some money, "Buy the three of us a couple of bottles of beer. I reckon we deserve it and I'll deliver this to the adjutant."

The lamp was burning in Captain Marshall's tent. He smiled as I entered. Before he could say a word, I heard, from the major's tent. "Captain, if Lieutenant Harsker is not here in thirty minutes I want him arrested."

I grinned and Captain Marshall shook his head. I handed the map and the report and waited. The major had obviously expected a reply for I heard his voice as he approached, "Captain Marshall did you hear…" He entered the tent and his mouth opened and closed.

"I have delivered the report and the map sir. Was there anything else?"

He snatched the report and the map and stormed out. Captain Marshall stood and shook my hand. "I take my hat off to you, Bill. You have got more nerve than anyone I have ever met but a word to the wise," he lowered his voice, "don't push him. It will not take much to send him over the edge."

"I think it has gone beyond that, sir. This is more than him just being a martinet. I can live with that but we have dead pilots and gunners now. That cannot be right. Can it?" He shook his head. "Any news from the colonel?"

"The last letter I had said that he would be leaving England in the next week or two."

"I just hope there is still a squadron for him to return to."

Chapter 5

The first week in July saw us spotting for the artillery. It had been decided to soften up the Germans. The rumours ran around the airfield like wildfire. This was going to be the start of a push. We would be attacking all along the front. For those of us for whom this was the second year of our war we were more sceptical. It might be a bluff. It might be a diversion. However, whatever was the truth, our task remained the same; we were to position ourselves over no-man's land and signal back to the gunners of the artillery below.

The major elected not to fly. His Gunbus was used by one of the pilots whose aeroplane had been destroyed in the bombing raid. We still only had eight serviceable aircraft and ten crews. It would be some time until we were at full strength again. The major put Billy Campbell in command. It was, of course, a snub to the three sergeant pilots but it did not bother us. Lieutenant Campbell was a good egg and he was sensible.

He sought me out before we flew. "Bill, I don't like this. You are a much better leader. The colonel made you Flight Commander; it should be you in command. You are a First Lieutenant."

I put my arm around his shoulder. "Don't worry about it. I don't. I think we all know how the major feels about me and the other two. It is a snub to us but you are good enough to lead Billy. I think he would put someone who had never flown over enemy lines in command before one of us. You have combat experience. It will be good for your career. You will command one day."

As we took off I realised that there was little to go wrong for Billy. We would be relatively safe from ground fire and we knew that our aircraft were better than the Germans we faced.

We reached our allotted sectors. We were all within sight of another two aeroplanes and could mutually support each other. We spotted the fall of shot and Sergeant Sharp would flash back if they were on target. The Royal Artillery gunners were good and it did not take too many erroneous shots for them to find their range. We then just had to fly up and down watching the shells rain down upon the enemy wire and trenches. We could have gone home but our orders were to stay for an hour and so we did.

It was close to the end of the hour when the Germans came. It looked to be a mixed Jasta. They had Fokkers and Aviatiks. Our problem was that we were spread out and they came in three flights of four each one targeting an individual aeroplane. We were nicknamed Gunbus for good reason and we had little to fear, unless they found our blind spot. Billy Campbell showed that he had what it took when he fired the flare to signal a retreat.

As it happened I was the rear aeroplane when they attacked. They found my blind spot. I felt the bullets crack behind me. I pulled hard on the stick and went into a steep climb. I had enough fuel to be able to use the maximum revs. Two Germans tried to follow me but the others went for the next aeroplane in the line. I heard the guns as they chattered but I was too busy trying to escape from the Fokker and the Aviatik behind me. I glanced over my shoulder and saw that they had fallen back a little. They would expect me to turn west, towards our lines. I did not do what they expected and I banked and dived east. It took them both by surprise.

Charlie was ready with the Lewis and, as we plunged down through the air he gave both aeroplanes a burst. He missed the Fokker but struck the cockpit of the Aviatik. I saw the gunner slump in his seat. I yanked the stick to bring us back on course and behind the other Germans who were pursuing my comrades.

I saw that Lieutenant Holt's aeroplane was pouring smoke. There were two Aviatiks beneath him and they were riddling him with bullets. I had the advantage that I was diving with a superior aeroplane and, cocking the rear Lewis, I dived on to the tail of the first one. Sergeant Sharp emptied his magazine into the first one. He took off the spent magazine. The gunner in the Aviatik saw this and he began to swing his gun towards us. I fired a short burst from my gun and I saw the bullets stitch a line from the cockpit towards the engine. Oil began to spit out over the pilot and he took evasive action. The second German turned his attention to us. I emptied my magazine towards him and then Charlie opened fire. The tail was shredded and the aeroplane began to spiral back towards the east.

The other aeroplanes had been beaten back and had to run the gauntlet of British small arms fire as they headed towards the safety of their own lines. I scanned the skies. Holt was in trouble and I stayed close to him as he took the aeroplane down in a shallow dive. He could not remain in the air. He would not make the airfield. He bounced the aircraft down on a short ploughed field. How he had found it I did not know. I thought he had made a good landing until the nose wheel broke and the right wing caught the ground. The Gunbus slewed into the ground. I brought our bus around and breathed a sigh of relief when I saw the pilot and gunner emerge, somewhat unsteadily, it has to be said, and wave at me.

"Right, Sharp, let's go home."

As soon as we landed I saw the senior sergeant, "Sergeant Jackson, you had better get a lorry. Lieutenant Holt has crashed in a ploughed field about six miles away. They are both walking and I think we can save the engine."

"Right sir, if we keep going on like this we'll have to begin building aeroplanes ourselves."

I left Sergeant Sharp and the mechanic to repair the holes in the bus and to service her. I had a report to write. I was half way through when Lieutenant Campbell came in. "That was a bit of a shambles today."

I gestured for him to sit on my cot. "Don't be daft, man. Holt is a young pilot. He will get better and you got the rest back, didn't you?"

"I suppose so but what can we do when they come on our blind spot like that? Head on or flying alongside we are superior but once they get below us even the Aviatik can have a pop at us."

I had been thinking about this. "The problem is, Billy, if we loop it works in their favour, they can fire at us as we go up and around and I have never tried to loop the other way. I suspect we might lose a few observers."

I put the report to one side and took out a fresh piece of paper. I drew a crude FE 2. "Let's try to visualise it." I drew a Fokker beneath and behind the Gunbus and dotted lines to the engine. "Well that is the problem. The question is, how to solve it."

When I had left home after my last leave my dad had given me a short pipe. He had been so pleased with his Christmas present that he had a spare which he wanted me to have. "It's a good little smoker and, when you smoke it, it will remind you of home." He had given me some bar tobacco. I had smoked it a couple of times already and, as well as making me think of home it helped me think. I filled the pipe while Billy looked at my drawing.

He took my pencil and said, "Do you mind sir?"

As I puffed I said, "Go ahead."

He drew another FE 2 attacking the Fokker. "Now if we could do that then we would not have a problem."

The pipe was drawing well. The pipe seemed to slow me down but that, in turn, made the brain work better. At least that is what I thought.

"Of course, that wouldn't work. The other Gunbus would have to be flying in the opposite direction."

It suddenly dawned on me. "Not necessarily. Here give me the pencil." I took the paper and drew a circle of aeroplanes. "If we flew in a circle this would work." He looked at my drawing. "When I was in the cavalry we had a manoeuvre we sometimes used. It had a fancy name that I can't remember now but it basically involved the troop riding in a circle and each man firing when they reached the same spot. We were all protected by the man behind. If we flew in a circle we could still move forwards but just a little slower. The gunner in the front could fire on any German which attacked another."

Billy pounced on the paper. "It wouldn't be a flat circle it would be like a spiral so that the vulnerable aeroplane; the one on the bottom would only be there briefly and another Gunbus would come up to help him."

"Damned good idea!"

We must have been making a noise for Ted and Gordy came in. "Are you two ladies having a party in here and if so why weren't we invited?"

Lieutenant Campbell proffered the sheet of paper. "Bill has just come up with a way of eliminating the blind spot. Look."

"Actually lads, we both came up with it."

Billy nodded his thanks and explained to the two of them how it worked. They looked at it and I said, "Well?"

"It will work but I don't think his lordship will wear it."

Ted's comment deflated us. "You may be right but the four of us know about it and if we are jumped then we can try it. The beauty of it is that the system works as long as you have at least four aeroplanes. More would be better but it gives us more of a chance and we might avoid ending up like Johnny Holt in a ploughed field."

They nodded their agreement. Gordy put his right hand out, "We'll be the four who watch each other's backs."

We all put our hands together and a bond was formed that night in the lamp lit tent. When I went to sleep later that night I felt much better. I no longer felt alone. The camaraderie of the cavalry was back; hopefully it would not end in the same slaughter as that experience had.

There were only four aeroplanes ready to fly the next day and as luck would have it those four were ours. We were ordered to patrol the front line and prevent enemy aeroplanes from observing our lines or attacking our field. Perhaps they had the same damage as we had because, disappointingly, no German aeroplanes appeared and we had no opportunity to try our new idea out.

The major had been noticeable by his absence and we almost had a normal squadron life. By the end of the week, when the eight aeroplanes we had were serviceable, all of that changed. The two pilots without aeroplanes were sent back to England to collect their new Gunbuses and to bring back the two replacement pilots. The rest of us, including our observers, were gathered in the large mess tent.

"There is going to be a big push in about a month or so." We all looked at each other. There had been rumours running around the squadron for the last few weeks. "Quiet down! You sound like a bunch of excited school girls." We were all suitably chastened and looked at his board again. "Our task is to prevent the German reconnaissance aeroplanes from observing the movements behind our lines. We have been given twenty miles of the front to cover."

Captain Marshall marked on the map where the sector was.

"Your route will be a square. You are not to cross no-man's land and you are not to initiate combat. If German aeroplanes attempt to cross our front lines then you can engage but I want to make it quite clear, gentlemen, that you will not take your aeroplanes to attack the Germans on their side of the front." As he was staring at the three of us, 'the old sergeants', we knew that he meant us in particular. "We have the chance to build a great squadron but we need well trained pilots who gain the right sort of aerial combat experience. Not just lucky pot shots. Be patient gentlemen."

I rolled my eyes at Gordy as we left. Words were immaterial. He was having another dig at us and attempting a rousing speech for the troops. He failed in both. The lieutenants did not look inspired and we were now immune to his criticisms.

Johnny Holt walked with me to the aircraft. "I say, I am to fly next to you. I feel safer already, Bill."

Since I had watched over him when he had crash landed he had become my semi-permanent shadow. He was immensely grateful for what he saw as a lifesaving intervention by me. He had made too much of it. It was what soldiers had always done; watch out for their comrades.

"Don't worry Johnny. You will find it much easier today. The first combat is always the hardest. If you see any Germans just make sure they can't get in your blind spot. How is your sergeant?"

"Oh, he is a good sort. Still he is not as good as Sergeant Sharp but I have high hopes for Bert."

I wagged a finger in his face. "Now do not let the major hear you being so familiar with the staff!"

He laughed but added, in a quiet voice, "You know when I joined the squadron I was so excited to be serving with the major. During training, he was terrific. He was kind and understanding but out here… well he has changed."

I nodded. "It does that to a man. Now you have to learn to be a combat pilot and that is totally different from training."

"I know but you are next to me and you are the leading ace in the squadron."

It was the first time I had heard the term although the newspapers were filled with the idea of someone who could shoot down enemy aeroplanes. The papers were full of praise for Major Lanoe Hawker who had shot down or destroyed more than seven aeroplanes. "Don't let the major hear you say that. He would not be happy. Now fly safe Johnny."

We took off. Once we reached the correct altitude I heard Sharp say, "I managed to acquire some extra magazines sir. They are just behind my seat. The balance should be fine but let me know if you need them moving."

"Righto." Sharp had put them in the best place. We did not want them at the front, even though they would have afforded some protection from a head on attack.

We had been flying for half an hour when he pointed towards the German lines. What do you think they are up to sir?"

I saw where he pointed and there were two aeroplanes; an Aviatik and a Fokker. They appeared to be flying lazy circles about fifty feet above the German lines. "I have no idea Charlie unless they are doing what we are doing and watching for us."

"No sir, I think that they would be higher." I liked that in Charlie he was a thinker and not afraid to contradict me.

Just them we heard the unmistakable chatter of a German machine gun. There, just five miles away was Johnny Holt and he was being attacked by a Fokker which had come from the west! The young pilot headed east.

"The bastards! It is a trap Charlie. They are driving Mister Holt towards the other two. They will be able to rake him when he flies over them." There was a heartbeat when I considered obeying orders. "Let's go and help him!"

"Yes sir!"

I heard the delight in Sharp's voice. I began to climb. I needed the extra speed that the dive would give me. Johnny was doing his best to avoid the monoplane which followed him. He climbed, he dived and he banked but the Fokker kept after him like a sheep dog. No matter which way Johnny attempted to go he was forced further and further east and the two waiting vultures.

"Charlie, I want you to fire as soon as we are in range. We have spare ammo and I can fire the rear Lewis while you change magazines."

"Sir!"

If I could fire then Holt might realise I was coming to his aid and turn towards me. It was a race against time and we were losing. Before Sharp was in range the two waiting aeroplanes had opened fire from below. I saw Holt's gunner throw his arms in the air and then slump forward. Bert would fly no more. The Lieutenant took evasive action by heading south; away from us. He could not have seen us. As we were the last two in the patrol we were both heading away from friends and any help that might bring.

Suddenly Charlie opened fire. He did not hit the Fokker but made the pilot turn. I had noticed that they had a tendency to yaw and this one did just that. It meant that he was no longer firing at Holt. Unfortunately, the other two aeroplanes had done the damage and smoke was coming from the FE 2's engine. I wondered why he did not head back to our lines when I saw his tail. The rudder had been shredded by the Fokker. He could not turn even if he wanted to.

Sharp had fitted a new magazine and this time he did strike the Fokker which peeled away towards the east. I dived down on to the other two aeroplanes. I saw Sharp fire at the remaining Fokker and I fired at the Aviatik. They were both slower aeroplanes and, as they tried to turn to bring their guns to bear on us it allowed Holt to open a lead. The bad news was that he was heading into German territory but he might survive.

"Let's see how brave our German friends are. Hold on Charlie I am going straight for them."

As soon as I dived towards them I rendered both of their guns useless. They could not bring them to bear. The German ground troops were afraid to fire in case they hit their own aeroplanes. The two Germans split up to avoid being struck by my bus. I screamed over the lines at no more than twenty feet. Had we had a bomb or even a grenade then Sharp could have caused some damage. As it was I was just desperate to escape. The evasive action by the two Germans and my superior speed meant that it would take them some time to catch me. They would have to turn and gain altitude.

I began to climb and follow Johnny. He was easy to spot with a plume of smoke coming from his engine. He was going down.

"Charlie, I am going after him. When I land... if I can land then you keep watch with the Lee Enfield."

"Sir." There was a pause, "I knew I should have bought that German phrase book."

I could see that the damage to the Gunbus would make landing difficult. In addition, my young comrade would have little choice in his landing zone. He would have to put it down where he could and not where he wanted. I, at least, was undamaged and could choose my spot.

He was getting lower and lower. There were no hedgerows in this part of Belgium which was a saving grace. There were, however, drainage ditches running along the fields and the roads. I watched, in horror, as his FE 2 suddenly lurched alarmingly. He fought to bring it under control. He almost managed it but the tip of the wing caught and he cart wheeled, again. There was a cloud of dust and smoke and the aeroplane disappeared from view. There was a road running parallel with the field and I dropped down as soon as I could. The road was slightly bumpy but was infinitely smoother than a field. Our narrow undercarriage meant we could manage to avoid the ditches. In the distance, I could see my two pursuers. They were about three miles away. We would not have much time. I saw Holt hanging from the cockpit.

"Charlie, change of plan. Leap out and grab Mr Holt, I think the gunner is dead. Take the Very pistol. I will turn the bus around. Bring him back and then fire the aeroplane."

"Yes sir!"

I slowed the aeroplane down and Sharp leapt out. I slowly turned us around using the side of the field, which was mercifully hard, and the cobbled road. The two Germans were getting closer. I could see them in the distance but the position of their guns meant that they would find it hard to fire while we were on the ground. I quickly changed my magazine and then watched as Sharp manhandled the young lieutenant from the cockpit. When Sharp began to carry him back I knew that he was still alive.

The German aeroplanes were less than a mile away. I cocked the Lewis. As I did there was an almighty crump as the Very flare ignited the fuel spilled from the downed craft. It distracted the two German pilots and I took advantage spraying each aeroplane with a short burst as they flew towards us. I must have hit both aeroplanes for they veered away. Sergeant Sharp dumped the injured pilot in the front cockpit and then scrambled on board.

He began passing me the magazines he had stored behind his seat. "We'll be nose heavy with these, sir. They will help the balance."

He was right, of course. I began to gun the motor but the two Germans were already banking to come around again. They were trying to get on both sides of me where their machine guns would have a cross fire. "Hold tight Charlie!"

The speaking tube was not working and I would have to shout now to pass instructions to Charlie. I gunned the engine to maximum revs. If it had been the old la Rhone engine we would never have got off the ground but the Rolls Royce Eagle was a powerful beast and the nose gradually came up. I saw Sergeant Sharp struggling to fire the Lewis at the Aviatik which was flying almost alongside us. The Fokker could not bring his gun to bear yet and so I banked towards the Aviatik. My manoeuvre took the pilot by surprise and Sharp's burst struck his engine. It began to cough and falter. I immediately banked to port. To my horror the Fokker had banked to starboard. For one horrible moment, I thought that we were going to collide but, more by luck than anything else, I lifted my nose as he lowered his. He had the presence of mind to fire a burst at us and I felt the undercarriage shudder. He had hit us.

I used all the power I had to take us as far away from the two Germans as it was possible to get. We had suffered damage and we were overloaded. The odds did not look good. Once again, I began to climb. There would be ground fire ahead and I needed the height to avoid them. I also needed the speed I would gain from that height. When I reach two thousand feet I glanced astern. The Fokker had a game pilot aboard. He was trying to catch me even though we were faster at this altitude. He was still following me but he was now three miles adrift. He would not catch me unless we were hit by ground fire.

I was desperate to know how Lieutenant Holt was but this was neither the time nor the place for conversation. That would have to wait. The puffs of shell fire around us told me when we were over the German lines and I breathed a sigh of relief when it stopped. I was almost back in friendly territory.

The field looked huge and welcoming after landing on the tiny road. I remembered being hit and so I shouted, "Brace yourselves. This could be rough!"

Rough is an understatement. The undercarriage had been so badly damaged that as soon as we touched down it sheared. If it had not been for the nose wheel we would have done a cartwheel but it held long enough for the fuselage to slither and slew across the grassy airfield. The random thought crossed my mind that the ground crew would not be happy with the scar I would leave on the ground. Eventually we stopped.

I heard Charlie give a little cheer and kiss the front of the cockpit. I was aware of a large number of people waiting for us. A crowd of people raced over with hosepipes and medical equipment. I saw the doctor and his orderly as they helped the lieutenant from the cockpit and then Ted and Gordy helped me down.

As I clambered down I caught sight of the major and Sergeant Shield with two armed airmen. I wondered why they had their guns. I was about to say something about using one of my nine lives to Gordy when I heard the major roar angrily, "Arrest that officer immediately. Lieutenant Harsker, I did warn you, now you will have your court martial!"

Chapter 6

To say I was stunned would be an understatement. I had just saved a brother officer's life and I was now under arrest. I now understood why he had brought armed soldiers and Sergeant Shield; his pet guard dog and spy. They had surrounded me in an instant. Gordy and Ted began to protest.

"Sir, you cannot be serious!"

"Consider your position before you say another word, gentlemen. I will happily put you both in the same cell as the prisoner."

I almost laughed as the cell would be a tent. "Leave it lads, let the little man have his moment of pleasure."

The watching gunners and airmen began smiling as the major went bright red with rage. He spluttered, "You are making it worse for yourself! You, you, ex-sergeant!"

At that many of those watching did laugh including two of my erstwhile guards. I found I was enjoying this. "How am I making it worse? Will you arrest me twice and court martial me twice?" I turned to the airmen guarding me, "Well then boys, let's get on with it!"

"I give the orders!"

"Well give them then, I have had a hard day." I smiled, "I take it I will not need to write a report tonight?"

"Take him away!" His voice was so high that only dogs heard part of it.

One of the airmen said, "Er where to sir?"

"His tent, you imbecile!"

That made it even more laughable. When I reached my tent I said, "Thank you for the escort boys. I feel much safer with you to protect me."

"The prisoner will refrain from speaking with his guards, sir!"

"Really, Sergeant Shield and in which part of King's Regulations is that sentence to be found?"

His silence was eloquent. I had been taught well by my mentor in the cavalry, Sergeant Armstrong. The guard dog did not know the regulations; he just cherry picked them. I took off my flying gear and lay back on my cot. What a day! I could not have expected it would end this way but I knew that I would not change one of my actions. In a way, it was a relief. The major had constantly threatened me with a court martial. I was just pleased that it was for something worthwhile. I hoped that Lieutenant Holt would recover. In all the commotion, I had not had time to ask after him.

I heard the guards talking outside until Sergeant Shield roared, "You are on duty. If you speak again you will be on a fizzer!"

There was silence as, I assumed, he walked away. I heard one of the guards say quietly, "Pompous prick!"

Then there was silence. I knew that the rest of the officers would be in the mess. I closed my eyes and enjoyed the peace. I must have fallen asleep for the next thing I knew Captain Marshall and Gordy were standing over me. It was dark and they had a lamp and a tray of food.

Gordy laughed, "How you can sleep at a time like this is beyond me. Here we brought you some food and the Captain here will take you through the procedure of the court martial." He suddenly became serious. "It looks bad, Bill."

I swung my legs over the edge of the bed and took the tray. I looked up at the captain. "Well go on, sir, while the condemned man eats a hearty meal."

I could see that the cooks had gone out of their way to make the meal as hearty and appetising as they could. I doubted that Sergeant Shield and the major would approve.

The Captain sat on my camp stool while Gordy sat on the bed. "Let's get the charges out of the way. Firstly, that you wilfully disobeyed orders, by leaving your allotted patrol, secondly that you wilfully disobeyed orders by flying over the enemy lines and engaging German aeroplanes which were not attacking you and thirdly," he sighed, "that you went to the aid of Lieutenant Holt landing your aeroplane behind enemy lines and jeopardising yourself, your gunner and your aeroplane."

I continued to chew. Gordy said, "Well? Aren't you going to say anything?"

"What can I say? I am guilty. I did all of those things and I disobeyed standing orders. As for the wilfully… well I am not sure what that actually means."

They looked at each other. Gordy laughed, "What did I tell you?"

Captain Marshall shook his head, "The major has convened a court martial. He and two other majors from other squadrons will be on the panel. They will be chosen by the major. Lieutenant Hewitt, here, will defend you."

I slapped Gordy on the back, "That is excellent."

"The fact that I haven't the first idea what to do is irrelevant. I will have to muddle through."

"And who is the prosecutor?"

The captain looked uncomfortable. "Me."

"Oh."

"I tried to get out of it but the major insisted that we need a more senior officer than one of the lieutenants."

"Don't apologise sir. At least I know I will get a fair trial from you."

"That you will, Bill." There was real sincerity in his voice. I knew he meant it. "The thing of it is that I can no longer speak with you. There is only Gordy here allowed to communicate with you." He shook his head, "In case you influence the witnesses." He shook my hand. "Good luck, Bill."

After he had gone I put my tray on the floor and took out my pipe. Gordy lit one cigarette from the butt of his earlier one. "If the major is on the panel then he will influence the others. It is pretty much a lost cause."

"Don't say that, Bill."

"No, I don't mind. This will expose the major for what he is. I will be punished but I don't think that General Henderson and the other senior officers will want this to continue."

"You may be right but," he took a deep drag on his cigarette, "I think the major is going for a firing squad. It is war time and it can be used. So, you see we don't want you punished. We need you found innocent."

"Oh." I hadn't thought that he could ask for such a punishment. "Is the firing squad a likely outcome? I know it is war time and the death penalty is possible but…"

He shrugged, "I genuinely do not know and neither does the captain. This is new territory for both of us. We will have to bring as many character witnesses as we can. I will bring up your war record. That has to count for something. Your time in the cavalry will help as will the number of aeroplanes you have destroyed. Saving Lieutenant Holt's life has to count for something too. The worst part of this is that we don't know who the other two majors will be. It is highly likely that he will pick his friends so that, no matter what we do, no matter how good your defence will be, it will still end up with you being found guilty."

"You just do the best you can. When is the trial?"

"The day after tomorrow."

"Then let's get started on the defence now."

As we prepared my defence I discovered that Lieutenant Holt was not badly injured but he was upset that I had been placed in such a position by my action. His pleas had been ignored by the major who had successfully alienated all of the younger pilots. He had made me the hero and him the villain by his actions. However, if I was found guilty, that would avail me nought.

We had suffered another three damaged aeroplanes that day. The Germans were being slightly more strategic than we were. They were well thought out ambushes. Given that the aeroplanes they used were inferior to ours they had used their minds to defeat us.

We were both methodical thinkers and we went through each incident on that day one by one. We could not get beyond the disobeyed orders and so we decided to attack all of the standing orders which had been introduced by the major. I was exhausted when he left and I could get to my bed properly.

When Gordy brought me my breakfast he was quite excited. "You will never believe it but for once Ted has come up with a good idea which is not negative. He went through all the losses in the squadron since the major arrived and compared them with the days when the colonel wrote the orders. We have lost far more aeroplanes and men since the major took over. It is startling. If we attack the standing orders then we might have a chance."

"Define a chance."

"It might mean a lesser punishment."

I suppose when the alternative is the death penalty then a less charge isn't so bad. The trouble is I did not think I had done anything wrong and, apparently, neither did the rest of the squadron. I was saddened that the colonel's son had been wounded but his absence almost amounted to dereliction of duty. Men had died and been wounded and most of it was down to his absence. We worked until late in the night. Both of us were exhausted by the time we had finished.

"However, it turns out Gordy I want you to know that you are the best friend a man could have and you could not have done more for me."

He shook my hand, "Don't be daft. We both know it could have been me. It was only a matter of time. He had it in for all three of us. Ted told us that when we arrived. I am just sorry that it was you."

"Now you are being daft. I am a single man and you have Mary. It is better this way." I hesitated. "Listen if they find me guilty and, you know, the worst comes to the worst; will they do it straight away or wait a day or so?"

He looked shocked. "It won't come to that."

"But if it does? Let's plan. The thing is I need to write a letter to mum and dad. It would be a better letter if I knew what the outcome was. But if they are going to, you know, shoot me immediately after the court martial then I had better write one now."

"Now you are being daft. They will not shoot you. Get that into your head. Now get a good night's sleep."

A good night's sleep would not come. I tried to write a letter but there were too many unknowns. If this was the last letter that they would receive from me then it had to be right. John and Tom had not written before they had been killed. It was vital that I did so; if only to explain why I had been shot. I would write the letter after the court martial. I would write one even if they took me out to shoot me right away. This was too important to me. Sleep must have come for Gordy woke me the next day before reveille. I was not certain that he had slept much from the bags around the eyes and the smell of stale cigarettes.

"Right Bill, let's have a good breakfast and then put on your number ones. We have to look smart. Wear your cavalry sword. You never know one of the other officers could be a cavalryman too."

When we were quite ready I stood before Gordy. He nodded, "You'll do."

The guard outside said, "They are about ready Lieutenant Harsker. Two staff cars have just pulled up." There was a pause. "It wouldn't do to keep them waiting eh sir."

I stepped out and the sun was shining. It was a beautiful morning. The Flight Sergeant in charge of the detail snapped, "Attention." Two airmen stood behind me and two in front. The sergeant stood next to me and said, out of the corner of his mouth, "Sorry about all this sir. But don't worry it will turn our all right." Then he snapped, "Prisoner and escort, quick march!"

As we entered the mess tent I noticed there were airmen seated outside. I saw Lieutenant Holt and Sergeant Sharp amongst them. They would be the witnesses. Once again, I was thankful that it was Captain Marshall who was prosecuting. He would be fair.

Inside the tent there were four tables. Sergeant Shield sat at one with a sheaf of papers in his hand. He glanced up as we entered and grinned maliciously. There was a long table with three seats behind it. In front of it was a single chair and then there were two tables facing it. Gordy took us to a small table with two seats. Captain Marshall smiled as we passed him reading his papers placed before him on the desk.

Suddenly Sergeant Shield shot to his feet and shouted, "General Court Martial, attention!"

I watched as Major St. John Hamilton-Grant strode in. Behind him was a taller officer I did not recognise. However, he had the same look on his face as the major and my eyes dropped to the desk. It was as we had feared and Major St. John Hamilton-Grant had ensured that it was men like him who would judge my fate. I was aware of Gordy sitting and I joined him.

I heard the major's voice. It seemed to be coming from far away. I knew I should have written the letter to my parents explaining what I had really done and not what the newspapers would say.

"Would you read the charges, Captain Marshall?"

As the Captain went through the list I wondered if I would be able to begin the letter now. I was about to turn and ask Gordy for some paper when the major said, "How do you plead Lieutenant Harsker?"

Gordy nudged me to rise. I did so and brought my gaze up. The words, "Not guilty," were just coming from my lips when I saw the third member of the panel of officers. It was Major Burscough. Although his expression was as serious as the others I convinced myself that I had seen hope in his eyes.

"You may sit. The other two members of the panel who will make judgement toady are Major Burscough and Major Stuart." They both nodded when their names were mentioned. "Captain Marshall, you may proceed and we can get this over with." Major Burscough shot an irritated glance at Major St. John Hamilton-Grant. He had not liked the comment.

"The prosecution calls its first witness, Flight Sergeant Charles Sharp."

Charlie came in and was asked the predictable questions about the events of the day in question. I could see Charlie trying to make it seem as though I was really obeying orders but Captain Marshall stuck to his task. At the end of his testimony it was quite obvious that I had disobeyed orders and the court martial could have ended there.

Gordy stood. "Sergeant Sharp I just have a couple of questions for you. Did you object to risking your life to rescue Lieutenant Holt?"

Before he could answer, Major St. John Hamilton-Grant snapped, "What difference does that make, Lieutenant Hewitt? He is just a sergeant."

"In which case, his answer will not influence the panel will it sir?" There was no answer and Gordy said softly, "Just answer the question, Sharp."

"Of course not sir. It is our duty to help our comrades. I am just sorry we could not save his gunner Bert."

"A sentiment we all agree with. Now a final couple of questions for you and then you may leave. You have served with Lieutenant Harsker since you arrived in Belgium?"

"Yes sir."

"You have served in this squadron then all that time?"

"Yes sir."

"Tell me then Sergeant Sharp, if this had happened say, during the Second Battle of Ypres, would Lieutenant Harsker be on trial here."

Major St. John Hamilton-Grant almost exploded, "Captain Marshall, are you not going to object to this line of questioning?"

"I can't see the harm sir. It does not change the facts that Lieutenant Harsker disobeyed standing orders, your orders."

"Answer the question Sharp."

"Of course not sir."

"And why not?"

"The standing orders. The new ones stopped us from being airmen."

"Thank you, Sharp, no further questions."

"You are dismissed Sergeant. Lieutenant Holt."

As Charlie walked by he winked at me. It seemed to make me feel better for the three majors all had stony and cold faces.

Lieutenant Holt had a bandage around his head and his arm was in a sling. Captain Marshall stood and asked, "Would you like to tell us what happened on the day in question; the day you received these injuries we can see."

"Sir we were patrolling the front as ordered. We had been told to stop any German aeroplanes observing movements behind our lines."

Even as he was saying this I knew that it had been rehearsed. "I was the last aeroplane in the line and Lieutenant Harsker was on my port side. A Fokker E1 had managed to come from behind our lines and he attacked me in my blind spot below the engine. I took hits from him and I was forced to fly over no-man's land. Two other aircraft were waiting for me. They attacked from the German side. That was when Bert, my sergeant was hit. I was forced to fly south. Lieutenant Harsker discouraged the first Fokker and then took on the other two. My bus was losing power and I looked for somewhere to land. The German ground fire and the fact that my rudder had been shot out meant I had to go behind their lines. There was no chance of landing in No-Man's Land. The engine lost power and I tried to land. The wing caught and I blacked out. When I came to the doctor was watching over me and I was back at the airfield; here."

"So, let me make it quite clear, Lieutenant. Lieutenant Harsker deliberately attacked those three German aeroplanes in direct disobedience of his orders."

"Yes sir."

"He deliberately landed behind enemy lines, again in direct disobedience of the standing orders, to bring you back."

"Yes sir, although as I was unconscious I was not aware of that fact until later."

"Thank you, no further questions."

Gordy stood and walked over to the chair with Lieutenant Holt. "I have only one question for you Lieutenant. Did you disobey orders when you flew over enemy lines?"

Before he could answer Major St. John Hamilton-Grant shouted, "The Lieutenant is not on trial here!"

"Allow him to answer please, I would be interested." Major Burscough's voice sounded so calm after the rants of Major St. John Hamilton-Grant.

"Answer the question Lieutenant."

"Yes sir, technically I did. I did not want to disobey orders but with a Fokker on your tail and two others trying to ambush you, you have little choice in the matter."

"But Lieutenant Harsker did have a choice did he not?"

I saw the look of incredulity on Holt's face and the look of triumph on Major St. John Hamilton-Grant's. It looked as though Gordy was doing the prosecution's job for him.

Gordy said softly, "Answer please, Lieutenant Holt. You know the old saying, '*speak the truth and shame the devil*'." As he said it he glanced at Major St. John Hamilton-Grant.

Johnny nodded, "Yes sir. He had a choice. He could have left me to my fate."

Silence descended on the court. "And what would that fate have been?"

"I would be dead along with Bert."

The silence as Lieutenant Holt finished his evidence was eloquent. After he had been dismissed Gordy turned to Captain Marshall. "Sir, are your other witnesses going to be saying the same thing, that Lieutenant Harsker disobeyed orders?"

I saw Captain Marshall's lips move in a slight smile as he said, "Yes, Lieutenant Hewitt."

"Then I think we can accommodate Major St. John Hamilton-Grant's wishes and bring this to a speedy conclusion by admitting that Lieutenant Harsker disobeyed orders and put him on the stand."

He glanced at the panel. Major St. John Hamilton-Grant snapped, "Anything to get this damned trial over with quickly and judgement passed."

"Lieutenant Harsker, would you take the stand. I only have a few questions for you to answer." I sat and looked at the wall of the tent. I could only see Captain Marshall and Gordy. It felt strange. The panel was behind me.

"Did you deliberately disobey Major St. John Hamilton-Grant's orders?"

"Yes sir."

"Why?"

"Firstly, they were stupid orders." I heard the intake of breath behind me, "and secondly I am a soldier and it is a soldier's duty to save the lives of his fellows if he can."

"Even if that means disobeying orders and risking your own life?"

"It is what soldiers do."

"Would you do it again?"

"Without a second thought."

"Even though you now the result would be this court martial?"

"Yes sir."

"Did you disobey orders before this occasion?"

This was the gamble. "Yes, I did."

"Why? You knew it was wrong and would incur the major's displeasure."

"Each time my disobedience stopped us losing men and aeroplanes it was necessary. It was the standing orders which were wrong."

I heard Major St. John Hamilton-Grant almost explode, "I am not on trial here either. Strike the record of those comments Sergeant Shield."

Gordy was facing me now and I saw the ghost of a smile. The major had reacted the way we had predicted. "In that case would it please the court to hear how the previous standing orders worked?"

Major St. John Hamilton-Grant snorted, "I do not see the relevance. I now command this squadron."

Then I heard Lord Burscough, "Temporarily, Major, yes Lieutenant Hewitt I would like to hear."

"Go ahead Lieutenant Harsker."

"We operated in flights of three aeroplanes. It was the colonel's idea. Major Hyde-White led one and three lieutenants led the others. The orders were to fly together and to protect each other."

"And did you?"

I waited for a heartbeat, "I lost neither a pilot nor an aeroplane during that time."

"Whereas now...?"

"Whereas now, we have lost a large number of pilots, gunners and aeroplanes. We are down to less than half strength."

"I have heard enough. Captain Marshall, sum up for the prosecution. You may resume your seat Lieutenant Harsker."

As I took my seat I was certain that Major St. John Hamilton-Grant had not followed procedure and it was confirmed when I looked at the three of them. Lord Burscough and Major Stuart both had frowned heads together talking. As he sat down Gordy said quietly, "That went better than I hoped."

Captain Marshall stood and addressed the court. "There is no doubt that Lieutenant Harsker disobeyed orders. By his own admission this was not the first time and appears to me to show a flagrant disregard for the authority of Major St. John Hamilton-Grant." Although the major nodded I realised that the captain was trying to mitigate the charges and help me. "Lieutenant Hewitt has made a valiant defence but I am afraid that the fact which will determine the outcome of this court martial is that Lieutenant Harsker deliberately and knowingly disobeyed his commanding officer's orders."

"Lieutenant Hewitt."

"Captain Marshall is correct; Bill, here, is guilty of disobeying the major's orders." We had calculated that the use of my first name would annoy Major St. John Hamilton-Grant but make me seem more human to the other two. "However, he was acting in the spirit of the squadron. This squadron is one of the most successful squadrons on the Western Front and if we find Lieutenant Harsker guilty then the squadron might as well disband for all esprit de corps will be lost. We should not punish the lieutenant, we should reward him."

He sat down and I whispered, "No matter what the outcome that was well done, Gordy."

Major St. John Hamilton-Grant glared at us and he coughed before he stood. "Before we briefly deliberate on the outcome of this trial I would like to make a couple of comments." He looked at Sergeant Shield and nodded. His flunky had pen poised, "for the official record. My duty is to the Royal Flying Corps. I have tried to turn this shambles of a squadron into something which will reflect the skills of its pilots. I had much to do when I arrived and Lieutenant Harsker is typical of the obstacles put in my way. The sooner he leaves this squadron the sooner I can turn it from a pathetic shambolic republic run by an officer who should have been pensioned off into a…"

I could not see but I heard someone enter the tent behind me. The three majors all stood to attention; as did Sergeant Shield.

Then I heard Colonel Pemberton-Smythe's voice and I leapt to my feet. "Do carry on major, you were saying something about a shambles of a squadron and a commanding officer who should have been pensioned off. Do carry on and ignore me."

Everyone sat down and Major St. John Hamilton-Grant stammered, "Well I think we had better debate the issue. The prisoner can be…."

I had not heard Major Stuart speak before; he was a Scot. "I think we can make our discussion public major. I don't think anyone wants things done behind closed doors," he smiled, "or tent flaps for that matter."

"Well if you insist. I think he is guilty."

I watched as Lord Burscough looked him in the eye and said, firmly "And I know that he is innocent."

When Major Stuart looked over Lord Burscough's shoulder at Major Hamilton-Grant and began to speak my old captain never took his eyes from the now red faced major.

"And I agree with Lieutenant Hewitt. This young officer should be promoted and not punished. I have never heard such a ridiculous set of standing orders in my life. It is a miracle more pilots weren't lost." He pointed at Gordy and me, "And that is probably down to the likes of these fellows."

Major St. John Hamilton-Grant looked stunned. I heard the Colonel's voice from behind me. "Well major are you going to pronounce the verdict or not?"

He spoke through gritted teeth. "This court martial finds the defendant. Lieutenant Bill Harsker, not guilty."

There was a pause and then an enormous cheer erupted from around the tent. The colonel walked towards me, his hand outstretched, "I believe the whole squadron approves of the verdict. Well done, Bill. I am proud of you."

Then he walked beyond me and said to Major Hamilton-Grant. "Could I have a quiet word with you major?"

"Certainly, colonel but you must understand I was acting not only in the best interests of the Corps but also the squadron. Lieutenant Harsker…"

The rest of the conversation was drowned out by the voices of my friends.

Chapter 7

Captain Marshall and Gordy both pumped my hand. Major Burscough and Major Stuart came towards me with arms outstretched. Lord Burscough waggled a finger at me, "I told you that you should have come with me, didn't I?"

Major Stuart shook my hand and said, "Any time you fancy flying Bristols you can transfer to my squadron laddie. You have what it takes." He gestured over his shoulder with his thumb, "You have five kills already and yon fellow wants to court martial you! Unbelievable."

Suddenly we heard Major St. John Hamilton-Grant's voice raised in anger. "But sir I must protest! You cannot ask me to transfer. This was a travesty today. My methods will work. I am sure that when I speak with General Henderson he will see it my way. You must reconsider."

"Reconsider? After the way you mistreated my squadron and spoke of it in such disparaging terms? I think not. I expect you," he shot a dismissive glance at Sergeant Shield, "and any of those who owe their loyalty to you to be off the base by evening."

Major St. John Hamilton-Grant saw us looking. "I wonder which one of those traitors dragged you back here!"

The colonel smiled and proffered a letter, "Actually it was none of those men. All of them are men of honour. It was General Henderson who begged me to return from my son's bedside. He was alarmed by the fall in efficiency of this squadron since you took over. It went from the most efficient to the one with the highest losses. And bearing in mind the squadron has the only aeroplane which can match the Germans that is quite a remarkable achievement."

His shoulders slumped in defeat the major left.

The colonel turned to us. "I need to see the two majors and Captain Marshall. I think you two chaps need to go and show yourselves outside. I think the squadron would like to express their feelings."

When we left the mess tent it seems the whole squadron was gathered outside in the late June sunshine. The first one to greet me was Lieutenant Holt. "I could not have borne it had you been found guilty. I am delighted that you have been exonerated."

"Don't get carried away, Johnny, I was found not guilty but it will still be on my service record that I had a court martial. If I intended to have any sort of career then that would be the end of that."

His face fell, "Oh I say."

"Let's just celebrate. Come on Bill, Ted will be in the officers' mess opening a few bottles."

"I have to see Sergeant Sharp first."

I had seen Charlie Sharp hovering behind the officers. I strode over to him. "Thanks for what you said Charlie and I am sorry for nearly getting you killed."

He laughed, "Killed I can live with but I cannot break in another officer. You'll do for me sir." He gestured with his thumb towards the airfield. "I can get back to rebuilding the old girl now sir. You enjoy your party."

There was a party atmosphere. Everyone knew that the major had gone. I suppose when the colonel arrived they all knew what we, inside the tent, did not. There would be a sea change. There were just the eight officers in the mess but the noise we made seemed to make it appear like more. Ted had acquired some beer. Not enough for us to get roaring drunk but just enough to make us feel happy. I was pumped for information about my flight to rescue Johnny. The facts given at the court martial were dry and they wanted to know everything.

We got on to the relative attributes of the German and British aeroplanes. Gordy was on fine form, "Bill has proved that, if we act together we can dominate the skies. The Aviatik is slow and is really a reconnaissance aeroplane with a rear gun. The Fokker is a better bus and has a forward firing machine gun but it is hard for their pilots to fly the bus and fire the gun. Our only weakness is getting attacked from the rear."

There was raucous and lewd laughter at the double entendre.

"He's right. As soon as they try to make an extreme manoeuvre the Fokker becomes more unstable and yaws like mad. Our bus is not as good at looping and banking but it is stable, it is powerful and it is faster; especially at higher altitude."

The looks on their faces told me that they did not know that. I should have realised. They had followed the major's orders to the letter and that meant staying at a specific altitude. "Yes, once you get higher you can get up to ten miles per hour more. As we are faster than they are anyway it means you can get away from them."

Johnny swallowed off the last of his beer. "Yes, but they are sneaky bastards. That was a cunning ambush. If Bill hadn't been alert I would have been a goner." That was an excuse for more cheering and patting me on the back.

In the middle of it Captain Marshall appeared. "I say chaps, try to keep it down a bit. You are all behaving like fifth formers at the end of the summer term. The colonel sent me to fill you in on the future of this squadron. Major Stuart has a Captain Leach who is ready to be promoted to Major. He will be transferring here and Lieutenant Campbell will be going the other way."

Billy looked crestfallen. The captain said, "Take it as a compliment. He wanted Bill here and you were the next best choice so well done. Besides you are promoted to First Lieutenant so it is not all bad."

His face brightened at the compliment.

"The standing orders are now defunct." This time the cheer was deafening. "The old ones will be reinstated. The three flight lieutenants will resume their duties and tomorrow Lieutenants Thomas and Hewitt will take their sections to patrol the front." He smiled at the applause. "We are now back to normal and I for one am glad. Now then Ted, where is my beer. All that talking this morning has made me drier than Wales on a Sunday!"

I left after the next beer. I was still in my number ones and I needed to feel comfortable. I also had a letter to write but, before I did that, I needed to speak with Major Burscough. As I was walking to my tent I saw a staff car pull out. It was driven by Flight Sergeant McNeil. He was another of the major's spies. I had never liked him either. Sergeant Shield was next to him and in the back, was Major St. John Hamilton-Grant. The major's eyes swivelled in my direction and I knew that I had made an enemy for life. That was it, all of the bad apples picked out of the barrel. We could begin afresh. I glanced over to the field. We would be starting over with just six serviceable aeroplanes. There were another two, possibly three which might fly again and the rest were only good as spares. It would be a rebuilding job.

I changed and then began to head up my letter. I had much to say to my family. I had just dated it when I heard Captain Marshall's voice, "This is his tent sir. I'm sure he will be in."

The flap opened and Lord Burscough stood there. "Thank you, Randolph. I'll see you before I leave." As the flap closed he shook my hand again, "You had me worried when I was summoned to the court martial. Of course, when I read the charges I realised how ridiculous they were." He shook his head. "We are in great danger of losing this war because of the incompetents who are running things!"

"It all ended well though sir."

"It did indeed and you are one of the top pilots in the RFC. You have come a long way." He leaned in and said, quietly, "I shouldn't be telling you this but the colonel has put you in for a V.C."

I was astounded. This was the highest honour in the British Army. "I was just doing my job sir." I paused, "You wouldn't have left a man behind the lines would you sir?"

"No but the damned fool orders put you both in an impossible position. If you ever get a command Bill then use your mind. Some men just use a rule book. Anyway, I must be off. Keep doing what you are doing. People think highly of you."

After he had gone I wrote the letter to my family. Had he criticised me in any way, shape or form, then I would have written it differently. As it was I was able to tell the truth and let them know, no matter what they might hear from others, that I had done nothing wrong. And now I could get back to flying- when Sharp had rebuilt my aeroplane.

There seemed to be a bounce in everyone's step the next day. It seemed as though a cloud had been lifted. Ironically, we all seemed to work harder than under the beady eye of the martinet Major Hamilton-Grant. The new pilots, gunners, mechanics and aeroplanes began to arrive. Gordy and Ted had easy patrols and were able to bed in their new flights well. I was looking forward to my first patrol.

Lieutenant Holt had begged Captain Marshall to be in my flight and he agreed. The third member was Lieutenant Carrick. He was a fresh-faced boy from Scotland. He had the bare minimum hours in an

Avro trainer and none at all in a Gunbus. Holt was a veteran by comparison.

When the new Major arrived, I sought him out immediately. Not only because I wanted to start on a good footing but also because I wanted to ask a favour. I liked Archie from the first moment he spoke. He was a genial officer and much younger than any other Major I had met.

"I have heard that you are a pilot with a killer instinct Lieutenant Harsker."

"I think I have had more luck than many other pilots."

"They say a good pilot makes his own luck. Now I know that you are a man who comes to the point, the Captain told me so what would you like to ask me?"

"Am I so transparent? Lieutenant Carrick is as green as grass. Not only that, he has not been up in a Gunbus. They require different skills from an Avro trainer."

"Quite right. We fly Bristols. I think I might struggle with a pusher."

"I'd like to take him on one flight as a gunner. If he understands the problems of a gunner then he will be a better pilot."

"You were a gunner once weren't you?"

"Yes sir and it stood me in good stead."

"I think it is a good idea but it will mean just you and young Holt on patrol. How will that be?"

"I know the sector well I will find a milk run."

"Good. Let me know how it all goes."

When I found the lieutenant, he was busy in conversation with Johnny. They both stood to attention when I reached them. "Come on chaps, I am the same rank as you."

Johnny grinned, "No sir, you are the Flight commander. This is Freddy."

"Pleased to meet you Freddy. I understand you haven't flown a Gunbus?"

"No sir."

"As an aeroplane, they are stable and fast but, because you have a gunner in the front, they need a different flying technique. Isn't that right Lieutenant Holt?"

"It is indeed sir."

"Can you fire a Lewis gun?"

"Of course, sir."

"Good then before we let you loose as a pilot you can be my gunner and give Sergeant Sharp a day off. Johnny, you will watch my tail."

Holt grinned, "Yes sir!" Poor Freddy looked terrified. "Don't worry Freddy, you will learn a great deal the lieutenant is a cracking pilot."

Of course, Sharp was less than happy with the arrangement but he saluted, said, "Yes sir," and then took the new lieutenant through the speaking tube, the Lewis gun, the Lee Enfield and the Very flares.

When he had finished he nodded and I said, "I don't expect you to spin the prop but you will need to know how to do that too." He nodded. "Now get on board." I turned to Lieutenant Holt whose aeroplane was next to mine. "We'll head over the German lines. Fly at two thousand feet and keep a watch for the Huns. They have been a little quiet in the last few days."

As we bobbled along the airfield I heard Freddy say. "I say sir, you are damned close to the ground up here and there is no engine in front of you."

I laughed as I lifted the nose. "Just wait until you fire that Lewis behind you!"

He glanced over his shoulder. "Surely you are joking sir."

"No, Carrick, you have to stand, brace yourself on your seat and hang on for dear life." I allowed that to sink in. "Now do you see why I am giving you a little trip as a gunner?"

"Yes sir."

Perhaps because I had a passenger, and Carrick was all of that, I was more alert and I saw the three Fokker monoplanes as they climbed towards us.

"Carrick, cock your Lewis and keep your eye on those three Germans."

"I can't see them." I leaned forward, tapped him on the head and then pointed to the little black crosses in the distance.

I waggled my wings to get Johnny's attention and then made the signal for return to the field. He nodded and I saw him looking ahead. His gunner pointed. He had seen the Germans too. That was the difference a couple of months at the front made. You saw things quicker. The Fokkers would never catch us. I began a lazy bank around and then saw that the Germans had laid a trap for us. Five hundred feet below us and climbing were three Aviatiks. They began to bank to follow the same course we were taking. Their three machine guns would converge on me. I pointed down urgently. I hoped that Johnny would see.

"Right Freddy we are going to have a crash course in aerial combat. I am going to dive towards those three Germans below. Do not fire until I order you to and then only a short burst. You will not have time to change magazines. Got it?"

"Yes sir."

The one advantage we did have was speed. Diving from altitude meant that, if we passed the Germans they could never catch us before we reached home. I cocked the rear Lewis. I could see that there would be a point of convergence. I decided to aim the bus between the first and second Germans. The fact that they were firing close to one of their own might make them make an error.

Their bullets began to fly up at us. They were missing. "Ignore the bullets. Just aim at the gunner in the first aeroplane. You'll be fine."

I heard a, "Yes sir." But he did not sound confident.

We began to take hits but luckily, they were on the wing. We were a hundred and fifty feet away. "Now Freddy! Short burst! Stop! Short burst! Stop!"

"Sir the gun has jammed!"

"Clear it and keep your head down." I fired a short burst from my gun. We were so close that I could hardly miss and I saw the gunner throw his arms up. I banked left, across the second aeroplane. I could hear Johnny's Lewis rattling behind me.

"It's clear sir."

"Good watch for the next target." As we swooped over our lines I saw the Tommies firing their rifles at the Germans. I lifted the nose and glanced behind me. I saw that the three Aviatiks had turned tail and joined the three Fokkers. The trap had nearly worked.

"Well done Freddy."

I heard the noise of my new pilot being sick. Poor Sergeant Sharp would be even less happy now.

We landed safely enough. Lieutenant Carrick looked white. "Sorry about that sir."

"Don't worry Freddy. This was you first combat and that is a frightening place to be. Believe me I know."

Sergeant Sharp wandered over. "I see you took a few hits sir."

"Yes Sergeant, more work for you."

Lieutenant Carrick said, "Sorry Flight but I was ill in the cockpit."

Sharp leaned over and nodded, "Don't you worry sir. I have come close to that a couple of times. The first time up I hurled over the side." He shook his head, "I can't wonder what the Germans thought when that lot fell on their heads. It will clean up. Leave this to me sir."

As we strolled over to the mess I noticed that Johnny Holt gave us the space and time to talk. "That sergeant of yours seems like a good egg sir."

"He is. That is why I let you fly in that position. You can see that you are a team. You have to trust each other." I turned and pointed to the bus; Sharp had already emptied the front cockpit to facilitate cleaning. "When I was a gunner one of the pilots I flew with did a loop while I was standing on the cockpit and firing behind us."

"How did you stay on?"

"Luck, I think. The point is that when I became a pilot I made sure that if Sharp there was standing then I did slow and gentle manoeuvres. It means we get hit more but we are also more likely to get back down in one piece."

We reached the mess. It was almost empty. The other officers were either flying or making sure that their aeroplane was ready to fly the next day. We picked up a mug of tea each. Johnny wandered in and I waved him over.

"That was close eh, sir?"

"This is the second time they have tried that ambush."

Freddy, whose colour had a returned, looked puzzled. Johnny explained with a cup and a sugar bowl. "The Gunbus is a good aeroplane but it has one weakness; the Germans can come up behind the engine, underneath us and we can't see them. As we fly faster than they do they have to catch us unawares. We don't expect them to come from our lines."

"And that is the puzzle we have to solve and soon." I gratefully sipped the hot sweet tea. "Now when we fly Freddy you will be between Johnny and me. Johnny here is a good wingman and will watch your tail. You watch mine. Imagine it like a game at school; follow my leader. Whatever I do then you do. You will have a new gunner and you will need to tell him to fire in short bursts and not shoot my tail off."

We drank in silence for a while and then Lieutenant Carrick said, "Sir, how do you fire the rear Lewis and fly at the same time?"

"We do not do that very often. The rear Lewis is handy if we are attacked from above and behind. Luckily the Germans find it hard to do that. The Aviatik only has a gun at the rear and the Fokker's gun is aligned above the propeller. They can make mincemeat of you if they are below you but a Fokker above you is, largely, impotent."

Johnny drained his tea. "There must be a way to protect our blind spot."

I remembered the conversation with Gordy, Ted and Billy. "Lieutenant Campbell and I came up with an idea." I placed the three empty cups in a circle. "We would fly in a circle so that we each protected the rear of the others. It would mean that we would progress slower as we would be circling but, at a pinch, it might save us."

"Has anyone tried it yet sir?"

"No Freddy. If we have to use it you will know because I will fly in a circle around to Johnny's tail. It is the same principle, follow my leader."

I went to see Captain Marshall and the colonel. I explained about the ambushes. "You see sir, they have someone over there who is trying to use the poorer aeroplanes they have to wrest the advantage from us. I think we played into their hands before because we were single aeroplanes. They were using five or six to one to guarantee a kill. It would be a war of attrition and they would wear us down."

"This could still happen though, Bill. Even with a flight of three of our aeroplanes they would outnumber by two to one. And they still have the advantage."

"The point is, Captain Marshall, that the worry that Bill, here, has is that they are coming from behind our lines. How?"

I had been thinking of the problem. "Unless they have an airfield behind our lines, and I have ruled that out, then they must be coming over early."

"Wouldn't the ground troops hear them?"

"Not if they flew high. Then they could turn and drop to a much lower altitude and watch for us."

"And that means that they must be waiting somewhere close to the airfield."

The colonel stood and examined the map. "Then tomorrow we will try to trap those Germans ourselves. Captain Marshall I want an officers' briefing before dinner tonight."

We took off before dawn. We had two lines of mechanics lining the field with hand held oil lamps to mark the runway. We risked the German aeroplanes seeing the lights but we had not devised a better way to take off in the dark as yet. Major Leach's flight had not taken off with the rest of us. They would be the bait. The three flights headed west. We did not fly high; we had no need to. We flew with a four-mile gap between us. We would wait well behind our own lines. I was given the southern sector as I had the least experienced flight. We assumed it would be Gordy's flight in the middle who would engage the enemy.

We watched the sun rise before us and the glorious July morning showed us an empty sky. There was nothing. We flew a box pattern at a thousand feet. Below us we could see in the distance the men in the trenches coming to life. Tendrils of smoke from fires trickled into the air. We saw movement along the communication trenches. But of the Germans we saw nothing. Then I heard Sharp's voice. "There, sir, to the north. It looks like Lieutenant Hewitt has spotted them."

I looked where he pointed. I could see the Fokkers fleeing east, hotly pursued by Gordy and his flight. They were heading towards the south east. "Let's see if we can cut them off then."

I waved my arm and headed due east. We had superior speed, height and the Fokkers were flying into our flight path. They seemed unaware of our presence as they jinked around the skies trying to out fly the Gunbus. They did have the advantage of more manoeuvrability. That only worked so long as they were not hit. I saw the bullets from Gordy's gunner strike the tail of one of the Fokkers which was forced to peel off north. The third aeroplane in Gordy's flight swooped on to its tail.

We were now over the German lines and their soldiers were trying to help their aircraft by firing their rifles at us. We were in more danger than Gordy because we were still some way from the Fokkers. We were, however, gaining hand over fist. They seemed to be drawn towards us.

"Whenever you are ready Charlie, have a pop."

"Sir!"

When the Lewis opened fire, it seemed unnaturally loud. The bullets flew over the cockpit of the first Fokker. The second took evasive action and headed north east. I glanced to my left and saw Gordy peeling off after him. We kept on after our victim. He tried every trick in the book. He rose and then dived, he flicked left and then right. He even tried to bank right and that was his undoing. Johnny's gunner gave him a burst and I saw pieces fly from the tail of the Fokker. Never the most stable of aeroplanes it began to yaw and pitch. That made it a more difficult target. Sharp gave another burst but the bullets flew over the top of the Fokker as it pitched, alarmingly, towards the ground. It was hard to predict where it would turn next.

Suddenly it flew in front of Freddy's aeroplane and his gunner stitched a neat line along the fuselage. The pilot tried to bank and turn away but, as he did so, he brought his aeroplane directly into Sharp's sights. He emptied the magazine. The tail disintegrated and the aeroplane began to spin towards the ground. The brave pilot could not have survived the impact, the concussion of which threw us into the air.

I waved us back home. The flight had their first Fokker. I was pleased. They had both followed orders and kept their heads. I doubted that the Hun would try that trick again. However, as we headed home, I was under no illusions: they would come up with something else. They had inventive minds.

Chapter 8

Gordy accounted for a second Fokker and the third had limped lamely home. It meant that July and August proved to be quiet months. The Hun appeared to have had enough in our part of the front. Holt and Carrick became well bedded in and gained a great deal of confidence from the success of their one combat and our success as observers.

In those first two weeks in September we ruled the skies. As we later discovered that was not necessarily true across the whole of the Western Front but for us, in our sector, it was. The Germans just used anti-aircraft fire to discourage us as we observed for the artillery and bombed the roads leading to the front. Now that we were freed from the shackles of Major Hamilton-Grant's orders we could fly to our target at a higher altitude and give mutual support. We did suffer damage; the German gunners became more accurate. We did not, however, lose any aeroplanes and that was important.

During the last week in August I was summoned to the adjutant's office. The Colonel, Major Leach and Captain Marshall were all there. "We have just had the letter back from the War Office, Lieutenant Harsker. I am afraid that they have turned down your V.C. I am sorry. I think it was that unfortunate court martial which coloured their judgement."

I shook my head. "You can't miss what you never had and besides I think the ones who receive that honour are far braver than I was."

The Colonel shook his head, "Your modesty does you great credit sir. However, what is in my remit is to promote deserving officers. Congratulations, Captain Harsker."

I was stunned. The Major and Captain Marshall shook my hand and said, "Well done."

"I don't know what to say."

"You say nothing." Captain Marshall handed me the extra pip. We had all gained our second pip when we had become Flight Commanders but this was something entirely different.

I left the tent, stunned. Gordy and Ted were just leaving the officers' mess and, seeing my face, assumed it was bad news.

"What's up Bill?"

"Bad news?"

I forced a smile, "No, just the opposite. I have been promoted to captain."

There was a second while they took the news in and then they snapped a salute, "Sir, yes sir!"

"Now don't you two start."

They laughed, "No, Bill, we are pleased for you and when you get that V.C..."

"No, Gordy, they turned me down. The court martial."

"That bastard, Hamilton-Grant. Even though he has gone he is still messing things up for us. Well never mind. We'll have to celebrate. The next pass we get we'll take a car into Boulogne and have a jolly boys' outing."

I brightened. That would be an excellent idea. With no activity on our front the colonel gave permission for the three of us to have a two-day pass. Major Leach was happy to be left with all the younger pilots; he had heard of our idea for a defensive circle and was keen to practise the manoeuvre while the front was so quiet. We borrowed the colonel's car, a Lanchester, which purred along beautifully. I was given the honour of driving, of course. Sergeant Sharp was philosophical about having to remain behind. "Well sir. I thought that I could try to make the front a little more bullet proof. It feels awfully exposed up there."

I did not envy him his task. He had to use a lightweight material which would stop, or slow down a bullet. Unless he had an alchemy set I did not think he would succeed. I was just happy that he was thinking about improving our machine. Up in the air it was the only thing between us and certain death.

As we boodled along the quiet roads of northern France it was hard to imagine that there was a war on. While Belgium and the Franco German border was a muddy morass of trenches barbed wire and machine guns, here, in the Pas de Calais, all was peace and calm. I gestured with my arm. "It is hard to believe that just less than a year ago I was riding across this very land with the Lancashire Yeomanry."

"You had a real war before you ever got in the air. Do you miss those days?"

"I miss the fact that when you went into a fight your comrades were so close you could speak to them but I do not miss the slaughter. The back of a horse is no place to be when someone is machine gunning you."

There was silence until Gordy asked, "Do you think we can win this war?"

"And I thought I was the pessimist. Of course, we can win this war."

"No Ted, you miss my point. I mean can anyone win this war? No matter how good we are in the air, and, let's face it, we have the Germans beaten in the air at the moment; the war is stuck in the trenches. We have seen the infantry trying to walk their way across the mud. All you need is a few dozen machine guns and no infantry in the world can cross No-Man's Land. That means German or British or French. We could be here for years."

I laughed, "Ted is right you have switched bodies overnight. I have to believe that we will win. Our cause is right. It was the Germans and the Austrians who started this war. They were the ones who invaded Belgium. The Belgian army was a joke. They couldn't have withstood an attack by a Yeomanry battalion let alone regulars. The Germans saw it as an easy way to get into France by the back door. Our mistake was not flanking them early in the war and now we are stuck here. But we will win. We have an Empire. There are Australian and Canadian squadrons ready to fight. India is sending thousands of men. The problem is the Germans look to be making it a war of attrition and we will win but only because we are the last man standing. I fear we will go home to a land without those lads we grew up with."

Gordy had deflated us like a barrage balloon punctured by .303. However, when we saw the sea ahead we brightened. Our French was not perfect but it mattered not a jot. There were so many English troops passing through that most people spoke English or at least understood us. We acquired rooms at a pleasant hotel up in the town. It afforded a view of the castle and the port. It suited us. We had money to burn and did not question the prices.

Our mood really improved when we walked along the front and saw the sea lapping on the beach. We could just make out the coast of England. It was our home. It was where our families lived. We were stopping the Germans from hurting our homes and destroying the land as had been done in Belgium. That was good enough. It was a reminder of why we were fighting.

The brisk stroll down the beach gave us an appetite and we found a bar with a couple of tables outside. This was something we would never have done in England but, here, it seemed appropriate somehow. We ordered beer and moules frites. It was as near to fish and chips as we could get. The steaming mountain of mussels seemed daunting at first but we made short work of them. Mopping up the garlicky juices with the baguette made us think that we were miles away from any war. Another two icy beers later and we were relaxed. We could have been three gents on holiday before the war. As I sipped the beer I had no idea how the owner kept it so cold. I suspected a deep dark cellar.

"You know lads," Ted leaned back as he smoked his cigarette, "the war has done one thing for us. It has broadened our horizons. I mean if the war hadn't come along would we be here; in France drinking beer and eating moules frites?"

I tapped my pipe out and began to clean it, "You are right. I would have made Blackpool for a couple of days if I was lucky. The rest of the time I would have been on the estate."

"Can we go back to that?"

Gordy had taken me aback. None of us had thought beyond the war. Could I go back to saying yes sir no sir three bags full sir? I was used to giving orders. I loved horses but I could not do what my dad did. What the hell could I do? What would any of us do? It made me think about the future for the first time in a long time.

Just then we heard the noise of soldiers coming down the street. I glanced over my shoulder and saw that there were about ten young men strolling and playing around as they promenaded. They were being loud and the officer in me frowned. Then I turned back to my beer and my pipe. I was in grave danger of becoming Major Hamilton-Grant.

I heard a voice as they closed with us. "Watch out lads some officers ahead."

"I don't give a bugger! I am on leave and I don't have to yes sir to them."

He was wrong of course; in the British Army, you could dress a donkey in a uniform and if it was of higher rank then you saluted it. More importantly I recognised the voice. I stood and turned as they came near our table.

"Attention!"

They were all well trained and they snapped smartly to attention. I saw the bemused look on the faces of Ted and Gordy. I winked. I turned and glared, "Who is the one with the mouth?"

They all looked at one young private who was trying to hide beneath the peak of his cap. His head came up slowly, "Me sir I... Bill!"

My brother Bert threw his arms around me to the astonishment of his fellows. I smiled, "At ease lads I am, Bert's brother. I was just having fun with you."

The relief on their faces was palpable. They seemed to see our uniforms for the first time. One of them said, "You are pilots?"

Even as I was nodding another said, "You are the one who shot down all those German planes. You are a hero!"

I sat down and laughed, "I don't think so. Would you lads care to join us?" I said that as the owner had come out to see what the fuss was all about.

Bert said, "There don't look to be enough chairs Bill."

I turned to the owner. "More tables and chairs and beer for the boys." I held out the money.

He smiled and took the notes, "Of course sir."

Bert took a chair from a nearby table and sat down. "This is my little brother Bert of the Royal Engineers and this is Gordy and Ted, two of the officers from my squadron."

He suddenly saw my extra pip. "You have been promoted! Well done, our Bill." I saw that the hero worship was still there and it explained the comments of his comrades.

Gordy asked, "Where are you stationed, Bert?"

Bert pointed north, "We are in a holding camp north of here, sir. We go up the line tomorrow."

"It's Gordy, son. You are our mate's little brother. Where are you off to then?"

He looked around furtively, "We aren't supposed to say."

Ted laughed, "I bet if I asked the owner here he would know."

Just then the owner came out with the foaming beers. "Where are these lads off to tomorrow then?"

He grinned, "Brebis, not far from Lens and Loos!"

Bert looked dumfounded. "There, I told you."

Bert grinned and began drinking his beer. "Go steady with that little brother."

Gordy said, "If he is old enough to fight he is old enough to drink."

"Oh, we don't fight. We dig holes and we tunnel."

It was my turn to be dumfounded. "I thought you were a driver or a mechanic?"

He shrugged as he took out a cigarette, "So did I but they decided I was small enough to tunnel and I would still be able to drive the lorry with the equipment."

I looked at my little brother who had grown up overnight. He was in the army, smoking and drinking yet, to me, he was still the little lad who followed me around at home. He had a more confident look about him and was assured. His mates all shouted cheers when their beers were brought and Bert acknowledged it as though he had paid.

Gordy and Ted allowed the two of us to fill each other in on our lives since we had joined up. Inevitably we spoke of home. During one of the silences I heard Gordy telling Ted of his plans for him and Mary once the war had ended. Now I understood his pessimism. He wanted a life with Mary so badly that it had changed his outlook on life. I hoped it would not cloud his judgement once we were up in the air. Aerial combat was not a forgiving environment.

One of Bert's mates shouted, "Eh up, Bert we best be getting back. T'sargeant major'll have our bollocks if we are late."

Bert stood and shook my hand. "I'm right glad to have seen you, our Bill. And I am proud of you too." He shook his head, "A captain no less."

His mate who had chivvied them to return said, "Aye, you're alright for officers."

Gordy laughed, "Well thank you for that; you cheeky little bugger."

They trooped off towards their camp. I noticed that the afternoon had worn on. "Come on you two, let's see a bit of this place. We'll be back at the airfield the day after tomorrow."

We made the most of our two days. We ate well. We drank well. We bought knick knacks for home. We bought wine for the mess tent and we bought some fine leather coats for the aeroplanes. I had a good one but it was showing the signs of wear and tear. If we were going to fly at altitude then I wanted to be warm. I also took the opportunity of buying some good tobacco. The tobacconist happily allowed me to try a few new blends I had not smoked before. I found one I really liked and that I was certain dad would like. I bought a few ounces for me and had a quarter of a pound sent to the Burscough estate; our Sarah would see that dad got it. It would be a pleasant surprise.

By the time we were heading back to the airfield my pockets were almost empty but the colonel's car was filled with our purchases and none of us regretted a single item. We had seen how swiftly death could come. It was better to live for the moment and worry about the bills later on. I did reflect that I would have to find out how much more pay I would be getting as captain. I was not mercenary, but it would be nice to know.

We had only been away for two days but things had happened which had major implications for us. As soon as we had returned the colonel's car we were summoned to an emergency briefing.

The colonel nodded as we entered; we were the last. "A timely return gentlemen for I have some serious news to impart. I have just returned from a briefing of all squadron commanders. It is, indeed, fortunate that we have only had one patrol out and that involved the whole squadron. It seems that the Hun has managed to fit the Fokker Eindecker with a machine gun which fires through the propeller."

He sat down. There was little point in trying to talk over the hubbub of noise from the younger officers. We three sat and said nothing. Talk would not defeat such a fearsome weapon. Eventually the colonel stood after Major Leach had attained silence throughout the tent.

"They are flying in Jastas and pouncing on any aeroplane flying alone. This has been going on for a week. The squadrons who lost pilots and aeroplanes put it down to bad luck but one pilot managed to land his badly damaged aeroplane and told his commander of the problem."

He smiled. "It seems I reinstated the flight system just in time. However, in light of this situation I believe that we just divide the squadron into two. Major Leach will lead one half and Captain Harsker the other. We will have to hope that our six aeroplanes can stop the rot."

One of the younger pilots, Lieutenant Lightfoot asked, "Sir what difference does it make? I mean they had a machine gun before."

Major Leach looked at the colonel who nodded. He stood. "You are correct Mr Lightfoot. However, the gun was mounted on the wing and aimed above the propeller. Now whatever the pilot sees he can hit. He aims his monoplane and he is aiming his gun. He moves his aeroplane he moves his gun and he only needs one hand to do so. In addition, he will remain seated too. We all know how difficult it can be to stand and fire the Lewis. He does not have that problem." He scanned the room. "We are all lucky here. In my last squadron, we had Bristols and they had a gun on the top wing. At least our gunners are in a good position to counter the attack."

Ted stood, "Yes sir but this also means that our blind spot is an even greater weakness. They can just aim their Fokkers at our engines and fire until they have no bullets left. We have no answer to that; even with six aeroplanes and twelve machine guns."

For once Ted had not been the pessimist. He had been the realist.

The colonel stood. "Gentleman the other news I have to give you is that we are about to start an attack at Loos. This squadron will be supporting that attack. Tomorrow we will see just how effective these

Fokkers with the new machine guns are. Get a good night's sleep; you will need it."

As we walked back to our tent Gordy said, "Loos, isn't that where young Bert and his mates were headed?"

I nodded. As soon as I had heard the name my heart had sunk. I wondered now just what tunnelling engineers did, apart from tunnel obviously. How close did they get to the enemy? Would they be under fire? I had never heard of the unit until Bert had mentioned. However, I now had different issues. I had Gordy and his flight under my command and I had to make decisions.

"Gordy, do you think your lads could manage the defensive circle we talked about a while ago?"

"I had forgotten that. Major Leach said he was going to practise it so they should have an idea."

"We may need to use that sooner rather than later. My lads are happy about using it. They will just follow me."

"In that case I will follow your number three and tell my men to follow my tail. How will we know that you are using the formation?"

"Actually, Johnny Holt pointed out that if I was flying in circles they would have to follow me. The trick is going to be to move the circle forward. Anyway, mention it to them tonight and I will see my lads and Sharp now."

The two Beer Boys had found the experience of flying with so many other aeroplanes exciting and frightening for it was very easy to misjudge height and distance. When I told them that we would be flying with Gordy's flight they felt reassured. "At least I will have Lieutenant Hewitt watching my tail."

Sergeant Sharp had come up with a novel way of protecting the front. He had found that the cooks and the Quartermaster were throwing away corrugated cardboard boxes once they had emptied them. He had packed the front of the nacelle with four inches of them. He had opened and flattened Bully Beef tins and put those between the layers of cardboard, and finally he had bound them together with the baling wire they used to keep the ammunition boxes closed. They were all light materials but there was some metal with the cardboard. I thought it was ingenious. "I don't think they will stop a bullet but they might slow it down. It is not heavy and it is cheap."

He had shrugged his shoulders. "It is worth a try."

"It looks like we might need them sooner rather than later. Some bright spark in the German Army has fitted a machine gun which fires through the propeller. The next time an Eindecker comes at you he will be firing at you with nothing in the way."

He shook his head. "I'll just find a few more pieces of cardboard, sir."

I smiled as I went to check the aeroplane. Since Major Hamilton-Grant had gone I felt much more comfortable checking my own aeroplane. I trusted Sharp and the mechanics but I felt better knowing I had given it the once over too.

Chapter 9

Our patrol was in an area we did not know well. It was only fifteen miles or so southwest of our airfield but Loos was in France and we had only patrolled Belgium hitherto. As I taxied I realised that the pilots we had fought before had known us. The fact that they had kept to their sides of the lines meant that they feared us a little. The pilots we would be facing over Loos knew nothing of us but they did know that they had an aeroplane which could fire through the propeller. That would make them confident. When Gordy had asked me could we win the war I had not thought of this outcome. A gun which could fire through a propeller could win the war for Germany.

I forced myself to concentrate. Our task was to stop fighters attacking the Avro 504 reconnaissance aeroplanes which would be spotting for the artillery. The Avro was unarmed but could keep station for a long time. The observer could transmit information to the gunners on the ground without worrying about firing a gun. But they were vulnerable to an attack of any type.

Major Leach had decided that we would fly south to north over the battlefield and keep five hundred feet above the Avros. It gave us the advantage of height and kept a kind of umbrella over our comrades. It was good to be ordered around by a flier once more.

When we saw the shells begin to land behind the German lines I warned Charlie to be on his toes. We were the lead aeroplane and we would see the enemy first. The Fokkers did not let us down. A whole Jasta fell upon the Avros which flew west as fast as they could; they had heard of this new Fokker and did not wish to be fodder. They were a slow aeroplane and two Avros were hit almost immediately. The major and his flight were closer to the stricken aeroplanes and they dived in to attack. Three Fokkers went after the Avros while the other nine climbed to engage the major and his aeroplanes. The Germans would be attacking from below. They had the advantage.

I had my first decision to make. Did I attack the Fokkers chasing the Avros or help my squadron? I chose my squadron but, in hindsight, that was the wrong decision.

I peeled off towards the Fokkers. They had not seen us and that gave us an edge; they had no observer and, largely, looked forward. I felt the shudder from the Gunbuses as the Fokker's machine guns tore into the aircraft. Major Leach's gunner died instantly and he was damaged badly. I watched as he began to glide towards our lines. The next two suffered almost the same fate. One exploded in the air while the other began to pour smoke and spiralled down to the ground. Ted and his flight were on their own.

"Charlie, fire when you think that you can hit something."

Charlie was a good shot. He might hit something when other gunners might miss. His gun crackled away and I saw the bullets strike the tail of one Fokker. At the same time Ted and his flight opened fire with all of their six guns. Ted must have prepared his men for this eventuality. Miraculously they hit a Fokker which began to limp away east with a smoking engine. It somehow gave us all heart. Gordy and his flight had moved slightly right of me so that we had two flights arriving simultaneously.

Gordy had the first confirmed kill. His gunner emptied a whole magazine into the tail of the second Fokker in the line. It began to spin towards the earth. I saw the pilot hurl himself from the aeroplane as it fell to avoid a flaming death. He still died but on his terms.

Sharp emptied his magazine at a second Fokker. Suddenly the neat lines of the two opposing sides disintegrated as it became an aerial melee. Aeroplanes suddenly appeared from every direction. You needed your wits about you to avoid flying into another craft, both German and

British. I was just looking for the black cross and a single wing. I knew that Sharp was reloading and, having already cocked my Lewis, I gave a burst as a Fokker drifted across my sights. I saw the bullets strike the lower part of the fuselage, the pilot shuddered and the aeroplane began to drift slowly east. It was damaged.

I felt Parabellum bullets thump into the engine and the Gunbus suddenly faltered, we had been hit. "We're hit Charlie. I am heading home. Get on the rear Lewis."

I banked left. I hoped that Freddy and Charlie would know why I was leaving and I prayed that they would not follow me. The Fokker which had hit us was on our tail. I felt the bullets as they continued to strike us. This new development was frightening. Then Sergeant Sharp opened fire. Perhaps the Fokker had been over confident and got too close, I do not know but Sharp's bullets struck the engine and parts of it must have flown back and hit the pilot for Sharp suddenly shouted, "Got you, you bastard!"

I was too busy concentrating on keeping the Gunbus steady. The engine was dying. I trimmed the engine to save as much fuel as I could and I began to glide down towards our lines. If the engine cut out then I did not want to fall from a high altitude.

"Come on old girl. Hang on!" I found myself sweating as though in a Turkish bath. The ground was so close I could tell which of the Tommies was close shaven and which had a moustache. When I saw the windsock I almost kissed the dashboard. The engine was coughing and spluttering like an asthmatic but she got us down. As the bus groaned and grumbled to a halt I looked over and saw them lifting the dead body of Major Leach's gunner from his aeroplane. The rest of the squadron was fighting for its life under the command of two First Lieutenants. So much for my promotion.

Archie came over to me. "You came right on cue Bill but these Eindeckers are deadly. You do not even have to be a good shot. You just aim your aeroplane and fire."

We both looked up as we heard the cough and the splutter of a dying engine. It was Johnny Holt. I was pleased that Freddy was on his wing watching him. There was little he could do but I knew that Johnny would be reassured that he was not alone. The undercarriage was sound and the FE 2 rolled along the ground and then the engine died. Freddy taxied next to him.

The two of them walked over to us. Johnny pointed over his shoulder. "One of Lieutenant Thomas' boys, Lieutenant Jones bought it. The rest are coming in now."

I saw them. Gordy had brought them back as low as he dared. It meant that there was no blind spot for the Fokkers to attack but it took great nerve and skill to be able to fly that low. As I expected Ted and Gordy were the last two to land.

I clapped them both on the back as they joined us. "Well done the pair of you. That was a good kill, Gordy."

The major looked at Gordy, "You shot one down?"

"Aye. There were four of them hit and limped off but only one was downed." He shook his head. "The Avros didn't stand a chance and how many did we lose, two?"

"Three."

"A quarter of our force. If this goes on then we last another three days and the Germans will rule the skies."

Gordy's words chilled us. He was correct for another three of our aeroplanes were damaged and this was just the first day of the attack at Loos. We could not afford this number of losses.

"Well chaps we had better report to Captain Marshall and then get our buses ready for tomorrow. I think that we will fly as one squadron tomorrow. What remains of the squadron, at any rate. We will, at least, have protection of numbers."

"Yes sir, but will there be any reconnaissance aeroplanes to spot for the artillery? Those Avros took a beating."

Captain Marshall already had the news. "I have just had Headquarters on to me. They are sending a squadron of BE 2 aeroplanes tomorrow. Our job is to support them." He looked sadly at our unhappy faces. It must have been hard for him to watch us put ourselves in danger and then wait for the results. "It might be easier tomorrow."

Ted stubbed his cigarette out with some force, "And then again, sir, it might be more of the bloody same."

The BE 2 was an old and a slow aeroplane but it did, at least, have a couple of machine guns. The Fokkers might not find it so easy.

Major Leach led us the next day with Ted and his flight following. My flight was given the task of being tail end Charlie. The mechanics and Sharp had performed miracles to get us back in the air. Luckily the damage had just been a damaged oil line and they could be replaced. We joined the eight BE 2 reconnaissance aeroplanes as they headed ponderously towards the battlefield. They were a slow aeroplane and it was hard to fly that slowly.

When we reached the spotting area I was amazed to find it clear of German aeroplanes. Had they thought that they had driven us from the skies? Even as the thought entered my head I dismissed it. The Germans were too efficient to play that game. No, it was more likely that they were waiting to see where we would patrol. That way they would save fuel. The spotters managed to send back their information for fifteen minutes before we saw the unmistakeable cross like profile of the deadly monoplane.

They came low over their own lines and I could see that they had thought this through well. They would be attacking the spotters from beneath and the gunners would find it hard to bring their guns to bear. Even though we were just five hundred feet above them, the climbing Fokkers struck the first of the BE 2. The Parabellum bullet had a steel jacket and they tore through the flimsy biplane. The first one almost disintegrated as it was shredded by the first of the Fokkers. The pilots of the spotters were brave but when three had been hit in the first encounter they began to head west as fast as their ancient engines would take them.

We peeled off to attack them in three lines. We had worked out, the previous night, that we stood the best chance if three of our aeroplanes attacked one of theirs. I dived down, more confident now that Johnny and Freddy would be able to emulate my every move. The Fokker Eindecker I targeted was so focussed on finishing off the BE 2 that he failed to notice us as we dived down and Sergeant Sharp began to pour .303 rounds into his fuselage. He banked away from the danger however the second Fokker began to fire at us. Sharp switched the Lewis to attack the new danger. The profile of an attacking monoplane is much smaller than that of a biplane and Sharp was missing the rapidly moving German. Johnny's gunner came to the rescue. He was firing from the side where the Fokker was a bigger target and, between them, they drove the German away. However, there were more Fokkers and the next two attacked Freddy who was now isolated in the rear. I banked and climbed to go to his rescue. I heard Sharp shout. "Gun's jammed!"

I cocked my Lewis and watched in horror as the two Eindeckers poured bullets into Lieutenant Carrick's craft. His gunner's head disappeared in a bloody mess and smoke began to pour from his engine. A monoplane came into my sights and I emptied the magazine. I had been aiming at the pilot but I struck the engine. I saw the propeller slow and then stop. The aeroplane began to glide back to the east. Had the situation not been so dire I would have followed him down and finished him off but there was a second Fokker. Lieutenant Holt opened fire. His bullets struck the undercarriage. The Fokker wobbled alarmingly and then, it too, headed east.

Freddy waved to show that he was still alive and he headed his stricken bird west. With Johnny watching my tail I turned to seek out other foes. The sky around us was empty. I could see burning aeroplanes on the ground and, to the east and the west there were smoke trails showing where damaged aircraft had departed.

As we approached the airfield I counted the aeroplanes. Unless there was another one behind us we had lost a fourth craft. Rolling along the turf I saw that most of the aeroplanes had suffered damage of one kind or another. I saw two shapes covered by tarpaulin. Freddy's gunner had not been the only casualty.

That evening in the mess the euphoria of my acquittal had dissipated. We had suffered too many deaths in a short space of time. Even older pilots like Gordy and Ted, who had both lost a pilot each were affected. For the younger ones, it was a harsh lesson in flying. A little over a week ago we had ruled the skies and now we flew at our peril. The previous day we had shot down one aeroplane for the loss of three of our own. Today we had shot down none for the loss of two. As we all looked around the mess tent you could see the pilots wondering who would be next. Two or three pilots would die the next day and soon we would be a squadron in name only.

It was with some relief that we were stood down the following day. It was not of our choosing but the attack had been halted while the small gains the infantry had made were consolidated. I wondered if Bert had been involved. I knew nothing about tunnelling and so I had no idea what he would have done in that battle. We spent the next few days repairing our aeroplanes and conducting the regular maintenance. Every day I was grateful for the Rolls Royce engine. I was convinced that it had saved us on more than one occasion.

The colonel returned from a hastily convened meeting of senior officers. Archie let us know the outcome. "We got off lightly. Whole squadrons of the BE 2 were decimated. Even a couple of the FE 2 squadrons were badly handled. It seems we have to patrol now in groups."

Gordy nodded, "Which is what we were doing anyway."

Archie grimaced, "Unfortunately some of the squadrons just used single aeroplanes to patrol. They were able to cover a wider area."

"So, what do we do now?"

"Regroup and wait for the new pilots and gunners. There is no point putting our head in the lion's mouth until we have to eh?"

Sergeant Sharp and I had discovered that his improvised bullet proofing had not been a total failure. We found one spent 9mm shell in the bottom of the nacelle. If it had come through then it would have struck Charlie. The problem was that it made the front cockpit crowded but Charlie was happy with the discomfort.

Chapter 10

We flew again during the first week of October. All twelve aeroplanes were involved. The Germans had been using Aviatik aeroplanes to spot for their artillery in an attempt to retake the small amount of land they had lost near Loos. They were protected by the Eindecker. We were going to prod the lion. It was a nervous bunch of pilots who gathered before dawn on the chilly October morning.

"We will fly together but attack in four flights." Archie nodded towards me, "Captain Harsker now has the most experienced flight. He will be leading the attack." I saw pride and fear in equal measure on the faces of Johnny and Freddy. "They will attack the spotting aeroplanes. I am gambling that they will head for home. The rest of us will take on the Fokkers. We know that they will try to attack from underneath and behind. For that reason, I want Lieutenant Thomas' flight to leave a gap so that they can attack any aeroplanes who attempt that." He picked up his pipe and began to fill it. "Let me make it clear gentlemen, I want all of you to return to the field today. Anyone who does not return will be given a detention!"

We all laughed, before the war Archie had been a school teacher in Scotland. Many of the new pilots were young enough to remember school vividly.

"I say sir, this is quite an honour."

It is Johnny but I know you realise it is also highly dangerous. I have decided, therefore, that when we attack Freddy will lead, you will watch his tail and I will be at the rear."

"But that is the most dangerous place!"

"I know but I have the most experienced gunner. Sergeant Sharp knows how to deal with the Hun in the sun. Anyway, I have made my decision. Make sure your guns are in perfect condition. The last thing we need is a jammed gun and take spare magazines. Good luck." Lieutenant Carrick would have the spare gunner. So far he had had nothing to do but now he would earn his sergeant's pay.

As we did the final check I told Sharp of my plan. "It makes sense sir, just promise me that you will warn mc if you are going to loop the loop!"

The German shells were peppering the British defences as we flew up. It was only when you saw their accuracy that you realised you had to take on this almost suicidal mission for thousands of men's lives were at stake. We were just twenty-four men. In the scheme of things that was a drop in the ocean. Archie had told us that over twenty thousand men had already died at Loos. I had prayed that Bert was not amongst them. Johnny and Freddy had their gunners standing on their cockpits with their rear Lewis gun. This was partly to see me when I gave them the order to attack and partly practice. We were flying straight and level and no one was firing at us. As soon as I waved my arm to attack then they would resume their seats; probably gratefully! Sergeant Sharp had taken them both through the problems and pitfalls of the standing position.

I saw the Aviatiks; there were six of them and they were spread out for a distance of a mile and a half. I signalled. I saw the two gunners wave and then sit down. Lieutenant Carrick swooped down like a bird of prey. He was seen and they began to take evasive action. The first one was too late. Freddy Carrick had had his first kill. Unfortunately, his gunner must have been over excited for he emptied the magazine. I saw Johnny Holt's gunner rake the second bird and smoke began to pour from the engine. It began to limp east. Out of the corner of my eye I saw the black crosses which identified the shape of the Fokkers. They were hurtling towards us like sheep dogs protecting their charges.

Lieutenant Carrick opened fire himself on the third Aviatik. It was a good effort but he failed to knock it from the air. It too made its way east. We were forced to turn and follow them which would bring us on a head to head course with the enemy fighters. Sergeant Sharp saw his chance and his bullets thumped into the side of the fourth Aviatik. I saw the pilot drop and the aeroplane plummeted to the ground.

And then the Fokkers were upon us. Their guns savagely tore into Freddy's aeroplane. The gunner disappeared in a bloody mass. Lieutenant Carrick banked to starboard and his bus was struck again. Lieutenant Holt's gunner came to his rescue and began hitting the Fokker which was forced to turn away. Johnny followed the German around and added his own gun to the fire of his sergeant. It was then I saw a Fokker flying directly at us. I felt his bullets strike the aeroplane. Brave Sergeant Sharp returned fire. I gritted my teeth and kept my bus as level as I could. At the last moment, the German flew over us. The sky before us was suddenly empty save for the fleeing scouts. Major Leach and the others had come to our aid. As I looked around for another enemy I saw that the Fokker which had flown beyond us had done the impossible; it had managed to turn on itself and was now descending on to our tail. It was the manoeuvre which became known as the Immelmann Turn. I do not know if it was Max Immelmann himself who was flying, although Sergeant Sharp later swore that it must have been. At the time, I was too busy taking evasive action.

"Charlie, get on the rear Lewis. He is on our tail. I shall slowly bank right." If we carried on in this direction we would be over enemy lines and I did not wish to become isolated. I felt the bullets as they struck our tail. The rudder became sluggish. Charlie braced himself and then let rip with the Lewis. We had spare magazines now, in my cockpit; this would be our first opportunity to try reloading during a dog fight. We were marginally faster than the Fokker, at the top of its turn the pilot had had to almost stall the aeroplane and his air speed was not as fast as ours. And then we had our first piece of luck. His gun jammed. Charlie's hand came out for a magazine and I handed him a spare. He managed to change it; how I do not know for he needed both hands but he had become quite adept at balancing.

After a long burst he shouted, "He's leaving!"

I looked to my left and saw the pilot wave as he headed east. At times, the combat was almost civilised back in those early days of the war in the air. I had no chance to follow him as my turns were restricted by the damage to my rudder. I waved Sharp back to his seat and slowly turned west. Most aeroplanes were dots in the distance. I could not tell where my wingmen were and I headed west.

Sergeant Sharp reconnected his tubes. "That was a hell of a turn from that Hun sir. He very nearly had us."

"Yes, Charlie, but you very nearly had him too. Well done."

Our day, however, was not over. I saw a Fokker monoplane heading for us. I saw Charlie cock his Lewis. I was grateful that he had not used the full magazine on the last one. We might need both guns.

"Charlie, aim for his engine!"

"Yes sir."

As we hurtled together at a combined speed of almost two hundred miles an hour I readied my Lewis. I would have one chance at this and one chance only. I would need lightning reactions. As with the other Fokker, just before we would have struck he began to climb. He would try the same manoeuvre; I do not know how I knew but I could almost sense it. As I was expecting it I was able to hit him when he was directly in front of me. My bullets must have penetrated his fuselage, his seat and finally his body for the aeroplane flopped around and fell from the sky. I watched as he spiralled to the ground.

I was elated. We had downed one of the vaunted Fokkers. We had been lucky, I knew, but it was a victory. "Well done, Charlie, we got him."

I heard coughing and then Charlie said, "Well done, sir but I think he got me first. Sorry." Then it went silent. His head was slumped to the side. I had to get back as soon as I could. I pushed the stick forward to get as much speed out of the damaged bus as possible. It seemed an age, and yet was only a few minutes when I saw the field ahead.

Other aeroplanes were taxiing and I had to pick my way through them to land. I kept the engine going and headed for the first aid tent. I think they must have known that such an uncharacteristic landing meant I was in trouble for the doctors and orderlies raced out. I shouted. "Sergeant Sharp has been hit!"

They manhandled the inert form and rushed him into the makeshift hospital. I jumped down and ran to the tent. An orderly stopped me. "Sorry Captain. Let the doctor and the lads do their job. You will only get in the way. Go and get a cup of tea eh sir?"

I was about to push my way through to the theatre when I realised he was right. "You are right orderly. Let me know how he is."

"Of course sir and don't worry. Doc Brennan is the best there is."

I saw Ted and Gordy as soon as I entered. Normally they would wave me over to join them but Gordy gestured to the right. I could see Lieutenant Carrick and he was distraught. Lieutenant Holt was reasoning with him. I grabbed a mug of tea and sat on the other side of Freddy.

"Sir, I am a jinx. That is two sergeants who flew as my gunner and they are both dead. Look!" he spread his arms and I could see that his flying coat was covered in blood and parts of his dead sergeant. Even as I stood to help I realised I couldn't remember his name. He had only been with us for the shortest time. "Let's get this off." I undid his bloodied buttons and my mind was taken back to the day when poor

Caesar had been slaughtered. The leather coat was almost like Caesar. I removed the coat and dropped it behind him.

I saw Johnny give a shrug. He knew not what to say. In truth neither did I but I was the Flight Commander and with that rank came responsibility. "Have you had a cup of tea yet?"

"Sergeant Higgins said he was very fond of tea."

"Good then he would want you to drink to his memory." Holt looked shocked at my words but we could not tip toe around what had happened. I spooned three more sugars into the tea and stirred. I put it into his hands. "Here's to Sergeant Higgins." I nodded to Johnny who raised his mug too. Freddy complied and drank the hot sweet liquid. "Lieutenant Carrick you are not a jinx. If anyone is to blame for the sergeant's death it is me. I should have been leading the line but I thought the most dangerous place was at the rear. Well I have learned my lesson and from now on I lead the line. So you see, it is me who should be apologising to Sergeant Higgins and not you."

Freddy stared at me, "You sir? No, sir. It wasn't your fault. But my gunner is dead and it is the second time this has happened in almost as many days."

"Who is the best Flight Sergeant in this squadron?"

Freddy said, "Sergeant Sharp, we all know that."

"Well right now Lieutenant Carrick he is fighting for his life. The last Fokker hit him. Is that my fault?"

"No sir. It was the German who shot him."

"Right. And next time you fly you make damned sure that it is the German who doesn't come back. You are a good pilot Carrick and you have your first kill." I nodded to Holt. "Carry on Holt."

He smiled, "Yes sir. I think I have the words now."

I took my tea and joined Gordy and Ted. I slowly filled and lit my pipe. It allowed my hands to stop shaking. I was not used to having to be a mother and a nurse. "That was a rough one."

Gordy nodded, "We lost another aeroplane and pilot. Lieutenant Grundy."

He had been one of the new ones. "Sharp was hit. He's with the doc."

Their faces fell. Charlie was popular with everyone. He gave advice to other sergeants and was a wonder with the engines. "How bad?"

I drew on the pipe and shook my head, "They took him away as soon as we landed." I banged my hand on the table. Everyone looked around. "Dammit! We need armour plating for the gunners. They are totally exposed there."

Ted shook his head, "It would make the aeroplane too heavy and too slow. It is something we have to live with."

"Or the gunners to die with."

Gordy changed the subject. "Did you see the turn that Hun did?"

Ted nodded, "That was really impressive and frightening. Still now that we have seen it we can prepare for it."

"If there are any of us left alive at the end of this. We have lost seven pilots in a week. We can't go on like this. We can't keep training them."

Gordy drained his tea. "Perhaps we need to do what we did before we started being pilots." Ted and I looked at him. "Train the gunners." He leaned in. "Between the three of us I think that you make a better pilot if you have been a gunner first."

He was right. "I think you have something there. When Charlie… if Charlie recovers I will suggest it to him."

"Don't be so pessimistic. If it was bad they would have told you."

I knew that I would not be good company and I left the mess to wander over by the medical tent. I peered in through the flap. There was a huddle of people around a table and I assumed that would be Charlie. One of the orderlies turned to throw a bloody rag into a bowl. He saw me and spoke to the doctor. The doctor turned and gave me thumbs up. I hoped that meant Sharp would survive. I knew that for a doctor saving a life was all that was important. Would Charlie lose a limb? That would end his career in the RFC and, in all likelihood, in any career after the war was over.

I strolled down to the Gunbus which stood forlornly with the other damaged aeroplanes. If Sharp had not been wounded he would already be working on it. I went to the front. It looked as though moths had been at it. The front was riddled with holes. Sharp was lucky to be alive. I leaned in and saw the blood but I also saw the cardboard. It had done a job of some kind for there were some 9mm shells in the bottom of the cockpit. I saw that some of the bullets had continued on and exited close to my feet. I could have been hit too.

There was little point doing anything and so I went back to my tent to get changed. The change of clothes made me feel cleaner outside if not within. As I came from my tent the medical orderly who had spoken to me earlier strode up to me. "Doc Brennan says Sergeant Sharp will be all right sir. We saved the leg but he will need to go back to Blighty for a bit."

I felt relief surge through me. "Thank you. Can I see him?"

He shook his head, "He's out like a light sir and, if you don't mind me saying, you ought to get your head down too."

"I will and thank you for taking the time to tell me."

He looked at me strangely, "It was no problem, sir and well done for the Fokker today. It's about time we started hitting back."

As I went to the headquarters tent I knew that I had been lucky. It had been an instinctive shot and Lady Luck had been with me. I could just as easily have missed. The monoplane was in front of my gun for the briefest of times. That was why the monoplane had the advantage. The pilot of a Fokker just had to aim his aeroplane.

Captain Marshall was busy filling in reports. He looked up at me expectantly. "Sergeant Sharp will survive but he will need some time in Blighty."

"Excellent. That was a good hit today. It boosted morale."

"It was lucky. They are whittling us down. We need fighters like the Fokker with a mechanism for firing through the propellers."

"I think they have chaps back in England working on it but it will take some time. What we need is to capture an aeroplane and examine it."

I laughed, "We are damned lucky to hit the buggers! Capturing one is a pipe dream."

The colonel came out of the inner tent. "Good news about Sharp. Captain Marshall, we had better get a new gunner, temporary of course, for Captain Harsker."

"I am surprised you get any volunteers to be gunners in a Gunbus. It seems to me that with these new monoplanes and their gun a gunner does not have great odds for survival."

The colonel shook his head. "We have no problem with volunteers. Where is that copy of The Times that the General sent over?"

"Here sir."

Captain Marshall proffered the newspaper to me. "There you are, Bill. Read that and you will see why we have no problems with volunteers."

The newspaper had been folded so that there was one story visible. I began to read.

British Gunner Becomes a Hero

Sergeant William Harsker RFC has shown us all what it takes to defeat the Huns. After bravely serving in the Yeomanry and fighting at the Marne, this plucky farm worker volunteered for the RFC where his skill as an air gunner has resulted in many downed German Aeroplanes.

Newly promoted to Lieutenant and a pilot Lieutenant Harsker has five downed German aeroplanes to his name. He is an inspiration to all

and an example of British pluck
and determination.

I handed the newspaper back. "But why an article about me sir? Gordy and Ted did the same."

"Propaganda dear boy, propaganda. This was written after you were vindicated in the court martial. It was seen as a way of attracting volunteers for the RFC. You are right, they could have chosen anyone but I think your story of having served in another unit was the one they were looking for. The General told me that there are hundreds of men in the infantry and the cavalry volunteering for the RFC. If they have fought over here, like you, then they will be better airmen. So you see, you are making a difference and we will be getting volunteers. A new batch is due any day now. By the time your aeroplane is repaired we will have another gunner for you."

Chapter 11

I went in to see Sergeant Sharp as soon as he was awake. There was a tent of sheets over his damaged leg and he looked pale. He smiled at me when I approached. "I am to be sent home then sir."

"Yes Charlie. You enjoy the rest."

"How is the bus sir?"

"Don't you worry about the aeroplane. She'll be fine. That cardboard looks to have saved both of us."

"Yes sir. The doc reckons another inch either way and I would have lost my leg."

"Is there anything you need?"

"No sir, the other sergeants have sorted my tent out and packed for me. When the new batch of replacements arrive, those invalided out will be sent back in their lorries."

It never ceased to amaze me how caring soldiers could be for their comrades. They might argue, fall out, even fight but when the chips were down they rallied to help each other.

"Well if there is anything you need then just let me know."

"I will do, sir, and I will try to get well as soon as I can. Tell the new chap he is just keeping my seat warm for me."

"Of course!"

I felt a little better when I went to the mess for breakfast. Charlie would not lose his leg and it looked as though he had not lost his nerve either. Captain Marshall had shown the newspaper article to Gordy and

Ted. They could not resist mocking me. As I sat down Gordy nudged Ted. "We are honoured today Ted. We have a real hero with us." He knuckled his forehead and Ted chuckled.

"You can cut that out for a start."

They jumped to their feet grinning and gave me a backwards left-handed salute. "Sir, yes sir!"

The young lieutenants laughed and I shook my head. "I should have known you pair would take the Mickey. I didn't write the bloody thing!"

Gordy smiled and said, "We know and we couldn't resist. It is good for the RFC."

"I told the colonel that the story could have been about any of us."

"No, it couldn't. You served in the first battles. Some people at home think that the RFC is full of people like Major Hamilton-Grant. Your story shows them that anyone can become an officer. It is not like the old days." Gordy was a thinker. If he stayed in the Corps then he could attain a much higher rank.

"Aye well, the replacements arrive today. Will the major be taking a patrol up?"

Ted gestured with his thumb. "He came to see us last night. We are going up a little later than yesterday. He wants the Germans to think that they frightened us off."

Gordy pointed to Johnny and Freddy who were sat by themselves. "Your flight is stood down. I think he wants you to go out tomorrow but I daresay he will tell you himself. It will probably be for the best. Young Carrick was shaken up and you only have one gunner between the three of you."

"Well if you are up today, watch out for that turn."

"I'll tell you something Bill that takes some nerve to almost stall the aeroplane like that."

I too, had thought that. We would all have to become better pilots to counter the German threat. We had ruled the skies and dominated the Germans now we feared them and tiptoed around the clouds.

Sergeant Sharp got a good send off. The sergeants who were on patrol had given those who remained a number of gifts for him. There were cigarettes and tins of sweets as well as letters for him to post in England. It was one way to beat the censor. No one would give any information away but I knew that the men did not like the idea of an officer reading their affectionate letters to loved ones. I suspect they also did not like the idea of their English being judged. The replacements looked at the stretchers as they were loaded and I think they wondered what they were getting into. After the lorries had departed I sought out Lieutenant Holt and Lieutenant Carrick as well as Holt's sergeant.

"We are getting our replacements soon." I saw the nervous look on Freddy's face. It would take a lot of effort to get him through this trauma. Having nearly lost Sharp I felt that I understood him a little better. "We will have no time to train them for Major Leach has told me that we will be patrolling tomorrow."

"Tomorrow sir! Isn't that too soon?" I saw fear on Freddy's face. He had fallen from his mount twice but he had to get up a third time or he would never get back up at all.

"It might be, Lieutenant Carrick, but the war does not stop because we both lose a gunner. We have to get on with it and do our duty."

"Sir." I saw his backbone stiffen. He might make it.

"Sergeant White, you will need to tell the new gunners what to expect. Give them the truth. Show them my aeroplane and Lieutenant Carrick's they might as well see the dangers and then the three of you can repair the two buses. You will have the rest of the mechanics to help you so use them. The major work on the engines has been done. Now it is down to fabric and wood."

"Yes sir."

"Oh and have a look at Sharp's cardboard. It looked to have helped a little although he did find it a little cramped."

"I know sir. He told me about it. It sounded daft but I have seen the front of the aeroplane and something must have saved him."

"Well you cut along to the aeroplanes and we will bring the replacements when they arrive." I turned to the other two. "The colonel knows we have had a rough time lately. All we have to do tomorrow is to discourage the Aviatiks. At the first sign of the monoplanes we run. Until we have worked out how to stop the Fokker we are wary. No heroics. And remember that turn we saw yesterday. It has been created to attack a Gunbus. It brings the monoplane into the perfect position below and behind us."

My new gunner was Airman Hutton. He was a tubby little chap with a wide grin. He saluted cheerfully and said, "Airman Hutton. Me mates call me Lumpy!"

I was intrigued. "Why Lumpy?"

He shrugged, "I have no idea sir but the name has stuck!"

He was a likeable chap, "Welcome Airman. This will only be a temporary posting until Sergeant Sharp recovers from his wounds."

"No problem sir. I just want to do my bit and kick the Hun, sir." He smiled, "I read about you sir, in the Daily Herald. Can I say it is an honour to serve with you? When I write to me mam and dad they will be over the moon."

I detected his accent when he said mam and dad. "Are you from the north east then, Airman Hutton?"

"Aye sir, a little pit village close to Durham. I was in the Engineers, tunnelling but after I read about you I fancied a bit of fresh air."

It is strange the way that fate works. My little brother was in the engineers, tunnelling and this son of a miner was in the RFC. "So you have never flown before?"

"No sir. We were given a course in the Lewis, how to start the engine and so forth but they had no time to get us up." He grinned, "It looks like good fun, sir!"

Lieutenant Carrick had an older gunner. He snapped to attention smartly, "Airman Jack Laithwaite, sir."

He looked to have served before. "And did you join the Corps directly or were you in the services before?"

"Like you, sir, I was in the cavalry." He shook his head, "I didn't like to see the poor animals slaughtered like they were and I transferred."

"I know what you mean. What regiment?"

"The 17th Hussars."

I smiled, "A proper regiment then not like the Yeomanry in which I served."

He had a wise old head on his shoulders. "It didn't seem to make a difference to the machine guns whether you wore a fancy uniform or not, sir."

"Quite right. Well let me take you to the aeroplanes and we can set you to work. We fly in the morning so I am afraid you will not have much time to adjust to life at the front."

Lumpy grinned, "Suits me sir. The sooner we are in the air the sooner I can start shooting down these Germans. You know sir, they shelled Hartlepool and killed women and bairns! It's not right!"

His indignation made me smile. "Right then, Lieutenant Holt, take them to your sergeant eh?"

Left alone with Freddy I said, "I think you have dropped lucky Freddy. Here is a man who has served. I think you will make a good team."

"I hope so sir, I hope so." He looked marginally less fearful than he had been. I prayed for an easy patrol.

I spent the next hour with Captain Marshall going over the maps. The Captain had been adding information from our reports and we had a detailed map now of the front. We also had an idea of where the German airfields were. That was important as it gave us the likely direction from which they would come. The Aviatik had a longer range and their airfields were further away. The closeness of the Fokker fields meant they could reach us quickly.

After we had finished we both lit our pipes. "You know, Randolph I think we ought to have a go at bombing their airfield. We know it hurt us when they destroyed those aeroplanes on the ground."

"Isn't that a risk? Suppose they are waiting?"

"I thought about that. If we attacked after they had patrolled, when they were landing then they would not be fuelled and armed. We could catch them with their trousers down, so to speak."

"Ah so you would use six aeroplanes to keep them occupied and have six in reserve?"

"That's about it. If half the squadron took off forty-five minutes or so after the first half then the combat should be over. They wouldn't have to engage closely just get them to use up their fuel and let them chase our lads back here. We would follow and bomb the field just after they had landed."

He smiled, "From the word 'we' I assume that you would lead?"

I grinned back, "My idea."

"Well I think it is a good one. I will mention to the Colonel and the Major. It would be good to take the initiative. I hate this defensive posture. It does morale no good at all. Speaking of morale, how is Lieutenant Carrick?"

"Tougher than he looks sir. Yesterday was a bad time for him but I think the new gunner will do him the world of good. Just in case I have Johnny keeping an eye on him. He is turning into a good pilot."

"And that reflects well on you, Bill. You have trained them well."

"I just copied Lord Burscough's methods, they seemed to work."

"It is Colonel Burscough now. He has two squadrons under him."

"So he has stopped flying?"

"You know the man; do you think he could sit behind a desk? No, he flies but he has a new Nieuport. A nippy little thing by all accounts."

I was pleased that he had done well for himself. He had been the direct opposite in bearing and character to Major Hamilton-Grant. If every aristocrat was like Major St. John Hamilton-Grant then I think I would become a Socialist!

We watched, at noon, as the squadron limped in. I counted and was relieved to see that there were nine aeroplanes. None had been lost although a couple were trailing smoke and they all had damage to them. I saw the replacements look up from their work as the aeroplanes bumped along the field. Doc Brennan and his orderlies ran from their tent ready to deal with any casualties.

As was to be expected it was the gunners who had been hit. One of the new pilots had lost his gunner while Ted and two others had wounded gunners. I strode to speak with Major Leach. "No losses then sir."

"No, Bill, but they got away Scot free. The Fokkers were above the Aviatiks when we reached them. The biplanes headed east and the Fokkers attacked us." He smiled, "We tried that circle that you and the others came up with. It seemed to work. We took the casualties before we made the circle."

Gordy joined us. He lit a cigarette. "Aye me and Ted have named it the Gay Gordons!"

Archie nodded seriously, "A fine Scottish dance; that'll do for me." He turned to me, "Tomorrow, Bill, it'll be just your flight. I want you to get there early and see if you can frighten them away. Don't engage the Fokkers."

"You want them to think that the rest of the squadron is waiting to pounce like we did the other day."

"Aye, it's not just the Germans who can be sneaky. Of course, it might not work but we canna go on losing aeroplanes at the rate we are. This autumn has been a disaster for the Royal Flying Corps. Apart from Colonel Burscough and us the other squadrons have been torn apart."

I nodded and walked over to my aeroplane. I needed to speak with the gunners. They would have a difficult job and for two of them it would all be new. It would be, quite literally, a baptism of fire.

We left before dawn. I had impressed upon the two pilots that we were not to risk fighting the Fokkers. If we could draw them on to our guns then so much the better but our aim was to drive the spotters away. We flew low and at the slowest speed we could. By dawn we were approaching the British lines. We knew from our flights over our lines that they stood to for an hour before dawn in case of an enemy attack. They would now be having their first brew of the day.

I was leading. I had spent some time explaining to Hutton how the speaking tube functioned. He seemed quite amused by it and kept chuckling, "Well I never. Who would have thought?" He seemed an unflappable and easily amused airman. However, he did have good eyes and he spotted the Aviatiks, there were two of them. "Over there sir, about a mile away. The two aeroplanes were silhouetted against the dawn whilst we, coming from the west and low down were almost invisible.

"Arm your weapon!" I cocked my Lewis and, as I began to climb, glanced over my shoulder to see that the other two were following me.

The German spotters came on steadily, blissfully unaware of the Hun-like trap we had set.

"Wait until I give the order before you fire."

"Righto sir. Will do!"

As we climbed I peered up into the sky. I saw the Fokkers. They were about five hundred feet above the two spotters. We might just be able to drive the two Aviatiks away. Because we had no moving propeller at the front to attract attention we were hard to see. However, when we were two hundred feet away, they saw us and they panicked. The nearest pilot jerked his stick to climb over us.

"Fire!" As Hutton fired so did I and the bullets converged below the cockpit. We must have killed the pilot instantly for the nose dipped and it spiralled down to crash in no-man's land. With almost a full tank of fuel it was an inferno and the observer would have known nothing about it.

As I banked west I heard the guns of the other two aeroplanes open up. Lumpy leaned back to watch and he shouted. They have him sir! He's having to land." Then, in almost the next breath he shouted, "Those one-winged aeroplanes you warned us about. They are diving!"

I dared not risk him standing. We had Lieutenant Holt in the rear of the line and Sergeant White would have to protect us all. I saw arms waving beneath us and knew that we had crossed the British lines. I heard the unmistakeable fire of the German guns followed by short burst of Holt's rear facing Lewis. Then the ground beneath erupted as the Tommies took pot shots. We were flying fifty feet from the ground and they must have thought Christmas had come when the Germans came in so low.

"Hutton, have a look behind. Are the other two all right?"

"Yes sir! Go on bonny lads!" There was a scream which nearly punctured my ear drums. "Gotcha, ya bugger!"

"Hutton!"

"Sorry sir. The lads on the ground have brought down one of them Fokker things."

That was great news. With luck, the machinery which enabled it to fire through the propeller could be salvaged and we might have a clue how to replicate it. We taxied to a halt and it seemed the whole squadron was waiting to greet us. The sun had barely risen above the horizon and we were already home. The Major, Captain and Colonel all waited by the headquarters' tent but the other officers and sergeant crowded around.

Ted pointedly examined my aeroplane for damage. "You didn't bother going on patrol then?"

I smiled and allowed Johnny Holt the pleasure. "We destroyed the two spotter aeroplanes and then the men in the trenches shot down a Fokker."

The atmosphere changed in an instant. Everyone knew the importance of salvaging the aeroplane. Gordy grabbed Johnny, "Right sunshine. You come with me. Flight Sergeant Richardson! Get a lorry! We may have a Fokker to salvage!"

Everything seemed to be happening at once but I was aware that we had two new gunners. I waved them towards me. "You two did very well today, didn't they Lieutenant Carrick?"

The young lieutenant did not look as nervous and diffident as he had a few days ago. "I think they both did very well sir."

I pointed at the aeroplanes, "And as there was no damage the two of you can get your heads down. We'll service them this afternoon."

Airman Laithwaite said, "If it is all the same to you, sir, I would like to practise standing and firing the rear Lewis. I saw what Sergeant White did and it doesn't look easy. If I can manage it on the ground I won't be as afraid when I stand and do it in the air."

"Whatever you choose, airman."

Lumpy grinned, "I might as well join him. Tell me, sir, it is always as much fun when we go up?"

"You mean is it like that ever time? Yes, but we normally bring back more bullet holes."

Lumpy rubbed his hands together, "I'm right glad I volunteered!"

Chapter 12

When the armourer returned we had eaten and were eagerly awaiting him. He had managed to salvage the whole engine. They also had the body of the German flier. It was treated with due reverence. He would be buried in our small cemetery with our own dead and Captain Marshall would keep detailed records for later.

Headquarters had been informed and we knew that it was only a matter of time before our find disappeared. Percy and his men worked wonders. They disassembled the mechanism before the day was out. We had no need for one as yet but there would come a time when we would and it was as well to be prepared.

It was when they were working on it that I had my idea. I grabbed Lumpy. "Airman Hutton, while the armourers are working on the German engine, come with me." Intrigued he followed me. We wasted nothing and all of the engines, spare parts and weapons were stored in an old tent at the back of the main armoury tent. "I want the best Lewis gun we can find."

He rubbed his hands, "A bit of legal larceny too! Good oh!"

He was incorrigible. "No, we are merely conducting an experiment. I will inform Flight Sergeant Richardson of our loan later."

He rummaged around and after a short while he said, "Here sir, this one looks in good nick!"

"Right I want it fitting on the cockpit of our aeroplane." As we walked back I could see him puzzling.

When we reached it, he put the gun on the grass. "Sir, there is a machine gun there already."

"No Airman, that is the rear facing one. This one will be fixed to fire forward. I will be firing over your head."

That thought did not seem to put him out. "Oh I get you and that means you don't have to stand while you fire. Righto sir, I'll get on it right away."

"This might not have worked as well with Sergeant Sharp as he is a bigger man but I noticed, when we flew, that you sit lower in the seat and the gun had a clear line of fire. This also means that the rear Lewis will always be loaded for you."

"I think it is a good idea. But I can fit it so that it will fire over Sergeant Sharp's head when he returns. It will make it more stable too. There is never a dull moment here is there sir?"

I liked Lumpy. He was resourceful and imaginative. He and Charlie had much in common.

We had respite for the next two days. A horrendous storm came from the north and made flying impossible. I dreaded to think what it would be like for the men in the trenches. I wondered how Bert would fare in his tunnels. I would ask Lumpy what they did exactly. The Fokker engine and mechanism was taken away and we managed to finish fitting the Lewis. I was desperate to try it out. I did not know how it would affect the balance of the aeroplane.

While the storm raged I was summoned to a meeting with Captain Marshall, the Colonel and Major Leach. There was a bottle of whisky on the table and four glasses. "Take a seat, Bill." The Colonel waved a hand, "It is raining cats and dogs out there. We thought we would use this lull to talk about the next few weeks and as Archie here had a fine bottle of malt we thought we would do so in comfort."

"Aye, it's an Islay, it might be a bit peaty for you Englishmen but it's my favourite." He held up his glass, "The Corps!"

"The Corps."

I had learned to sip spirits and was glad that I had. It burned a little but it was a pleasant taste. I lit my pipe and found that the taste of the tobacco and the whisky went well together.

"Now Captain Marshall has mentioned your bombing idea and we think it has merit. We just need to plan it well. This weather affords us that opportunity. You talk us through it and we will throw in questions. Four minds might be better than one eh? Off you go. By the way, Archie, this is a damned fine Islay."

"Aye well go easy Colonel there's just one more for each of us and then we will be on the blended stuff."

I drew on my pipe and then began. "Six aeroplanes would take off as normal and patrol the front. My six would take off an hour later. We would climb high. By the time we reach the front the Fokkers should be ready to head for home. We would follow them."

"What if they have not taken the bait?"

"Then we will lose no aeroplanes that day and we would try again on another occasion. Fuel is cheaper than aeroplanes and pilots sir."

"Quite right."

"And why at high altitude?"

"Well, Major, the aerial combats normally end up at very low level. It would make us hard to see and they would not have enough fuel to climb and engage us. And we would be able to travel faster at higher altitude."

"Good but when you make your attack…."

I smiled, "I was just coming to that. Once we had crossed their lines we would descend to low level. We would follow the Fokkers in. With luck their ground defences would see what they expected to see, aeroplanes returning home. We would fly in two flights of three with sixty feet between wing tips. That way we would have more chance of damage. I would just use one pass. The gunners could hurl four bombs in that time and we could pepper their field. Then we would climb and return home at high altitude."

They all nodded and Archie poured our last glass of his precious potion. "The only problem I can see, laddie, is your new gunners. They haven't dropped bombs yet."

"I know but my two new ones seem very dependable and have not shown a tendency to flap. If I took Lieutenant Hewitt's flight too they have bombed before."

"The aeroplanes at the back would be in danger from the concussion and explosion from the ground. The first two aeroplanes would be beyond any chance of that but the last one..."

Randolph was right. I tapped my pipe out to give me time to think. Then Archie said. "If the last one in the flight comes in at a hundred feet higher then they can still bomb but will not be in any danger and they could watch out for any danger."

"Thank you sir, that would work."

The smiles on their faces told me of their approval but I asked the question anyway. "So we go ahead with the plan sir?"

"We go ahead. Brief your pilots and we will have bomb racks fitted while it is raining. We try this out as soon as the weather abates."

The advantage to the plan was that it cost us nothing to be prepared. We would be on patrol to stop their spotting aeroplanes anyway. Gordy was as pleased that I had suggested him as Ted was disappointed to be left out. "Huh, typical, I get to be bait again!"

We left him chuntering while I took all the pilots and gunners through the raid. "This will have to be planned beforehand. Each pilot must follow his instructions precisely. I will lead the formation. Once I begin to descend then Lieutenant Hewitt will fly alongside me. The last two aeroplanes in each flight will take up position a hundred feet above us. We will be dropping our bombs from fifty feet to maximise damage. The last aeroplane in each flight will have to judge where best to drop their bombs but we only have one pass to drop four bombs." I looked at the faces. There were three new gunners. "For three of you this will be the first time you have dropped bombs. You just need quick hands. We will return at high altitude" I paused, "Any questions?"

"What about the weight sir? We have extra magazines and you have your new gun."

Airman Hutton showed that he was a thinker. "Take off the rear facing Lewis. We will be leading and the other two gunners in flight can cover our tail."

And with that we were ready. Gordy joined me in the mess where we found Ted still sulking. "Cheer up Ted. Just think, while we are just bombing an airfield, you can be adding to your tally of Germans."

"Ha bloody ha! Well, when do you try this raid then?"

"The next break in the weather."

Gordy brought two teas over. "The skies look to be lightening in the west so I would guess tomorrow."

We sipped our tea in silence. "Have you heard from Mary lately?"

He shook his head, "No. And I know that she will have written."

"None of us have had any mail for a couple of weeks. Not that I would know as I never get letters anyway."

"You never know Ted, there will be some girl out there just waiting for you."

"Aye," added Gordy, "she'll be the one desperate to kiss a frog. So you never know…"

"I don't know why I talk to you pair. All I get is insults."

The weather had cleared and we watched as the Major and Ted took off with their flights the next day. The patrol had to be done but I felt guilty knowing that they were taking all the risks. The time ticked by very slowly as we waited for the hour to pass. Captain Marshall waved his arm and we began to taxi. The nose was slightly heavier than normal with the bombs and take off was trickier than usual. We began to climb and, again, it was slower because of the weight. We had filled the aeroplanes with as much fuel as we could. We did not want to run out on the way back.

We had crossed the British lines when we saw the others. They were to the north of us and were heading west. I counted six of them but I could see smoke coming from two of them. Four Fokkers were pursuing them and I could see our gunners standing on the cockpit fending them off. Ahead I could see the other monoplanes heading east. The four Fokkers turned around once the British trenches began firing at them. They had lost one to the infantry already and I knew that they would be wary of pushing their luck. They soon began to overtake us as I had the air speed as low as I dared. They did not look up and I was pleased I had thought of the higher altitude. This was partly to conserve fuel but also to enable us to arrive undetected. When we lost altitude, we would pick up speed closer to the target which is what we wanted.

The four Fokkers would not catch their companions and that suited us. With luck, we might be taken for other German aeroplanes. When I saw that we had crossed their German lines I began to descend. We had dropped five hundred feet, I saw Gordy next to me and he waved. He had the job of estimating the distance between us. We were in position. Soon we were just sixty feet above the ground. I glanced back and saw Johnny Holt a hundred feet above us.

If the monoplane had had an observer then they might have seen us. As it was they did not. They blissfully headed home unaware that they had company. Soon we saw their airfield ahead. To my horror I realised that they had another Jasta there. They were the ones lined up neatly along both sides of the runaway. The twelve aeroplanes might be armed, fuelled and ready to fly. I had the chance to abort the mission. I did not. We would have to hope to hit as many as we could.

"Lumpy try to hit those Fokkers that are neatly parked. They haven't flown yet."

"Right sir. This is like the coconut shy at the local fair."

"Well make sure you get the major prize!"

I waited, as we approached, for the sound of their guns firing at us, but they must have seen us as friendlies. I cocked the Lewis. It looked like we might need it and I wondered if we would regret removing the rear Lewis. I hoped not.

When they saw us, it was as though we had upset a nest of ants. They swarmed from their wooden huts and raced towards their aeroplanes. Lumpy began hurling the bombs. He threw to the left while Gordy's gunner threw to the right. The shrapnel would cover the ground between. Lumpy was a very quick thrower and I hoped that he had not thrown too quickly. Then I saw him cock and begin to fire his machine gun. One of the Fokkers which had just landed suddenly burst into flames as his bullets struck it.

Then I pulled back on the stick and began to climb. I banked left while Gordy would bank right. That way we would avoid any unnecessary collisions. It also gave me a chance to assess the damage. I saw Johnny Holt begin his turn. We were all safely through the maelstrom of flying metal.

I counted at least six burning Fokkers. It was obvious that some of the others were damaged. However, I saw four of them taxiing. They would follow us, hell bent on revenge. I pointed to them and Gordy nodded. We both began to climb. We would continue to fly in two columns for mutual protection. We climbed as high as we dared. When I levelled out I looked down and behind. There were four Fokkers climbing followed by a fifth. With any other aeroplane I would have taken those odds but not the Fokker. They could approach from below and pick us off one by one. Our rear Lewis would not help us and we could not use our circle, the gay Gordons as we would not have enough fuel.

It was a race now. Would we reach our own lines before they caught us? I saw the German support trenches appear below me and then I heard the stutter of the German machine guns. We had to lose altitude. I put the nose down and began to dive. Immediately we picked up airspeed. I saw Lumpy bring his gun around and watched as he fired at the Fokker attacking the last aeroplane in Gordy's flight. Although he missed I could see that the German pilot was aware of the danger.

There were four Fokkers attacking Gordy's flight and the last enemy was still labouring to climb and attack us. "Airman Hutton, I am going to swing around and attack the Germans. I will be firing my Lewis."

"Righto sir!"

I began to bank to port. The manoeuvre took the Germans by surprise. I headed for the middle two aeroplanes. "Lumpy go for the one on the right." I aimed my aeroplane at the one on the left. Perhaps the pilot had seen that we had no rear mounted Lewis and assumed he was safe but he soon thought differently. I discovered what it must be like to be a Fokker pilot. As the monoplane loomed across my sights I pulled the trigger. I hit the engine and then the pilot. It was as though I had swatted a fly. It dropped like a stone. Hutton had hit the other aeroplane in the tail.

I saw the last Fokker firing at me but his bullets went through the empty space behind the engine. Then Laithwaite and Flight Sergeant White began to fire at the last Fokker and he turned away, engine smoking.

I brought the flight up on Gordy's port side. I could see that all three of his aeroplanes were damaged but the last two Fokkers had seen enough. We were over No Man's Land; they had lost one aeroplane and had two more damaged. They cut their losses.

I let Gordy and his damaged flight land first but we were almost flying on fumes ourselves and we barely made the end of the airfield before the engines cut out. Five more minutes in the air and we would have all had to land in the trenches; not an easy task.

I looked at the Gunbuses. We had all suffered some damage but to the aeroplane and not personnel. We could repair the aeroplanes. Thankfully we did not have bodies for Doc Brennan to fix.

Gordy came over shaking his head. "Another Fokker!" He grabbed my hand. "Thanks Bill, you saved us back there. I owe you one."

"Don't be daft. It was my idea. I couldn't let you lads pay for that could I? Besides we are all in the same squadron and we watch over each other."

Chapter 13

The other flights had suffered damage when they had played bait but no deaths had resulted. It had been that rare thing in the squadron; a day without wounds or deaths. That evening we all celebrated in the officers' mess; for the first time we had managed to shoot down a Fokker and not lost an aeroplane. We had been lucky.

I had watched Percy Richardson with his hands on his hips watching me as I had taxied. He pointed to the Lewis and wagged his finger, "Captain Harsker, sir, if you had asked then I would have fitted one for you. You had no need to steal one!"

Lumpy strode up grinning, "We borrowed it, Flight, but you can have it back if you like."

The armourer sniffed, "Well while it is on... who fitted this?"

"I did Flight, anything wrong?" Lumpy sounded worried.

Percy clambered up and checked it over. He jumped down and wiped his hands on an oily rag. "It'll do, I suppose."

I laughed, "That means he thinks it is a good job!"

"I suppose they will all want one now."

"It does work Flight Sergeant and if we have spares..."

He nodded and wandered off to comply.

I had reported to the Colonel and the Major who were waiting. They were delighted with our success but when I mentioned two Jastas their faces clouded. "I know we have hurt them but we didn't hurt their pilots. They can churn out weapons and I would expect them at full strength next week or the week after."

"Luckily they are short days now and we can expect less action but even so we had better prepare the field for retaliation."

The party in the officers' mess was lively but it was as nothing compared with that organised by Quartermaster Doyle for the sergeants and airmen. We were anticipating a quieter time and this was a chance to let off steam. We also celebrated because we had letters from home. There was a backlog. We never discovered why but we were just grateful for the mail.

The day after the party was a drizzle filled day with low cloud. Flying was impossible although the colonel ordered all the airmen on the base to man the machine guns in case the Hun decided to bomb us again. I settled down in my tent to read my three letters. The first, from our Sarah told me the same as the other two letters but I read them anyway, three times each.

September 1915

Dear Bill,

I hope you are well. We read all your letters four or five times each. When we read them, it is almost as though you are there.

We were shocked to hear about you being put on trial. I am glad you were found innocent- not that I doubted you. Lord Burscough sent a letter to his wife and she told us that you had been badly treated. There are some awful people around but we are all glad that you are safe.

Bert is in the Engineers and has set off for the front. Mother is beside herself. She bursts into tears all the time. It doesn't help that our Kath has gone and married that curate, well he is a vicar now. I still don't like him. Anyway, they moved to his new church in Yorkshire, a little place called Masham.

The upshot is that mum only has our Alice at home and she is of an age where she wants a bit of excitement. I think both mum and dad worry that she will do what John and Tom did and run off to Manchester. They worry that she would end up changed like they were. I don't think so. She's not like them. She wants to do something different from the rest of us. She is very creative. She makes lovely clothes and dresses. Mum can't see beyond the estate. Out Alice will have to move away some time.

Some news to give you, and I think it is good news, is that I am expecting a baby. It is due in the New Year, probably January. Her ladyship has been good about it. I thought she would finish me but she and Lord Burscough seem to have a soft spot for our family. I think that has a lot to do with you. She said she will hold my job open and if mum looks after the baby when it is born then I can return to work.

Mum is overjoyed at the thought and it means I will be living at home for three or four months. It might make it easier on both of them.

Keep the letters coming. They mean more than you can know.

We pray every day that God continues to watch over you. Mum takes some comfort from the fact that flying an aeroplane makes you closer to God. Dad rolls his eyes when she says that but so long as she is happy then what is the harm?

Your big sister,
Sarah.

xxx

So I was to be an uncle. It felt good and I re-read the letter a few times. When I read the others, I saw the different sides to things.

Our Kath was a little put out by Sarah's attitude and I could see that she saw herself as something a little better now. She felt she had done well to marry into the middle class and was the wife of a vicar. I don't know what my brothers would have thought of that!

Mum's letter was stained with what I assumed were tears. In the letter itself she was putting a brave face on things but I could tell that the empty house was eating into her. From her letter, I discovered that Dad had finally retired but his lordship had allowed them to live in the cottage. She was more upset about Bert. She thought her little lad was too young to go to war. She was probably right. She never mentioned Alice and the problems there. She was probably protecting me.

Gordy was even happier than I was. From the moon struck face and the way he kept re reading the letter I assumed it reciprocated his feelings for the widow Mary. We did not know when we would be granted a leave but one thing was certain, Gordy and I would not be on leave together this time. Major Leach had decided that we needed at least three of the flight commanders on the base at all times. When we were granted a leave then it would be in rotation. I had asked for January so that I could be there for the baby. It looked likely that I would be granted it.

The rain gave us respite for another few days and then winter hit. It was heralded by icy winds from the east and then a chilling cold. It meant we could fly once more but we flew in icy conditions. If you forgot your gloves then you could lose fingers. Using the Lewis gun was a nightmare.

I made sure that Lumpy understood the conditions in which we would be flying. I didn't want to lose him to frostbite. We flew half squadrons. It was safer as we reduced wear and tear on aeroplanes and crews. Out first patrol was largely uneventful. The Loos and Ypres sector seemed to have quietened down. I had heard that we were running out of shells; what the German reason was I had no idea. However, I had learned to be suspicious of such things. The Germans were meticulous planners and did nothing without a damned good reason.

The Rolls Royce engine still purred, no matter what the temperature but I was glad for the fur waistcoat and good leather coat I had recently bought. My ears, despite the flying helmet, were still cold. I had misplaced my balaclava. Perhaps if I asked my mother she would knit me another one.

Lumpy was well prepared. He had so many jumpers, gloves and helmets on that he barely fitted in the cockpit. His balaclavas made communication difficult and I had to resort to tapping him on the head.

That particular day we saw a Fokker patrol. There were three of them but they stayed on their side of the lines. We patrolled parallel to each other. They had learned to respect us. We outnumbered them two to one and we were not the Fokker fodder that was the BE 2. No-one wanted to initiate a combat which would be likely to result in men dying for no good reason. I headed back to our airfield. If this was to continue for the next few months it might be boring but I would not lose any more aircrew.

November ended that way. No action but no deaths either. Sergeant Sharp sent me a letter. I had written to him suggesting that he might like to become a pilot. I did not want to lose him as a gunner but I had been encouraged to do so and, while it was still possible, I thought he ought to try.

November 1915

Dear Captain Harsker,

Thank you for your kind letter. I was touched to receive it. I know how busy you must be.

The leg is healing well and I will be fit for active duty again in January. As regards training as a pilot; I am not certain if I would like that but I appreciate your thoughts and your concern. I will wait until I return to active service and then decide.

Yours faithfully,

Chas. Sharp,
Flight Sergeant

It was typical of Charlie that he should be so thankful. I knew he had not had a loving family as I had. The things I took for granted he had never had. I would persuade him to train when he returned. Lumpy Hutton had worked out well. He was not Charlie Sharp but I knew that, eventually, we would be given single seater fighters like the Germans used and then I would need neither a gunner nor an observer. I would have to fly alone then anyway. As the Fokker had shown aeroplane design was improving rapidly.

It was December when we received our first alert. The sector close to us, towards the south, was occupied by the French. Their aeroplanes had been badly handled by the Fokkers and the Hun had gained air superiority.

"Tomorrow, gentlemen, we are on standby. The French sector is forty miles away. We can be there in half an hour. If the French and the British squadrons there strike trouble then we will go to their aid."

Ted raised his hand, "Colonel, if we are going to help them wouldn't it be better if we set off to help them before they got in trouble?"

"I can see where you would think that, Lieutenant Thomas, however we know how cunning the Germans are. They may have been mauling the squadrons down there to draw us away and then they could hit our airfield or our lines."

"Ted is right, sir, we may get down there when it is too late to do anything save pick up the pieces."

"Nevertheless, those are the orders and we will follow them."

As we went to the officers' mess Gordy shook his head. "It's always the same; some genius at Headquarters who doesn't know his arse from his elbow comes up with a plan which will only result in our lads getting hurt."

"We'll have to make sure we don't. If we fly higher we can gain ten miles an hour and be there five or ten minutes quicker and we would have height advantage. Remember we all have the extra Lewis now. As the only one who has used it I can tell you it makes all the difference. It is like flying a Fokker, what you see is what you hit. You aim the aeroplane and not the gun."

"I hope you are right or some poor sods will not see the New Year."

The telephone line to the front was working and, as we waited by the aeroplanes, we saw Captain Marshall come from the tent and fire the Very pistol. We set off south in two lines of six. I took my flights high while the Major went low. I worked out that we would get there slightly ahead of him but the Germans would see him first. I agreed with Gordy; I was not certain that the Germans would still be there.

Lumpy spotted them in the distance. "Sir, there are loads of them. Little crosses in the distance."

I saw what he meant. It looked like the two squadrons we had bombed some time ago. The other allied aeroplanes were heading west to avoid the deadly monoplanes. "Arm your weapon." I raised my arm to tell the others we were going into action and then cocked my Lewis.

I began to dive down. The speed approached a hundred knots as we screamed down from the skies. My plan was simple; I would lead my six aeroplanes through the middle. We would cut a swath through the heart of them and then Major Leach could attack from below. I no longer needed to tell Lumpy when to fire. He had worked that out for himself. We both opened fire at the same time. The first Fokker was easy. He had not seen us and was too busy destroying the BE 2 in front of him. His plane began to spin out of control and I saw a wave from the pilot of the BE2 as he limped west. A Fokker flew directly at us firing his gun. We had two and we both emptied them as we closed. I braced myself for the impact. He swerved to port. I pulled up the nose and, as I reached stall speed, turned the nose of the aeroplane so that we began to fall from the sky.

I heard Lumpy say, "Bugger me!"

I said quietly, "Come on old girl do not let me down now."

The engine fired again and we roared down to attack the Fokker which had swerved to avoid us. He was not expecting the manoeuvre and I saw his shocked face as Hutton, with a new magazine emptied it into him. He died instantly. I saw him slump in the seat. But his aeroplane kept ploughing through the skies like an aerial Flying Dutchman. I looked around for another target but the Fokkers, probably running low on fuel, were heading east. I saw three downed BE 2s and one downed Nieuport but I saw the remnants heading west. Many had been saved. I lifted the nose and gained altitude so that my flights could take station on me. I saw Major Leach doing the same. I counted my birds as they joined me. They were all safe and all of them waved the thumbs up.

Heading home I found myself actually believing that perhaps the planners knew what they were doing. We had trounced the Fokkers and made them flee. We had surprise on our side and we would not have that the next time but, as Christmas approached, I reflected that we had lasted far longer than I had expected. It was now over a month since we had lost anyone and that was a record.

The Germans punished us, or at least they tried to punish us. The weather, over the next few days, was not at its best but we could fly. The colonel decided to send out each flight on patrol. The next flight left half an hour after the first so that, by the time the first was ready to land the third was ready to take its place. Ted later said that made the colonel a witch. I thought it just made him intelligent.

We were the third flight out. We waved to Major Leach and his boys as they passed us. We were not expecting trouble. We had handled the Fokkers badly the previous day and we knew from experience that it took time to refit and repair damaged aeroplanes.

It was Ted and his flight which were slowly looping over the front at a thousand feet. The world of the clouds and the sky looked peaceful. I was wondering if this was a waste of fuel and thinking that an afternoon in the officers' mess with some beer and whisky might not be more pleasurable. My mental wanderings were stopped when I saw the line of aeroplanes heading west. There were eight AEG 1 bombers; we knew them. Then there were the ten Fokker monoplanes above them. It did not take a genius to work out that they were headed for our airfield. We were outnumbered.

I flew close to Ted. We had not worked out a system of communicating in the air and so I used hand signals. I mimed the bombers and pointed to Ted to take them out. He nodded and waved his hand in acknowledgement. We would find out if he understood when we engaged the enemy. I was also counting on Gordy arriving soon to give us better odds.

I began to climb. I wanted to have the advantage of altitude when we dived into the Fokkers. I knew that the AEG 1 was no match for Ted and his aeroplanes. I hoped that they would stop them before they reached our airfield but at odds of more than three to one I knew that we would, more than likely, be shot down in short order.

I looked astern and saw that my two wingmen were on station.

"Lumpy, this will not be easy. I will be moving around like a flea in a Geordie's long johns!"

I heard him laugh. "Dinna worry sir. I couldna move if I wanted to. I have more layers than an onion. We'll be alright."

With men as stout as Hutton on our side, how could we lose?

The Fokkers were in three waves. There were four in the first, four in the second and two in the rear. I decided to plough through the middle. We had six machine guns and could fire on two sides. I wanted to disrupt their formation.

"Lumpy, I am heading up the middle. Take the one on the right, to starboard. I will take the one directly ahead."

"Right sir!"

The German aeroplanes concentrated their fire on me. The problem was that they fired too early and they could not see if it was their rounds which struck us. I had the advantage that I knew if I was hitting my enemy. And I did. My bullets struck the engine of the first aeroplane. I passed so close that I could see the pilot struggling to make his Fokker remain in the air. I looked at the next aeroplane in the line. This time they were fearful of firing for their own comrades were close to us. Their hesitation cost them dear. My bullets struck the wing of the Fokker and he took evasive action.

I had emptied my magazine as the last Fokker came into view. He fired a few rounds and then banked. I drew my Luger and I emptied the magazine. He was so close I could see a duelling scar down his right cheek. One of my bullets must have hit him and mortally wounded him for his aeroplane went into a steep dive. I began to climb and bank.

I was feeling elated until I looked behind me. Both Freddy and Johnny had been badly handled. I could see that their wings were riddled with holes. Lieutenant Holt's bus had smoke coming from the engine while I could see oil trailing behind Carrick's aeroplane. In the distance, I could see Ted finishing off the bombers but of Gordy there was no sign.

"Lumpy, fire the Very pistol. We need to send the other two home and then try to buy them some time."

"Righto sir."

From his calm tone, you would have thought I had asked him what was for dinner in the mess. The flare arced high above us. I began to bank the aeroplane and saw the two Gunbuses peel away west. As I had expected two Fokkers tried to follow them. We swooped on to the tail of one of them and Hutton fired a burst which must have clipped the propeller for the E1 suddenly pitched and bucked like a bronco. The pilot fought to control it and I turned the aeroplane towards the one firing at Carrick. I saw the Fokker's bullets hit the engine and the oil began to flood. He was below the FE2 and Jack Laithwaite could not see him. I fired at the Fokker which swerved away to avoid my bullets. I followed him around and continued to fire. He was within my arc. Hutton was firing at the Fokker coming at us obliquely to catch us on our quarter. The magazine empty I watched as the Fokker, trailing smoke, headed east. I saw Hutton changing his magazine and I began a steep climb.

I knew that we had a better rate of climb at altitude and I wanted to drag the Fokkers away from Carrick and Holt. I began to think we had succeeded when I felt bullets striking the underneath of the aeroplane. We could not use the rear Lewis. Hutton would have fallen to his death.

"Lumpy, there is a Fokker underneath us. Can you get him with the Lee Enfield?"

I saw my gunner peering below us. "Not a chance sir, I would have to be a contortionist but I can try something sir. You keep us steady."

I saw him reach into one of the pockets of his coat and take out a Mills bomb. I had heard of this new hand grenade but never seen one. I would ask later where he got it. I saw him pull the pin and then drop the grenade. The bullets continued to hit us. I dipped the nose and then jerked back to throw off the German's aim. It must have worked for the bullets stopped striking us and then there was a crack and we were buffeted by the explosion. We were struck by tiny pieces of shrapnel from the grenade but they just punched a couple of tiny holes in the wings. I levelled out and saw the stricken aeroplane tumbling from the sky.

"Well done Lumpy. Now get that magazine changed."

"Yes sir."

I changed mine as we flew dangerously straight and level. The explosion and our climb meant that the other Fokkers were some way behind us but, as I looked at my compass, I saw that we were heading east! We were going the wrong way. The fuel gauge was also heading in the wrong direction.

"Hang on I am going to bank and dive. When I level out get ready to fire the rear Lewis."

"I'll try sir but it is a tight fit here in the front."

His layers of clothing, while keeping him warm made him less mobile. That decided me. We would hedgehop back to the airfield. That way they could not get below us.

I gave the bus all the power that was available. If I ran out of fuel I would glide. We were still descending when I saw the rear German trenches. As we levelled out, thirty feet above them they began to fire at us. I heard Hutton say, "Cheeky beggars!" I saw another Mills bomb dropped over the side. This time we were travelling so fast that we did not feel the concussion but I knew that the Fokker following behind would. It would buy us a few seconds.

Now I felt the engine labouring. I could not see behind me but I knew that we had been hit. I was losing oil or fluids. The fuel gauge was dipping towards empty as we zipped over No-Man's Land. When I saw the Tommies waving I knew we had reached our own lines. The question was, where would we land?

"Look for somewhere to land, Hutton. We have been hit and we are running out of fuel."

"All I can see is trenches and wire, sir. It'll make a right mess of us if we try and land here."

"If we run out of fuel we may have no option. Let me know when you see anything vaguely flat."

Even the roads had been destroyed in the barrage and all that I could see was pock marked with craters. They would be as lethal to us as the Fokkers which had given up the chase now and returned home.

"Sir, straight ahead! I can see a patch of green."

Even as he said it the engine began to cough and splutter. I too saw the patch of green. It was not as flat as I would have liked but it was the earth and we were going to hit it anyway.

"Brace yourself"

I heard him mumble, "For what we are about to receive…"

The engine cut out and we struck the ground. Without power, I had no control over the craft and I just fought the stick and the rudder to avoid obstacles. Hutton and our height meant that I could not see directly in front of the aeroplane.

"Sir! Rock!"

We struck the rock with our nose wheel. The rear of the acroplane rose alarmingly and then, thankfully crashed down. I heard something crack and break. We both clambered from the Gunbus. I reached the ground before Hutton who was struggling with his layers. We had broken the propeller, the nose wheel and the tail had broken off. However, as we walked away from the Gunbus I remembered what Ted had first told me when I had started to fly. *'Any landing you walk away from is a good landing.'*

Chapter 14

There was a farmhouse close by the field. We wandered over on the off chance that there might be an occupant. Although the wrecked door suggested that the farmer and his family had fled. The cupboards were bare and anything soldiers might be able to use had been taken. The only items which remained were the armchairs and couch and a couple of broken down beds. There were a couple of broken picture frames showing the family at a beach somewhere; they were dressed in their finest. It was a sad reminder of happier days.

"Well someone robbed these poor people and no mistake."

"I think, Lumpy, that the family would have taken everything of value. Their lives would be more important than possession. I reckon when this war is over some people at home might realise that too."

"For me they always have been, sir."

We found a road not far from the field and we waited. The road had to lead to the front and, sooner or later, a vehicle would come by. Eventually I heard the rumble of a lorry. It pulled up next to us and a young head popped out. "Captain Harsker! Bert's brother! What are you doing out here?"

"Do I know you?"

"You bought us a pint in Boulogne, sir."

"Ah yes. We crashed over there. Any chance of a ride back to our field?"

"Of course, sir. Jump on board."

After we had given him directions we headed along the road. "We saw your aeroplane not long ago sir. You were trailing smoke. The lads all wondered if you would make it. Bert will be made up when I tell him I met you."

I felt relief. I had wanted to ask the question but dreaded the answer. "How is he?"

"Oh he is fine. He is a Lance Corporal now." His face became sad. "We lost a few lads in the attack. The Hun countermined our tunnel and twenty of the lads were buried alive. Bert showed he could lead men when the chips were down and they made him a Lance."

I shuddered. That was a horrible way to go. There were no pleasant ways to die in this war but it seemed to me that with gas and tunnels we were making more horrible ways for a man to die than in the past. It only took twenty minutes to reach the field. Another five minutes in the air and we would have been home.

"Thank you for the lift, private. Tell our Bert to be careful!"

He laughed, "That is a bit rich sir, if you don't mind me saying so sir. You have just crash landed in a field and you are telling him to be careful. But I will pass on your message."

As we walked towards the mess tent Lumpy said, "He is right, sir. You do take some fearful risks."

We watched as Gordy's flight landed. The other pilots and gunners waiting had not noticed us, walking in from the road, and they crowded around the three aeroplanes as the crews descended.

We were thirty yards away and I saw Lieutenant Holt run up to him, "Any sign of Captain Harsker."

Gordy shook his head. Hutton cocked his head in their direction, "Shall you tell 'em sir or me?"

"Let me. Have you chaps lost someone?"

They all turned and stared. Ted shook his head, "Where's your bus then?"

"The field here was too crowded so we left it twenty minutes away."

Freddy Carrick said, "How on earth did you get away? When we looked back they were all swarming around you. We were convinced you had bought it."

"It was a little close but Airman Hutton here had a surprise up his sleeve. He has downed a Fokker with a Mills Bomb."

That brought a mixture of laughter and applause. He looked a little abashed by the attention from the other gunners. "I'll just go and change, sir. These layers are a bit warm when you are on the ground."

"Righto and well done, airman. Today you were outstanding."

I strode to the mess tent with Gordy and Ted. Major Leach had heard the commotion and he walked from the Headquarters' tent. "I suspect you have an interesting report to write, Captain Harsker."

"That I have sir." I gestured behind me to Lumpy Hutton who was now surrounded by his peers. "I would like to recommend Hutton for promotion and a medal. He downed a Fokker with a Mills Bomb."

"Did he by George? I think we might well manage the promotion but I don't think they have medals for other ranks; apart from the V.C. that is. The colonel had already mentioned promoting him and Laithwaite anyway. It seems an anomaly to have those two just as airmen when all the other gunners are Flight Sergeants. Come inside and tell us all about how you managed to escape."

The colonel came to listen too. When I had finished he said, "What could have turned out to be a disaster has been somewhat salvaged. Lieutenant Hewitt, what did you discover?"

"By the time we reached the front there were just a few burning aeroplanes and I could see the Fokkers heading east. We assumed that Bill had bought it as there was no sign of his aeroplane."

"I was hedgehopping. I was almost out of fuel. I hope they can repair her."

"Don't worry they will give it their best efforts. Well if you would write your report and then you can have a rest for a while. I think tomorrow we will just send out half the squadron and stay on our side of the lines. Their bombers were badly shot up by Lieutenant Thomas here."

Ted looked embarrassed. "We managed to shoot down three and damage two."

"Well done!"

"I know but we left you in the lurch. We could see them swarming all over you and knew that you were keeping them off our backs."

"Don't worry about it, Ted. It all worked out for the best. I was just worried that Johnny Holt and Freddy Carrick would have bought it. They took some punishment."

"Don't worry Captain, they will be mentioned in despatches." The colonel pointed to the tent wall, as though it was a window, "If the weather deteriorates much more then we will not have many more opportunities for such patrols. It will give us time to build up our strength again. Anyway gentlemen, thank you for your efforts today."

As we stood to leave, Ted asked, "Sir, is there any chance of some wooden huts for the winter? It is a bit cold for tents."

"I thought that myself. We have some Royal Engineers coming next week. They will make our home a little more permanent."

"And that, of course, means no one thinks the front line will be moving any time soon."

"Quite right Lieutenant Hewitt. The Loos offensive gained more ground than most but it was still only a couple of miles and bought with the blood of too many Tommies."

It took three days to dismantle and bring my wrecked aeroplane from the field and it lay forlornly on the grass while we waited for spares.

Before the Engineers arrived, we received a missive from Headquarters. It did not affect us directly but it showed the way the war had changed. There was to be no fraternising with the Germans over Christmas. I remembered that the first year of the war had seen Christmas Day football matches and the exchanging of gifts. That would not happen again. The war had become too serious. If we fraternised we might realise that we had much more in common than we knew.

The arrival of the Royal Engineers was greeted like a visit by the King. We were all keen to have them start work and so we watched their lorries as they arrived. To my delight I saw Lance Corporal Albert Harsker jump down and set to work. I decided not to embarrass him. I would wait until they had a brew and then speak with him.

Lumpy Hutton had become quite a celebrity since the hand grenade incident. He had proved himself to be a resourceful and resilient airman. Even some of the older and more experienced gunners sought his advice. He was a man who knew many things. He seemed to be a fountain of all knowledge; both useful and useless. Although as he told me 'There's no such thing as useless knowledge. It's just stuff you haven't needed yet!"

I suppose having been a miner he relished the open air more than most and took everything in good part. Life above ground suited him. Nothing seemed to get him down.

Our poor Gunbus was looking very sorry for herself. There was no propeller and her undercarriage was wrecked beyond repair. Laithwaite and a couple of mechanics were helping Lumpy who was whistling happily as he worked. He saw me coming. "Sir, this bullet proofing; it works but I can't move. I am going to just use the bully beef tins and one layer of cardboard."

"I'd hate to lose you, Lumpy. It works you know." I pointed to the holes we could see in the nacelle and the three 9mm bullets in the bottom of the cockpit.

"I know sir but I couldn't get to the rear Lewis and that nearly cost us. I won't take as many layers next time. Besides Jack here reckons thinner layers are better anyway."

"I leave that to you. Thank you Airman Laithwaite. I appreciate your efforts."

He smiled, "We Donkey Wallopers have to stay together sir!"

I heard the cooks shout, "Tea and Jippo!"

"Are you lads coming?"

Lumpy pointed to the Engineers. "Best let them get it first sir and that way we might have a warm billet for the night."

A wise man was our soon to be Sergeant Hutton. I strolled along to the mess that they were using. I saw Bert in the line and I waited until he had his tea and bacon sandwich. Of course, the men called it 'a bacon butty'. Back home it might be a bacon bap but whatever it was called the smell made you hungry. When I had spoken with Bert I would grab one myself.

I waited until he and his mates had collected their steaming mugs and were walking back to the building site munching on the steaming, greasy feasts before I approached him. "Now then Bert!"

He grinned from ear to ear. "I heard this was your airfield and wondered if I would see you. Cedric told me about your crash. You had better not tell mum she worries enough anyway."

"Aye well it is a good job that she knows nowt about what you do either. I heard that some of your lads were killed by a mine."

He shrugged as he finished the butty and wiped the grease from his face with the back of his hand. He pointed to the sky. "We are both in the same boat really. Something bad happens to you and you fall from the sky. Something bad happens to me and the sky, so to speak, falls in on us. Both are less of a risk than dying like Tom and John, charging machine guns."

He was right.

"Lance Corporal Harsker, stop bothering that officer and get back to work!"

I turned and saw a Second Lieutenant. He looked to be about fourteen and I was not even sure he had started shaving. "Thank you, Lieutenant, but my brother is not bothering me and," I waved my arm around at the other engineers who were on their break, "as you can see it is their break."

He blushed, "Sorry sir, I didn't know. Er carry on Harsker!"

Bert said drily, "Thank you sir. Very good of you I'm sure."

The officer beetled away as quickly as he could. "Who is that?"

"Lieutenant Smythe; he's not so bad."

One of his mates said, "Aye so long as he doesn't give any orders. He hasn't the first clue."

"That's enough Arthur. He's our officer and we support him." He rolled his eyes. "Anyway Bill, he's right we should get back to work. We have to get this done in two days and the ground is frozen solid. We'll chat again." He gave an exaggerated salute and a wink, "Sir!"

As I strolled off to get myself a bacon sandwich I found myself marvelling at the change in Bert. He had become a self-confident young man and had a maturity beyond his years. The army had been good for him. I hoped that the war would be as kind.

The wooden quarters were finished just in time. The weather got even colder and wetter. Christmas was almost upon us. Gordy was delighted and thankful to be the first one to be granted leave. He had a week. He had the shortest journey of any of us for Mary lived in London. It would be less than a day's travel whereas the rest of us would need a whole day just to get home. We would have a bare five days with our loved ones. That was the luck of the draw and none of us begrudged Gordy his extra hours with his young lady.

As we said goodbye he was like a puppy with two tails. "I am grateful that you lads decided that I could be the first to go on leave. I can't wait to see Mary."

"You ought to think about telling her your intentions Gordy."

"I told you; she has been made a widow once and I am not going to turn her into another one. This war can't go on forever. We will wait. I'll make sure we have a lovely leave together."

I was not sure. I had seen too many young men die and Gordy was not immortal.

The Engineers had done a good job. Each mess had a potbellied stove as did the barracks. The officers were quartered in separate bedrooms but we all shared one building, again warmed by a potbellied stove. I had forgotten what it was like to be warm and I found myself sitting on a chair before the stove smoking my pipe and not actually doing anything. I just luxuriated in the warmth of the cosy room. I realised that we took such things for granted when at home but they were precious and to be savoured.

Our aeroplane was repaired on Christmas Eve. I received permission from the colonel to take her up for a test. Johnny and Freddy insisted on accompanying me. Ostensibly it was to see how their own repaired aeroplanes had fared but I knew they were watching over me.

We headed for the front. It was quiet. The guns had been silent for a few days. There might not be a truce but the soldiers on the ground wanted a peaceful Christmas even in the damp and muddy trenches rimmed with frost. I had decided not to risk No-Man's Land and so we climbed to nine thousand feet. It was too cold to stooge around there too long and I took the flight down to a thousand feet. It was still cold but the aeroplane preferred it.

It was such a clear day that we could see behind the German lines. There appeared to be a lot of traffic on the roads. There were both vehicles and horses. I was tempted to go and see what it meant but I was aware that there were just three of us and I could not risk it. We landed and I told the Major of my discovery.

"Interesting. Do you think they are trying something? Perhaps they intend an attack during or just after Christmas?"

"I don't know sir. We know that they think things through better than we do and their generals appear to have some thought to their plans."

The Major gave me a wry smile, "It is sad to see one so young and yet so cynical. I'll have a chat with the colonel. Now you go and get a warm."

With a quarter of the squadron on leave it was a comfortable time to be in the mess. The Engineers had given us a sort of lounge with wooden chairs and a basic table and a door led to the dining area. The food was brought from the kitchens. It was a simple arrangement but there were only fifteen officers and it suited us.

I sat and read a two-month-old newspaper. It felt almost civilised. Ted joined me. "You know Bill we could do with a few comfortable chairs. I mean it is Christmas Day tomorrow. I don't fancy sitting around getting splinters up me backside!"

"You have such a way with words." I had a sudden idea. "Go and get a lorry, I think I know where we can get some."

Ted got on well with the sergeants and he honked the horn in no time at all. I grabbed my coat and was about to climb on board when Captain Marshall appeared. "Where are you two off to?"

"We are going to do a little bit of Christmas shopping."

I could see the puzzled look on his face as Ted headed for the gate. I directed him towards the front. "We aren't going to the German lines, are we? I mean I don't mind it in a Gunbus but not a lorry."

"Trust me we will get nowhere near the front." Ten minutes later I said, "Turn in here."

We pulled up next to the deserted farmhouse where Lumpy and I had crashed our aeroplane. I opened the living door and said, "Tara," like a fanfare.

Ted smiled. "I take the folks here have gone."

"This is about the only stuff worth taking. I don't think they would want it now." We carried the three armchairs and the couch and put them in the back of the lorry. We explored the house. We found other homely touches which we took: a small table complete with dirty lace cloth, an oil lamp and a padded footstool.

Feeling pleased with ourselves we headed back to the airfield. Most of the other officers were still busy with their aeroplanes or catching forty winks in a warm bedroom. Ted and I arranged the furniture. We stood back feeling well pleased with ourselves. Having acquired the furniture, we claimed the two armchairs next to the stove. I lit my pipe and resumed the reading of my paper. Ted lit a cigarette and stretched out his legs as though he was back home in his own parlour.

The door opened and the Major and Captain Marshall stood there. Captain Marshall began to laugh, "I see now what you meant about shopping! Where on earth did you get it?"

"There was a bombed-out farmhouse just down the road, close to where I crashed. Everything of value had been taken; apart from these."

Major Leach shook me vigorously by the hand. "You deserve a medal for this alone. I have a bottle of blended whisky. That seat is mine. I'll be back in a minute."

As the dusk fell the four of us sat with a glass of whisky in our hands feeling at one with the world. When the lieutenants came in their jaws dropped then they all fought for a place on the couch next to Captain Marshall. It was the last comfortable seat left. Freddy showed intelligence by grabbing the footstool.

Johnny asked the major, "Where did it come from?"

"Father Christmas!"

They looked at the major as though he was drunk. He shook his head, "Captain Harsker here got them. That is showing initiative. And remember you young men, these chairs are for you only when we are not here! Respect your elders!"

It all made for a much more pleasant Christmas. We had no parcels from the Royal Family this year but extra rations were sent and the cooks made a good effort to give us a pleasant and hearty meal. The colonel made sure that the older officers were around for the whole of the day. For most of these young men it was their first time away from home. Considering we were in France and a few miles from the enemy it was quite a jolly Christmas.

Chapter 15

Two days after Christmas the colonel sanctioned a patrol over the German lines to see what the activity had been. He impressed upon us that we were not to engage with the enemy unless it was impossible to avoid.

Major Leach led and I followed with my flight. Ted was the rear flight. The lines seemed quiet as we flew over. Every nerve was strained like the wires on our fuselage. We crossed No Man's Land and I expected the crump of guns but it was silent. There were Germans below us but they were not firing at us. The Major took us north, away from Loos to inspect the Ypres sector. The story was the same there.

I almost had a crick in my neck from looking over my shoulder. We saw not a single German aeroplane. It was weird. It was as though they had decided to stop the war for a short time.

After we had landed the colonel held the debriefing in the new and more comfortable surroundings of the mess. "So Archie, you are saying that they weren't being reinforced and they weren't planning an offensive?"

The major looked perplexed. "It was strange. I expected them to take pot shots at us but they didn't. It was all quiet."

Captain Marshall had been doodling. He did that to help him think. "Bill, you couldn't know if the Germans were bringing stuff to the front or taking it away, could you?"

"No. I just saw vehicles and assumed that they were reinforcing."

"And that is logical but suppose they were moving men and materials away from this front and this sector to reinforce somewhere else."

"That would make sense," Archie nodded his agreement.

We sat in silence taking it all in. "There is one way to find out you know sir."

"And what is that Captain?"

"Fly over to their airfield." I saw some of the lieutenants pale. "We would only have to get close enough to count the aeroplanes. There were two squadrons. Anything less means they have moved them. If there are two then it means they are up to something. We would only be travelling twenty miles further than we did today. If we go in at high altitude we should be safe."

The Major looked at the colonel and they nodded. Ted shook his head, "It is my turn to go on leave the day after tomorrow. If anything happens to me I'll have you, Billy Harsker!"

I laughed, "That is what I like the old pessimistic Ted Thomas is back."

It was another crisp and cold day when we took off. I led the flight as I was the one who knew the route better than the rest. I was happy with that responsibility. That way I could determine the height and initiate a retreat if necessary. When we had passed the front, I noticed that there were less vehicles parked and fewer tents. Men had been moved. As we neared the airfield we armed our weapons. I knew that Hutton had acquired another couple of Mills bombs. I didn't ask where from. It was, however, reassuring.

When I spotted the airfield, I noticed immediately that there were only eight aeroplanes lined up. I circled so that the major and Ted could confirm what I had seen and then I headed back to our airfield.

"Well it looks like they have moved a squadron. This could well be a quiet sector for a while."

The five of us who were the senior officers were all seated in the Colonel's office. "And I agree with Bill we saw fewer men in their secondary trenches. The front line was just as full of men as before but not the support trenches."

"Well then I will write a report for Headquarters but in light of this I think that when Lieutenant Hewitt returns the rest of you can take your leave. That way we will all be back here by the middle of January."

"And you sir?"

"I think I had plenty of leave when my son was ill."

"And how is your son now sir?" None of us had asked those questions before in case the answer upset the colonel but he smiled. "He is at home with my wife. He is recovering and so I will pay back the squadron for the time I was absent. I owe it to them."

Small things, such as an early leave, have the most amazing effect on morale. Already happier now that we had wooden walls and warmth the younger officers became like giddy schoolboys. I found myself watching their antics with the Major and Captain Marshall. It did not seem five minutes since I had been a young boy with the Yeomanry behaving much the same as the lieutenants were. The war was over a year old; I felt like I had aged much more.

Poor Gordy came back bouncing and full of joy at having had Christmas with Mary. His excitement was punctured like a barrage balloon when he discovered that the rest of us were off on leave. He would be left alone with his two younger officers.

I travelled with the other officers as far as London. We made surprisingly good time and reached London by early afternoon. I discovered that the only train which would get me home was a slow train which would only reach home in the early hours of the following morning. I decided to stay overnight in a hotel. The paymaster had just paid us and I was feeling flush. I decided to head down to the better end of London; towards Piccadilly and Mayfair. I would have a good night in a luxury hotel. I took a taxi from the station.

The cabbie was a typical Londoner; he complained nonstop about the traffic, the politicians and the conduct of the war. If he was running things, he had assured me, then the boys would soon be back from the trenches. I got out at Green Park somewhat relieved to be away from his barrage of vitriol. I was standing on the corner and lighting my pipe when I heard the honk of a car horn. I looked down and saw Lord Burscough pulling out of the Ritz's garage. Ignoring the honking horns, the major leapt out of his Singer and pumped my hand. "Bill! Damned glad to see you. Where are you off to?"

"The colonel gave us a week's leave so I was heading home. The only train gets in at two o'clock in the morning and I was going to get a later train tomorrow."

He grabbed my bag and hurled it into the back seat with his. "Well this is a fine thing. You will come with me. I can get us home quicker and you can spell me with the driving. Hop in!"

The major was always impulsive. I found myself next to him as we hurtled northwards on the A5. He chattered on nonstop. He had much to tell me. I discovered that Major Hamilton-Grant had been sent back to train pilots. I was not sure that was a good thing but, I supposed, it was better than having him risk their lives in combat. Lord Burscough also had a short leave for he was to take command of a new squadron flying a new aeroplane called the DH 2.

"It is very much like the FE 2. It is a pusher but there is no gunner. It is single seater." He had sounded, briefly, sad, "Those damned Fokkers cut my boys up pretty badly. The Bristol was no match for them. I know you chaps did pretty well against them. How many kills do you have now?"

"Six Fokkers and another two captured or shot down."

"An ace! I am honoured. I only have seven myself. Still with this new bus I reckon we can turn the tide. "

"Is it faster sir?"

"A little but it is smaller and that means a smaller target for the Fokker. The other thing is I will be able to turn and loop without worrying about throwing out the old gunner." He laughed and we both remembered how I had had to hang upside down from the guns when one pilot had tried that manoeuvre with me as a gunner.

I relieved him at the wheel and we thundered up the empty road. We almost flew along the black strip of tarmac. It was hairy in places as there were wet patches on the road but we managed to keep up a good speed of between fifty and seventy miles an hour. The major managed the seventy; I was more conservative during my stints behind the wheel. Four and a bit hours after leaving London he pulled up outside the cottage. The glowing lights inside looked welcoming.

"I'll be going back myself in five days. Shall I pick you up?"

"If it is not too much trouble, sir."

He laughed, "You are good company and we do it far faster. Enjoy your leave!"

His roaring exhaust and screeching wheels brought my dad to the door. "What the..." when he saw me his smile spread from ear to ear, "Mother, it's our Bill, he's home!"

There is something about walking through your own front door; it is an experience and a pleasure like no other. Memories of growing up, comfort and food all intermingled. I saw the welcoming fire and mum in her rocking chair knitting. Dad's seat was empty and next to it sat our Sarah looking as though she had eaten a whole goose for Christmas.

She went to get up. I held up my hand. "I think you might need a crane there, our kid. Don't get up!"

I went to hug her, "You cheeky little so and so." As I pulled away she said, "But I am glad to see you."

I went to mum and hugged her. I felt the salt tears on my cheeks but her face was filled with joy. She just stared at me and Sarah said, "Don't you look smart in your captain's uniform. You'll be fighting the girls off with a stick, our Bill."

"Chance'd be a fine thing. The nearest we get to a female is if one of the farmer's cows strays close to the airfield!"

Dad laughed as he resumed his seat. "Sit down, son. We'll have a chat and then we'll go down for a pint!"

"Father he's only just got home!"

"I know mother, but I want to have a nice sit down and chat with one of my sons and have a pint if that's all the same to you."

It was rare for my dad to be so forceful and mum just sniffed and said, "Well it will give me time to get some tea on then."

She began to rise and I said, "Let's sit and talk for a bit. It's good to be home."

I knew I had said the right thing when she beamed and our Sarah nodded her approval.

"Was that Lord Burscough's car we heard?"

"Aye dad, he picked me up in London and we drove here straight away. The alternative was a train which didn't get in until the middle of the night. He's giving me a lift back so I have five days here." I began to fill my pipe. "How long then our Sarah?"

"Any time. I've had a few twinges."

"Where's our Alice, I thought she would have been here to help?"

Mother's face darkened, "That little madam will be gallivanting about. She has taken to going into Liverpool with her mates of a night. She's changing!" I saw her put her handkerchief to her face.

"Now then mother, it is just a phase. She's all right is our Alice and when she knows our Bill is home she won't go out as much." Our Sarah was always the peacemaker.

"Well I hope so."

Dad had his pipe going, "Our Bert is over there now, you know."

"Aye, I met him." The relief on their three faces showed me just how much they worried about both of us.

"When?"

"The first time was just before the battle and the last time was a week ago. He and his Engineers built our quarters."

"He's safe then? We heard a lot of Engineers died at that battle."

"No, he's fine and he's a Lance Corporal now. You wouldn't recognise him. He's grown a lot. The war does that to you."

"Aye we know."

"Mrs Burns' son, Harry, he died at Loos."

Our Sarah nodded. I noticed that she was knitting all the time we spoke, "And Gerald, the under footman, he joined up and lost both his legs too." She shook her head, "He should have stayed at the house. What will he do for a living now?"

I couldn't answer and I knew that whatever I said would not make them feel any better. I knew she was thinking of her husband, Rogers, the butler and what would happen if he was in the army. I had no good news to give them. Things would only get worse. It was better that they did not know the horrors of the front. Whatever they imagined was a pale shadow of the harsh reality.

Dad stood, "Well get your coat and let's go. The lads'll be pleased to see you again."

Mother said, "Don't you want to change, you know, into ordinary clothes?"

"Our Bill is a hero. It said so in that paper. Let them see he is serving his country.

As we strolled down the lane to the village he said, "Our Sarah is wrong you know. It is every Englishman's duty to fight these evil Germans. I wasn't happy that Bert went but that was only because of his age. But I am proud of both of you. There are lads older than him and they are making a nice living here in the village and not risking their lives. It's not right and I tell them!"

I could imagine that. Dad was a real patriot. England, the King and Queen and his lordship; they were his world.

It was a cold evening and our breath formed clouds before us. The glow from the pub drew us like moths to a flame. I saw other men strolling for a Friday night in the pub. When the door opened we were hit by a wall of beer fumes, smoke and human sweat. It was a unique mix and I had missed it.

As soon as I entered I took off my greatcoat. I was about to take off my hat when Dad said, quietly, "Leave it on, son. You look smart. When we were recognised there was a roar from dad's cronies.

The landlord grinned and said, "Welcome home captain. The first drink is on the house!"

One of dad's mates said, "Tight bugger! For a hero, it should be drinks for everybody."

George, the landlord, pointed to the moaner and said, "When you shoot down German aeroplanes then you can have a free drink."

It was a pleasant hour we spent in the pub. I was bombarded by questions. They came at me as fast as a Fokker's machine gun. They had all heard of the Fokker Scourge. The newspapers had been filled with stories of British pilots falling foul of this new German weapon of terror.

"It is only temporary. Things move quickly in the air. I daresay we have some engineers devising an aeroplane even better than theirs. It's the way things go."

That seemed to please them. "Anything the Huns can do we can do better. They aren't even a proper country and their king is Queen Victoria's grandson! She'll be turning in her grave."

That began a whole heated debate about the rights and wrongs of the Royal Family and the Germanic connections. I sensed that dad was getting upset, "I'm starving. What say we get a couple of bottles from the outdoor and have them with our tea?"

He brightened. "George, a couple of bottles of brown ale to take out."

"Are you off already? Don't mind this lot Bill. I'd like to hear more about your flying. We didn't have aeroplanes in my day. We just fought the Boers with rifles and cannon."

"I am home for five days. I daresay I will be in again."

"Good."

I put the bottles in my greatcoat pockets and we left. The snow had started to flurry. It was always the same in January. We never got a white Christmas but you could guarantee snow in January. The frozen flakes on our faces made us hurry, as fast as dad could manage, to reach home.

There was a wonderful warm smell when we entered the house. Mum had made a rabbit casserole. She smiled when she saw we had returned relatively swiftly. "It's still got another hour to go but our Sarah made some fresh bread before and I have some nice butter we made yesterday. That'll go well with a bit of cheese."

I was home and that meant that mum waited on me hand and foot. I took off my boots and my tunic and loosened my collar. Dad poured me a beer and I happily ate fresh bread, homemade butter and some cheese made on the estate. Life did not get any better than that. When the food was ready I wolfed it down. Beer has a way of giving an appetite.

It was after nine o'clock when Alice arrived home. I was dozing by the fire and I was woken by angry voices.

"What time do you call this young lady?"

"It's only nine o'clock and I was the first one to leave!" I stood and turned. Alice gave a squeal and threw her arms around me, "Our Bill! Why didn't you tell us you were coming home?"

"If you had been in you would have known!" Alice flashed mother an angry look.

"I didn't know but I am home now for five days." I hugged her. She had grown into a pretty young woman. The last time I had seen her she had been little more than a school girl but now she was dressed in smart, fashionable clothes and I could see that she wore make up. No wonder mum was not happy.

"Good. Let me get my coat off and you can tell me all about it."

I sighed. This would be the third telling of my life as a pilot. Despite the harsh words mum went for a plate of the casserole and Alice ate, at the table while I recounted my exploits. I decided I would get more beer from the pub the next day.

Chapter 16

I did not get to the pub the next day. I was woken in the early hours of the morning by a scream and a shout. I leapt out of bed, catching my head on the door as I rushed to see what the problem was. Alice was standing there in her nightie. "Our Sarah has gone into labour. Put the kettle on, our Bill."

When I had put the kettle on to boil water I found the teapot and rinsed that out. The water would be for the baby but we would need tea. British families always needed tea to get through a crisis. Dad had dressed and he joined me. We sat at the table. "All we do now son, is sit and wait. They'll not thank you for interfering. Don't worry about our Sarah, your mother is the one the women on the estate send for when their times comes. She has soft hands. Sarah'll be alright."

Alice came down and went to a cupboard. She grabbed handfuls of towels. "Our Bill, bring that water upstairs."

You would never think she and mother had had a row a few hours earlier. They were now working together for our Sarah. It was the way of our family. We might have our differences but when our backs were to the wall then we all pulled together.

I climbed up the stairs. Alice halted me. "That's far enough. Put the water there and get downstairs with dad. This is women's work." She smiled as she said it.

In the kitchen dad had put the kettle on again and was warming the teapot. "This could take some time. Better put some bacon and sausages on." He smiled, "Your mother always gets them in for the weekend and I think there is a bit of kidney too."

The two of us pottered away both aware of the sound of footsteps on the floor above. When the tea had brewed I said, "Should we take a cup up to them?"

"I know you pilots are brave son but have you got a death wish? It's bad luck for a man to be there at the birth. You should know that."

"But what if it is a doctor?"

"They just do the fancy houses and they don't hold with such superstitions. No, son, you just wait here with me. That's Alice's job. She knows we have a brew on and she'll come when they are ready." He chuckled, "Besides the smell of the bacon'll bring the baby sooner."

There was still some of the fresh bread left and, when we had taken out the bacon and the sausage we dipped the bread in so that it became soaked in the bacon grease.

"Right son. Let's dig in. I've yet to meet the man that can walk by freshly cooked bacon."

The bacon in greasy bread was a treat and I bit into the bread feeling the juices run down my chin. Not the manners and behaviour of the officers' mess, but I was at home. I indulged myself. We washed it down with hot sweet tea and then lit our pipes.

"I remember when Tom and John were born. They were the first and I was up at the stables. Your mum was in labour for twelve hours with both of them. Your gran, her mother was still alive then and they were exhausted when they had finished. Mind, the tea was still on the table for me when I came from work. By the time you were born it was over in a flash. And Albert just took an hour." He gestured upstairs with his pipe. "This is her first so..."

I suddenly stood.

"What is it son?"

"Cedric, we haven't told Sarah's hubby that she is in labour. I know he can't be here but he should know."

Dad looked at the clock. It was just coming up to seven. "If you go up now the house should just be waking up."

"Right." I ran upstairs and threw some clothes on. Grabbing my flying coat and scarf I stepped out into the cold. Although the snow had lain it was a thin covering which would dissipate when the sun emerged. The ground was hard but I knew it was slippery underfoot. I went as quickly as I could to the big house, as we called it.

I saw that the curtains were open. They were up. Cedric Rogers was now the butler. In all likelihood, he would be the one to greet me. The gravel drive crunched under my feet. The snow had not settled here. I saw the Major's car, not so much parked as abandoned, under the huge portico. I pulled the handle on the bell pull and heard the ringing deep in the house.

It was Cedric who answered it. He had filled out since I had last seen him at the wedding. He looked surprised to see me and then he stiffened. "Yes, Captain Harsker? If you are here to see his Lordship he has yet to rise."

He sounded pompous. I had never been a fan of Cedric but Sarah loved him. I just wanted to prick his pomposity. "No, Cedric, I came to tell you something. Our Sarah is in labour."

For a moment, his mask fell and I saw the caring husband that Sarah loved. Then the fixed face of the retainer returned. "Thank you, Captain. I appreciate you taking the time to tell me."

It was obvious I was dismissed. "Well," I added awkwardly, "I will bring you news whenever I get it."

I headed back to the house wondering how I would be if I should ever have a wife and family. I hoped that I would show more concern than Cedric. Then I realised that our Sarah, as much as I loved her, was probably as bad. As housekeeper, she had a good job and it would be mum and dad who would be bringing up their child. I suspect the two of them had planned out their future carefully. I wondered if the child had been planned. I did know that my parents would love the child and he would be cared for and, at the end of the day, that was all that mattered.

When I returned and told dad what he had said he was not surprised, "It's just the way Cedric has been brought up son; service to the big house. It's how I was brought up but you, well, you would never have settled for that. Don't get me wrong, I am not putting you in the same boat as Tom and John but your mother and me knew you were destined for something more from the moment you were born. It's no secret that you were the cleverest. The school told us you were the brightest lad they had ever taught. So, you see, we knew you were different and your mum, well, when she sees you in your uniform she is so proud. She worries about you but she is proud at the same time."

I felt unsettled talking about me. "Should I see if they want tea?"

"No, I told you, that is No Man's Land up there and they don't need barbed wire. Besides our Alice came down for three cups and a bacon butty after she heard the door slam!"

Just then we heard the unmistakeable wailing of an infant. Dad grinned and jumped up. He shook my hand. I have no idea why. "There you are. The baby's born."

I heard feet moving and then, five minutes later Alice came through with a pile of soiled towels. She smiled but she looked tired. "You can go up now. Our Sarah and mum are ready for another cuppa."

We took a tea each and mounted the stairs. Opening the door, I saw Sarah with the new red-faced baby and mother standing beside her. It was a perfect picture of motherhood on every level. Sarah smiled as I entered, "Here is your nephew, William Rogers. William this is your uncle, the hero."

I looked down at the small bundled up baby who had been named after me and my world changed. I didn't realise it at the time but I was aware that something was different. I felt different. After I died there would be another Bill in the family. I wanted my own child and I wanted my own family. I suddenly envied Cedric and Gordy; they had what I wanted but I knew that I would have to wait until the war ended. I would not wish widowhood on any woman.

We were allowed the briefest of audiences and then ushered out. "I'll go and tell Cedric."

"I'll come with you our Bill, I need the fresh air." As we left the house Alice linked me, "It's good to have you back, big brother." She snuggled in. "Sorry about last night. Mum and I seem to butt heads the whole time. I don't mean to argue with her but she just seems to get under my skin."

I had been thinking about the problem and I thought I knew the reason for the arguments. "You know you are the only one left at home and the youngest. She is frightened that she will lose you. The arguments are her way of coping. Remember John and Tom? She worries that you will go the same way."

"But that's daft. I am nothing like them."

"I know but you need to talk to her. Dad is on your side, you know that."

"I know. I'll try."

"She will need more help than ever, soon. She will have the bairn to look after. That might help heal the differences."

She suddenly stopped and looked at me, "You have become wise, our Bill." She leaned up and kissed me on the cheek. "Don't you worry about me, love. What we are going through is nothing compared with what you and our Bert have to live with. Besides I know what I want to do. I am not like Tom and John. I don't just want to get out for the sake of it. I am taking a course at the technical college for design. I am quite good at it. I do a bit of work in a pub in Liverpool to make ends meet. Mum and dad think I am off gallivanting but I am not. You don't need to worry about me. I know where I am going."

I hugged her a little closer and kissed the top of her head. "I never doubted it for a minute, our kid."

Cedric still had the same po face when he answered the door. His face cracked a little when I told him that he had a son called William.

He smiled. It was not news to him. "We decided to name him after you. I hope you do not mind, Captain?"

"Of course not."

Just then I heard footsteps thundering along the hall. Lord Burscough threw his arms around me, much to the surprise of Rogers. "Did I hear you are an uncle? That calls for a celebration!" He suddenly seemed to see Alice. "Ah Alice and you are an aunt. Haven't you grown? You are a proper young lady now. Come in and we'll have some bubbly! Cedric get Lady Burscough. She is always asking after Alice here."

She shook her head, "I couldn't sir, I am not dressed properly."

He put his arms around us both, "Nonsense you are almost part of the family. Rogers we'll have it in the sitting room."

I knew that Alice was torn. She was delighted to be in the big house. She would see parts of it she had never seen before. Our sister was the housekeeper but we would be guests. At the same time, she would have wanted to look her best. Her clothes were presentable but not her finest. It is strange, but I felt completely at ease. I suspect it was because I had seen behind the façade and Major Hamilton-Grant had certainly coloured my judgement.

I was thankful, as we left, that Alice had been sensible. She had only drunk two small glasses of Champagne. Most of the time, she had chatted to Lady Burscough as though they were old friends. His lordship had picked a down to earth wife. Margaret Burscough was a modern lady and was very popular on the estate. She had to be for she ran it whilst his lordship was at war.

Strolling down the drive she snuggled into my arm, "You know Bill, John and Tom were both wrong. They hated being inferiors but you, well you and his lordship are almost equals and her ladyship is so lovely. She is just nice."

I laughed, "I wouldn't say that. He is a major and I call him sir."

She playfully punched my arm, "You know what I mean. I am even more proud of you than I was before. You have shown that we can change our station and we don't have to get married, like our Kath, to do so. I am going to make something of myself."

There was determination in her voice. She had always been clever and had done well at school. Now I knew that she was studying for a career in fashion I was happy. They earned good money. I think that was another reason for her and mum butting heads. It was an alien job to mum.

There was a slight frown from mother as we entered and I held up my hand, "Before you have a go, his lordship invited us in for a glass of Champagne to wet the baby's head. We couldn't refuse, could we?"

Mum glared at Alice, "Champagne?"

"She had one small glass." I used the firm voice I had learned to adopt when speaking to second lieutenants. It was the first time I had used it on my mum. Perhaps it was the Champagne which had given me the courage but it worked.

She smiled. "Your big brother looks after you well young lady. You should try to be more like him."

She gave my arm a squeeze and winked at me. "I'll try, don't you worry."

Chapter 17

We were nearing London and his Lordship and I had talked for the whole journey. He was excited about his new squadron and I was, well, I was excited about everything. I had a nephew. Alice had been sorted out and I knew where I wanted to be years from now. In addition, I was happy about the squadron. The Fokker Eindecker might be a scourge to others but I knew that my squadron could deal with them. For the first time in a long time I felt happy.

I was dropped at the station. "Keep in touch, Bill. If you ever want to transfer don't wait until you get an idiot like Hamilton-Grant."

"Right sir but we both know the Colonel is nothing like Hamilton-Grant."

"You are right. Damn your loyalty!" Laughing he roared off making everyone around turn and stare at the car.

It is strange; a couple of years ago, maybe even a year ago I would have been embarrassed if anybody turned and stared, first at the car and then at me. I had changed. Being stared at did not matter. It was not even important what others thought of me. I had sterner critics whose opinion I valued; the men I flew with.

I was one of the first back. That was largely down to the flying Major who had got me down for an earlier train than I had planned. I reached the base, courtesy of a lift with a lorry heading for Loos, on the evening before I was due to return. I must have looked keen.

I dumped my bag and coat in my room and went to the officers' mess. Gordy was in front of the fire with a glass of some spirit in his hand. He was more than a little drunk. "What the hell are you doing here? You aren't due back until tomorrow."

I smiled, "Major Burscough gave me a lift and I thought I would make your life a misery."

"Huh, it's that already. I had to leave Mary and then I have just spent a miserable week here with the bloody kindergarten." He found the young officers like schoolboys. Having been a sergeant for a long period and working alongside older soldiers had coloured his judgement. I noticed that he was slurring his words and looked flushed. He was drunk.

I pointed to the drink. "Well you have made yourself comfortable. What is that?"

His elbow slipped on the arm of the chair and a little of the amber liquid spilled on his arm. He lapped it like a cat. "Brandy! I found a village down the road and they sell it there. I thought it was a bit rough at first but I think that must have been a bad bottle. The last two have been fine."

I was shocked. I sniffed it. It smelled like petrol! Gordy was normally a beer man and to have downed three bottles of cheap brandy in less than a week was worrying. "Have the cooks finished for the day?"

"I just told them to make sandwiches. There is a pile in the dining room if you are hungry."

"Have you eaten?"

He shook his head, "Wasn't hungry." He had another sip of the brandy. I took a chair and filled my pipe. It was comfortable although I noticed that the fire had almost gone out. I turned to Gordy, "The fire is…" He was asleep and the brandy was perilously close to spilling. I took it and the half-smoked cigarette from his hand. I sniffed the brandy. It was one level up from paint stripper by the smell. I put the stopper back in the bottle and removed it from harm's way. After I had banked the fire up I sat down with a plate of sandwiches.

Two heads peered around the door. It was the two lieutenants from Gordy's flight. They looked worried. When they saw he was asleep they came in, looking relieved. "Did you have a good leave sir?"

"Never mind that, Dixon. Explain yourself."

They tried to look innocent. "What do you mean sir?" I didn't speak I just stared. Eventually Lieutenant Dixon said, "It's just that when Lieutenant Hewitt has had a drink he shouts at us a bit. After two nights, we decided to steer clear but it is warmer in here and he is normally asleep at this point."

I nodded, "Don't worry Dixon. He just disliked being on his own. The rest of the squadron is back tomorrow. There are sandwiches next door."

They looked at my pile miserably. "We know, sir, but we preferred hot food. Mr Hewitt said sandwiches were good enough for him."

"Did the colonel eat sandwiches?"

"No sir, the cooks made him the same meals as the sergeants ate."

"Righto. Give me a hand and we'll put him to bed."

The three of us manhandled the corpselike Gordy and put him in his bed. He never moved and snored away blissfully. I spoke with the cooks and asked them to cook a hot meal for the three of us. I left the two lieutenants in the mess and went to the colonel's quarters. The Royal Engineers had given him a bedroom and a small study.

I knocked on the door, "Come." When I entered he beamed, "Back early. A bit keen eh?"

"No sir, I got a lift with Colonel Burscough."

"Ah and have you eaten?"

"I had some sandwiches but I will eat with the lieutenants in a moment. Er Colonel, how has Gordy been lately? He seemed a little depressed to me."

He nodded, "I am glad that you are all back. He has been a little morose and, I think, drinking more than is good for one. I never judge and it seemed harmless but I wouldn't like it to continue." He gave me a pointed look. "You and Thomas are close to him…" He coughed, "I would prefer not to take disciplinary action. Do I make myself clear?"

I nodded, "Right sir." I saw he had a map in front of him. "Plans for us sir?"

"Yes, Harsker, we are going to be escorting bombers and spotters for a while. It seems that we are one of only a handful of squadrons who are holding their own against the Fokkers. Lord Burscough's new aeroplane, the DH 2, might be useful but they aren't even in France yet."

"Baby sitting eh sir?"

"Remember William, our job is to stop other pilots getting killed. It is damned expensive to train a pilot. The aeroplane is cheap by comparison. Some pilots are only lasting three hours over enemy territory. That is unacceptable. Even Freddy Carrick, our most junior officer has shot down a Fokker and lasted much longer than every other pilot who came out with him. The powers that be want to use that expertise." I turned to go. "Oh by the way the promotions for Hutton and Laithwaite came through. They are both in your flight, I'll let you tell them." He reached into a drawer and brought out two sets of sergeant stripes.

"Thank you, sir. They'll be pleased."

"They deserve it. Oh and I haven't heard yet about your medal. Damned pencil pushers."

"Don't worry, sir, you never miss what you have never had." I had already been turned for one medal I suspected with my record they would turn this request down too. I was just happy that my men had been rewarded.

I ate with the lieutenants and explained to them our new role. I think they appreciated it. Gordy had not been himself; that much was clear.

Gordy was hung over the next day and could barely remember speaking with me. "How did I get to bed?"

"Me and your lads put you there."

"Oh."

We were alone in the mess and I decided to take the bull by the horns. "Gordy, you have to be less aggressive with your flight."

I saw him stiffen, "Is that an order sir or just some advice which I can ignore if I choose?"

He was aggressive and I wondered if I ought to have waited until Ted was there. Then I realised that was the coward's way out. I decided there was no point in being subtle. It was for Gordy's good. "Actually, Gordy, it was advice from a friend but if you choose to ignore it then I will give you orders." It was then that I realised he didn't look well. His eyes had dark rings around them and he looked to have sunken cheeks. It was accentuated by the aggressive look he gave me and the way he balled his fists. "And I would warn you now to back off."

"Or what," he sneered, "you will put me on a charge?"

"No, we are old friends. I would take you outside and teach you a lesson." I leaned in to him and added quietly, "And you know I can do it." He glared at me for a moment and then sank back into his seat. "There was a time, Gordy, when I would never have dreamed of saying what I did but, at the moment, you are a wreck. I can't believe the change in you in just two weeks."

He suddenly changed. His face became haunted and his tone pleading. He spoke quietly, "It's Mary, Bill, and she wants to get married."

I smiled, "That is wonderful news, congratulations."

He shook his head, "You don't understand. How can I marry her when I might die at any time? Can I make her a widow a second time? I don't think so."

I nodded and began to fill my pipe. "I see, so instead you will become everything that you hated as a sergeant. You will be the bullying and uncaring officer who finds solace in the bottom of a bottle. You will break the heart of the woman who loves you. Yes, you are right; that makes perfect sense to me." I lit the pipe and puffed on it while I watched Gordy take in that information. He was breathing easier now. "Is she a bright woman, this Mary?" His eyes widened and I held up my hand. "I mean no offence but if she is, as I assume, intelligent, then do you not think that she has worked out that she could become a widow again and she is willing to take that chance>" He sat back with his mouth open. "You and Mary have a chance of happiness. Of course, you could get killed. We all could. If you do die then she will at least have the happy memory of the time you spent together. The longer you delay the marriage the shorter that time will be."

The door opened and Johnny and Freddy stood there with grins on their faces. They looked at us and the grins disappeared. Gordy stood and grabbed my hand. He shook it. He said, quietly, "Thanks Bill. I've been an idiot. Use the rest of that brandy as a firelighter. I have a letter to write." He left and closed the door behind him.

"What was all that about sir?"

I put my hands on my hips. "Nothing for Second Lieutenants to worry about." I smiled to take the sting from my words. "Did you have a good leave?"

"Oh yes sir. But it is good to be back."

I shook my head, "Oh to be young and foolish again."

The others all arrived together on the same train and the mess became crowded, noisy and smoky. The only absentee was Gordy and Ted took me to one side. "Where is Gordy? I have heard he was hitting the bottle and behaving like an idiot."

"He is fine now, Ted. He just needs his friends around him. There is nothing to worry about so don't mention it. It was a mistake to leave the three of them alone for a week. But we are back now and we can start to win the war."

The first night back was a party atmosphere but Gordy, noticeably, abstained. I too took it easy and the three of us sat and chatted whilst the younger ones told tall tales of their leaves and the hearts they had broken. Major Leach was the last to arrive back. He had had the shortest leave having travelled all the way to Scotland. He caught my eye and waved me outside.

"Let's take a wee stroll around the field eh laddie. A nice fresh night." Fresh was the word; it was freezing but I complied. "I take it you had a word with Gordy then?"

"Yes sir." I paused, "The colonel spoke with you and told you of the problem?"

"Aye, he let the lieutenant's behaviour slide but he was prepared to do something if you hadna had a word. Is it sorted?" He held up a hand. "You two are friends and I am not going to pry. I am asking as the officer who has to lead this squadron to war. Can I rely on Gordy?"

I looked him squarely in the eye. "One hundred per cent sir. You have my word."

He grinned and slapped me on the back. "You are a good lad, Bill. Well let's get back inside I am freezing."

Chapter 18

The next day we received our orders and the rest of the squadron received the news that we would be watching over some RE 7 bombers. We were going back to war. Before I went into the briefing I went to the aeroplanes where Laithwaite and Hutton were busy working on the buses. I took Holt and Carrick with me. They knew what was coming and wanted to be part of it.

"Laithwaite, Hutton, stop what you are doing and come here a moment please."

They both stiffened as though they had done something wrong. Lumpy asked, "Summat up, sir?"

I reached into my right-hand pocket and brought out the sergeant's stripes. "Not really but you have been promoted. Congratulations." I handed him the stripes. I was delighted to see that Laithwaite looked pleased for his friend. "And you too Laithwaite. Well done." I handed him his stripes. "I think we can get it backdated to the first of January. A little more money always comes in handy after Christmas eh?"

"Thank you, sir."

"Carry on."

As the engines were being warmed up, in this cold February morning, I took Holt and Carrick to one side. "I want to practise staying in formation today at high altitude. I want to try something different for us three. If it works we will try it with Lieutenant Hewitt's flight too."

Their keen young faces showed that they were eager to learn.

"I will fly in the middle, Johnny you will fly slightly behind to the right and Freddy, slightly behind and to the left. It means that I can see you both and give you better direction. It will not need to be follow my leader. I will use simple handle signals. I will point in the direction I want us to go. If I want you to do something different I will point to me and then the pilot I am ordering. Does that seem simple enough?"

"Yes sir."

"I want to give us more flexibility. There is little point in three of us chasing after one Hun and leaving the bombers to be attacked by hordes of the little beggars."

"Righto sir. When do we start the escort duties?"

"It could be any time, Johnny so be on your toes."

I returned to Captain Marshall's office. Since the new building had been erected we had an office where Randolph could keep the reports and maps. I would spend an increasing amount of time there. Major Leach was already there when I arrived. He waved a sheet of paper at me.

"We are popular fellows, Bill. It seems we are to escort two squadrons of bombers each heading for a separate target."

Captain Marshall walked to the map and put a red pin in the airfields of the two squadrons. I could see that they were further from the front than we were. One was to the north and one to the south. "From what I have been able to gather these birds have a slower speed, about ten miles an hour, at least, slower. They have a lower altitude as well as a shorter range."

"That is a good thing surely?"

Their faces told me that they did not think so.

"It seems to me that we can use the extra altitude and speed to wait above the bombers and hit the enemy fighters when they try to attack and our greater endurance means that we can watch over them when they return home."

Archie lit his pipe and sat on one of the seats. "You wouldn't fly next to them then?"

"No. We lose all surprise. The enemy can see us and attack our blind spot. If we are above the bombers we can see a greater distance. We might even be able to hit them before they get close to the bombers. That is where our speed comes in."

"Suppose they come from the rear. They have shown that they can be cunning blighters."

"We do not have to fly in the same direction. We have greater speed we could zig zag across them."

Archie smiled, "You know laddie, that just might work! Any more bright ideas?"

"I am going to try a formation with me in the middle and the others on either side of me. It might be I need to use them individually."

"Risky. Are the two lads good enough for that?"

"I think so and if we have Lieutenant Hewitt's flight with us they can fly the regular formation."

"Well give it a go then."

As I left the office a lorry pulled up. I saw Sergeant Sharp jump down from the back. I saw him wince slightly as he landed. "Charlie! Good to see you! All healed?"

"Getting there."

"I saw your face then Charlie. It still hurts?"

He nodded, "But it is getting better, sir."

"Good. Listen we are taking the flight out tomorrow. We will leave Hutton on the gun until we have completed that and then I'll take you up and we'll see how you manage. How's that?"

I saw relief on his face, "That's great sir. I want to get up again but I didn't want to let you down."

"You won't. Come on and I'll take you to the new quarters."

He spread his arm. "This is a bit better than tents eh sir?"

"It is certainly warmer. Have you given any more thoughts to becoming a pilot? This squadron will be your best chance."

"Yes sir. I have and I think I will try the colonel's test. If you think you can teach me."

I laughed, "It will not be a problem. When your leg is healed we will give it a go." We had reached the new barracks. "Here we are; the sergeants' Shangri-La!"

I was tempted to stay and see how Charlie and Lumpy hit it off and then realised that they were grown men. They would work it out. I found Gordy with his pilots and their gunners. They too were checking out their aeroplanes. That was a good sign. An even better one was the fact that they were laughing and joking.

They snapped to attention as I approached. "As you were. Just to let you know that we will be escorting bombers tomorrow. I intend to fly above them. I am trying a new formation with my flight but you can use the normal line astern. If mine works out then you can try it too."

Gordy nodded. "Any idea where we are off to?"

"The railway lines just east of the front from what Captain Marshall told me. It doesn't really matter as we know it will be behind the enemy lines. You know what that means?"

Gordy nodded, "We will be closer to their airfields and they can get more aeroplanes to attack us in a shorter time."

"Exactly. I intend, if we are attacked, to buy the slower bombers time to get back. We know we can handle the fighters but they would be Fokker Fodder! If we have to we will use the defensive circle."

"Only the younger officers have tried that!"

There was an edge of criticism in Gordy's voice. I understood it. We would be gambling with an untried strategy. I shrugged, "If it looks like it isn't working I will fire a Very flare and it will be every man for himself."

We were up before dawn. The rendezvous with the bombers would be at eight thirty but we needed to make sure that we were ready. This was a new bomber and carried over two hundred and fifty pounds of bombs. It was important to get things right.

Sergeant Sharp was at the aeroplane with Hutton when I arrived. "You could have had a lie in Charlie."

He laughed, "I need to get back into the routine besides the nurses at the hospital took great delight at waking us at the very crack of dawn!"

"How is the bus?"

They both nodded and Lumpy tossed a Mills bomb in his hand. "She's ready to go and I have a couple of these."

Charlie laughed, "They have their own chart in the sergeant's mess sir. Lumpy here is top."

"A chart?"

"Yes sir. How many enemy planes each sergeant has downed. I have a target when I rejoin you."

I saw a flash of disappointment on Hutton's face but he soon hid it as he busied himself inside the cockpit. We took off into the rising sun. When we finally reached our cruising altitude we went into our new formation. I realised that we looked like an elongated arrow. I was the tip and the last Gunbus in Gordy's flight was the tail.

We circled the rendezvous until the eight RE 7 bombers arrived. They were single engine and a biplane. A little bigger than us, I saw that they only had one Lewis for defence. There was no gun for the pilot. I could see why they needed protection. The leading aeroplane waved and I waggled my wings and we followed them. It seemed ponderously slow although we were only flying at ten miles an hour slower than we normally did. We passed our lines and then No-Man's Land. The German guns opened up at us when we crossed their lines. The shell bursts looked perilously close to the bombers. I would have flown at a higher altitude had I been their leader.

Once they reached their target they went into line astern and began their bombing run. I took my arrow in a large loop above them keeping a close watch to the east and the German airfields. I heard the crump of the bombs striking the ground and when I looked down I could see that the railway lines, the bridge and the road were wreathed in smoke and flames. It only took five or six minutes for the eight bombers to offload their cargo and then I saw them head west. I kept my fight above the burning bridge while we watched for the enemy.

The last bomber had just turned to follow his companions when the Fokkers appeared. It was a squadron. It looked to me that they had taken off as quickly as they could for they were strung out in a ragged line. We had an advantage. For once we would outgun them.

Gordy would be playing follow my leader but I pointed forward to my two wingmen and we dived, head on, towards the Fokkers. "Lumpy wait until you cannot miss."

"Sir!"

I hoped that Holt and Carrick would have the nerve and hold fire too. The Eindecker was climbing at a slower rate than we were diving. He would struggle to make the turn we had seen the others do. In addition, I had three more Gunbuses behind me. I began a slow turn to starboard. I wanted the Fokkers to face a wall of fire from all of the aeroplanes in my flight. Hutton opened fire a heartbeat after the German did. The difference was that Hutton could continue to train his gun as we turned whereas the German was firing into empty air. Lumpy and Laithwaite were able to concentrate their fire and they struck the engine of the first Fokker. It stopped and the stricken craft plummeted to the ground.

The next aeroplane climbing to meet us was hit by the combined fire of three aeroplanes and it too fell from the sky. We had now made our turn and were heading west. I led my aeroplanes down to a low altitude so that the Fokkers could not get below us. As I levelled out I said, "Lumpy get on the rear gun."

I heard the sigh before the, "Yes sir!" He hated having to turn and then stand. If he had thought about it he would have realised that his low centre of gravity made him safer.

When he was in position and his face was just in front of me I shouted, "Can you see them?"

"Sir, they are chasing Lieutenant Hewitt's flight but they are all strung out."

I glanced at the ground below me. We had passed the German lines. The desultory crack of rifles and machine guns below us showed that the Germans were awake but, thankfully, not accurate. Once we had passed No-Man's Land I breathed a sigh of relief. Two Fokkers had been destroyed but, more importantly, we had not, as yet, lost an aeroplane.

As we approached the field I saw that Major Leach had not been as fortunate. I counted but five aeroplanes and the cluster of people around two others suggested injuries and damage too.

I landed and taxied my flight to the opposite side of the field. Since we had been bombed we had spread the aeroplanes out to minimise damage in case of an attack. I waited for the other pilots to join me. Laithwaite and Hutton were congratulating each other. "That's at least half an aeroplane each."

Gordy's gunner joined in, "But what about the other? At least four of us got that one."

Lumpy snorted, "That's easy; a quarter of a kill each."

I nodded to my two wingmen. "Well done you two. I should have warned you that I might turn and attack across their guns."

Johnny nodded, "I thought it was risky but I had my eye on your sir and when I saw your wing dip a little I knew you were turning. That formation really works sir."

"Yes, Johnny, but next time they might take off earlier and be waiting for us. They could meet us in a line of their own. Then we might be in trouble."

Gordy clapped me on the back; he was getting back to his old self. "That felt good. We caught them with their pants down there."

"But they will be up and about the next time. It will not be as easy."

He nodded towards the other aeroplanes. "It looks like the others were banged about a bit eh?"

"I know. Let's make our report. They won't want the attention of our smiles and grins." I pointed to the two sheet covered bodies. "They have lost men."

The others heard my words and saw the bodies too. The grins and smiles left their faces. Our joy had been short lived.

We had just finished writing our report when the major came in. His face told the story. Captain Marshall asked the question which was on our minds. "What happened, sir?"

"The RE 7 squadron managed to bomb well enough and then the Fokkers hit us. They got my gunner before he got off a bullet. Then they got the second aeroplane in the line. Stephenson didn't stand a chance. The bullets went through his gunner and hit him. They crashed in No-Man's Land. Then they got Lawson's gunner and we got back here as soon as we could. Thomas did well and his men covered us but they were knocked about a bit too."

He seemed to remember that we had been on a raid too. "How about you? I saw six of you land."

"The bombers did their job and we were jumped too but we hit them with my new formation. We downed two and then headed back home. Hutton and Laithwaite are deadly with their guns."

He smiled, "It seems we need to watch and learn. Charlie Sharp is back, isn't he?"

"Yes sir," I said, warily.

"I'll take Hutton from you and we will have to try to get another replacement."

"But sir, I am not sure his leg is healed."

"I'm sorry, Bill. If the hospital released him then he is ready. We can't afford any passengers here."

I found Sergeant Hutton and Sergeant Laithwaite in high spirits. "Sergeant Hutton, may I have a word?"

He beamed as Sergeant Laithwaite headed for the Sergeant's Mess, "Yes sir, what can I do for you."

"You could regard this as promotion, Lumpy, you are to be Major Leach's gunner. His gunner died today."

To say his face fell would be the understatement of the year. He nodded and held out a hand. "Can I just thank you, sir for all that you have done for me. I had never even flown before I became your gunner and now I am the top gunner in the squadron. I owe it all to you. I may be going to the senior pilot but I am not going to the best pilot." He nodded, "And you and Charlie, well, you are a team. I knew I was just filling in but it was worth every minute sir."

"And Sergeant, I have learned much from you."

He walked off slowly and then, as his natural happy nature took over, he began whistling and there was a bounce in his step once more. Charlie of course was delighted to be gunner again. When I mentioned his leg he shook his head, "No sir, it is fine. I must have landed heavily jumping out of the lorry. I am as right as rain today."

"And a consummate liar. You might want to have a look at your cockpit. Lumpy was a little larger than you and he took out some of your bullet proofing."

"Righto sir."

The message from headquarters was that the raids had been unqualified successes. A handful of dead men and no bomber losses was their measure. I am not sure that it was mine. The colonel was also pleased. He had the major and me in his office the following day. "Archie here told me about your innovative formation. Do you think we should all give it a go?"

"Well sir, Gordy's flight flew in line astern which gave us the best of both worlds so I am not sure. The best thing about it is the flexibility. We have been using three aeroplanes as one when sometimes they would have been better if we had given them leeway."

"Well Archie?"

"I reckon we will try out the new formation. It can't hurt. You can't argue with success and young Harsker here is either the luckiest pilot on the planet or he knows something we can all learn from."

Chapter 19

We were called upon to help four days later. There was a bridge which carried a railway line and a nearby road. They were both supplying the Germans. We were in a war of attrition. If we could make them divert resources to repairing roads and railways whilst putting their men on short rations then so much the better. We later discovered that the Germans were about to attack at Verdun. Our little raids were only pin pricks but they drew resources away from where they were needed. That was the problem of being one small fighter squadron; you never saw the big picture.

The major would only have four aeroplanes at his disposal. I had the luxury of two full flights. Lumpy Hutton waved cheerfully at Sharp and me as we went to our aeroplane. The nights were now marginally shorter and we left that little bit earlier than we had done previously. We were escorting the same bombers but we had a different rendezvous point. Gordy was trying out my arrow formation. I had his aeroplanes a little lower than ours and we circled the slow bombers as we flew across empty skies towards the target.

Sharp saw them first; the distinctive little crosses that were the monoplanes. They were in two lines. This would not be as easy. I estimated that they were over our target. We would have to try to disrupt them. I saw that there were just ten of them and I worked out that it had to be the same Jasta we had encountered earlier. They would know of our new formation. I waggled my wings to attract Gordy's attention and then pointed at the Fokkers. We had one advantage; we were six aeroplanes but we had twelve guns. I had already discussed with my pilots how we could use our forward machine on the attacking aeroplane and the gunner to rake the sides of other aeroplanes. This would be the day when we would try that out.

The bombers must have been worried at the sight of so many enemy aeroplanes. If we failed then they would die but they were brave men and not one of the eight turned around. There was little point in travelling at the slow speed of the bombers. We had altitude and we used it. I pushed the stick forward and we leapt towards the Fokkers. This time they were at a slightly higher altitude and we came together at almost two hundred miles an hour. Combat is over in the blink of an eye at those speeds and I hoped that Sharp had not lost his edge.

"Remember, Charlie, I will go for the head on Fokker. You choose one to the side."

"Right sir." There was a pause. "I won't let you down."

"I know."

We hurtled towards the first one. It was a hard job to estimate the best time to fire. I cocked the Lewis and made the slightest of movements to starboard and then corrected. It would not affect Holt and Carrick but it might make the Fokker think I was banking. He fired and my manoeuvre meant he only struck the upper wing at the tip.

I held my nerve and, as he climbed to do the sneaky turn, I fired and ripped through his fuselage. I had no time to see what damage I had caused for the monoplane whizzed above my head. Sharp was pumping bullets into the side of one of the other Fokkers and Holt's gunner was doing the same. I began to bank to starboard. I did it slowly to give Johnny time to react. It also allowed Freddy and his gunner to add to our fire power. Gordy and his flight kept going straight. We had gone from one arrow of six to two arrows of three and I could see one downed Fokker and one limping away.

I continued my bank to starboard and glanced down at the bombers. They were in line astern beginning their bombing run. I banked to port. Once again, I made a slow start to allow my wingmen to see the move. It took the Hun by surprise. They were engaging Gordy and his flight. We arrived on their port side with six machine guns blazing. This time the speed was slower for they were moving up to attack Gordy and his men from beneath. My magazine was empty. I drew my Luger and emptied the magazine into one of the Fokkers as we passed above him. I had no idea if I had struck him but I was close enough to make him look up.

As I passed above them I saw that Johnny and Freddy had, quite rightly, taken evasive action. I could make tighter turns now that I did not have to worry about them. All semblance of formation had now gone and aeroplanes were coming from every direction. I heard bullets as they thumped into our rear.

"Charlie. Get on the rear Lewis, someone is on our tail."

I dipped the nose slightly in case they were beneath us. When the bullets hit the tail, I knew that they were not. Charlie cocked the Lewis and began to fire. Perhaps because we had not used it before the German pilots appeared to have forgotten about our sting in the tail or maybe they thought it could not hurt them. Whatever the reason, Sharp managed to hit the Fokker which began to spiral to earth. And then we were alone in the sky.

I checked the compass and saw that we were heading east. I banked around and saw the bombers heading west. It was almost the same as before except that there were three Fokkers chasing them. I could see the other Gunbuses engaged in aerial duels of their own.

"Charlie, get back on the front gun!"

As I pushed the stick forward I watched as the rear bomber was attacked by a Fokker. The gunner did his best but, when the second Fokker opened up he had no chance and the aeroplane began to fall from the sky. I used my knees to hold the stick steady and changed the magazine. We were gaining rapidly on the enemy. The disadvantage with the monoplane was that you had no idea what was going on behind you. Sharp timed his shots perfectly. He began firing halfway along the fuselage and tracked the bullets until they smacked into the back of the pilot. He had to be dead but the aeroplane did not know that and it continued to fly in a straight line. I flew over the top of the dead German. Sharp was not as lucky with his next shots. The Fokker moved to port to bring his guns to bear on the next bomber and Sharp's bullets missed, alerting the pilot to the danger.

I instinctively turned to port too and the Fokker came across my gun sight. I fired a short burst and saw the bullets stitch a line along the fuselage. Oil began to pour from the engine and he swung his aeroplane around towards the east and safety. The last Fokker was shredding the tail of the next bomber. Sharp emptied the magazine at the same time as the gunner on the RE 7 fired at the Fokker. He was caught between two fires and then I pulled my trigger. His fuselage looked like a piece of Swiss cheese and he turned to starboard and safety.

We began to climb above the bomber so that I could get a view towards the east. The gunner waved cheerfully as we rose above it and banked to starboard. I saw a couple of Gunbuses hurtling towards us. I assumed they would be my flight. I could not see any other aeroplanes. Where Gordy and the Fokkers were I had no idea.

As I had enough fuel I began circling. The bombers, those that remained, were safe now. We had lost one and nearly a second but that could not be helped. We had been seriously outnumbered and they had been waiting for us. I saw that it was Freddy and Johnny and both had taken hits. They waved to show that they could fly and took station on me. I had about ten minutes fuel left and then I would have to head for home. I decided to wait.

I saw a trail of smoke appear from the east. I saw that it was an FE 2 and there were four Fokkers chasing it. I wondered where they had come from. I had lost track of the damaged and destroyed aeroplanes. If these were four Fokkers from the same squadron then Gordy and his flight had been badly handled.

I saw that the smoke was from one of the Fokkers but the FE 2 was moving erratically about the sky. It was Gordy! I dipped my nose and we began to dive towards them. We closed the gap rapidly and, as we drew close, the four Germans fired a last burst at Gordy and then headed east. I flew around the stricken aeroplane and saw blood on the fuselage near to the cockpit. Either Gordy or his gunner was wounded. I signalled the other two to keep on station and we shepherded Gordy back to the base.

It soon became clear that it was Gordy who had been wounded for the plane rose and fell alarmingly. I saw the gunner look around to see what was wrong with his pilot. When we were a mile from the field I said, "Charlie, a flare!"

The Very light soared into the sky. Doc Brennan and his team would be forewarned.

We allowed Gordy to land and then with fuel tanks almost on empty we dropped to the ground. I saw that all of the Major's aeroplanes had landed. We were now down to eight aeroplanes again. The pendulum had swung in the opposite direction. The Germans had had the upper hand.

Doc Brennan was leaning over Gordy when we reached him. "Stand back, you fellows. He'll live but not if you lot suffocate him."

I pulled his gunner to one side, "Tell me, Sergeant, what happened?"

"We followed you in sir and it was going well. Lieutenant Hewitt banked left to go after the Fokkers and Mr Hardy didn't see him. He pulled the stick too hard or something and the Fokker ripped him in two. They outnumbered us then. My gun jammed and Lieutenant Hewitt ran out of bullets. That was when they got young Mr Penrose. They came after us. We looked around and I saw your two lads heading west. I got on the rear Lewis and then, well you know the rest."

I patted his shoulder. You did well now before you do anything else strip down and clean all three Lewis guns. We both know yours should not have jammed." He nodded and I could see that he was upset. "These things happen but only the once eh?"

The Lewis was a reliable gun. Sharp and Hutton made sure that our guns did not jam by taking them apart after each flight and completely cleaning them. It was still possible for them to jam but at least the gunner knew that he had done everything in his power to prevent it.

Doc Brennan had taken Gordy away and I went to the office. Archie took one look at my face and said, "Now stop that, Laddie! You have nothing to reproach yourself about. That was a good operation. I spoke to young Holt. You destroyed at least three and possibly four aeroplanes and damaged two more. Yes, they got a bomber and two of our lads went down but we came out on top."

"From what Gordy's gunner said one of the aeroplanes went down because of pilot error. I still blame myself. I should have made Gordy practice that formation I did with my lads and it made all the difference. If they had flown line astern then both those young lads would still be alive."

"Might be still alive. There is distinction. Combat flying is not a science, we know that. Good God man, there aren't many pilots who can take on the Fokkers and come away successfully; you do it more than most. Now write your reports and then take some time off." He paused and smiled, "By the way, Lumpy is quite a character. I can see why you two got on so well."

"I am pleased he is working out."

Ted was waiting for me in the mess. "I just went in to see Gordy. He won't need to go to the base hospital. Doc Brennan reckons he can fix him up here. They were clean wounds and the bullets went through his arm and clipped his cheek. He's lucky the German bullets make clean wounds. God help the poor devil who gets hit by one of our .303s."

"You had a better time today then?"

He nodded, "But we still got knocked about a bit." He gestured with his thumb at the airfield, lined with aircraft. "I know these are only a couple of months old but they are taking some hammer. We are going to start to feel it soon."

"It's the men I worry about more." I lowered my voice, "Gordy nearly cracked and he is one of the most down to earth blokes I have ever met..."

"I heard. It surprised me. I could see you cracking up. You fly on the edge all the time but Gordy seemed more stable somehow."

"He was and he will be again. It was just a difficult part of his life and he suddenly had to think about a future. That's always hard."

We sat down on our armchairs. The lieutenants had vacated them when they saw us. "This is my future, Bill. I like this life. Even after the war I think I will stay in."

"No family then?"

"Nah, besides who would have a miserable bugger like me?"

Despite our losses our raid had been successful and the bridges and railways lines destroyed. We were stood down. We visited Gordy, briefly, in the hospital. He was still doped up and didn't say much. The Engineers had done a good job and this was one of the reasons we did not need to send the wounded back to Blighty. We had room. As Ted and I wandered over to the field he commented wryly, "Of course a couple of nice nurses would make it even better."

"I thought you didn't want a family?"

"I don't but I ain't a monk my friend!"

We checked that the few remaining aeroplanes were in good order. Gordy's gunner, Cyril came up to me. "I cleaned out all the guns sir. They won't jam again." He looked a little shame faced. "The lads from your flight had a go at me, sir. I am sorry I let Mr Hewitt down."

"Don't worry Sergeant he will be fine and it is a lesson learned. You will be a better gunner after this. Did the sergeants tell you to load the magazines yourself?"

He looked surprised that a pilot and an officer would know such things. "Yes sir."

"Good. You have to be as careful about our weapons as you do about the engine. Carry on."

Captain Marshall waved us over to the office; he looked excited. When we entered the office the major and the colonel were both beaming like the cat that got the cream. The colonel strode over and shook my hand. "Congratulations. You have been awarded the Military Cross."

Ted's normally dour face was split by a beaming smile, "Well done mate!"

"Thank you, sir."

"You will be awarded the medal by the King but that will not be for some time; probably nearer to the summer but the award has been made. We are all delighted."

Archie shook my hand, "This will do wonders for morale. After the recent losses, we need something to give the lads the spring back in their step."

Captain Marshall added his congratulations and said, "It will be back to patrols tomorrow. We can only manage two flights. We will have a morning one and an afternoon one." He smiled. "I assume you will be celebrating tonight and your flight has the afternoon one tomorrow."

"Thank you, sir. Do I have your permission to teach Sergeant Sharp how to fly?"

The colonel looked surprised. "Aren't you happy with him as your gunner?"

"Of course, but he would like to be a pilot. No disrespect to the younger pilots, but someone who has been an air gunner makes a better pilot." I suddenly realised how arrogant that sounded, "I mean he…"

The colonel laughed and held up his hand, "You do not need to explain we agree."

"And I daresay you would want Hutton back?"

"Well sir he is your gunner now."

"I can do without, '*Captain Harsker did it this way*' and '*Captain Harsker likes to…*' ringing in my ears the whole time. No, you can have him back whenever Sharp manages to convince the colonel that he can fly."

And so I began to teach Charlie in the old Avro. It had been kept serviced for one never knew when it might come in handy. So far, we had not had to bring it back into service but the mechanics enjoyed working on a different type of aeroplane.

I found it harder to teach than to learn but our shared experiences made Sharp a little more forgiving of my acidic outbursts than another trainee might have been and, once I saw what I was doing wrong, I was able to correct it. He was a fast learner. We went out either on the morning or the afternoon depending upon our patrol times. We would head towards the coast and then back. By the middle of March, we were ready for him to try the Gunbus. This was a much faster aeroplane and a pusher. I sat in the front cockpit for the first time in a long time and it felt strange.

He managed it well.

"Well Charlie, I think you are ready. Take the Avro out yourself tomorrow. Go solo. Then we will see the colonel and ask him to test you."

"Thank you, sir. Do you think I can pass?"

"Of course."

We both looked up when we heard the engines coming from the west. It was the replacement aeroplanes and pilots. Lorries had been bringing spares, gunners and mechanics for a week and we knew that something was up.

"And it looks as if you have chosen the best time too. Something is up."

The despatch rider who roared in was my warning that there was an important message for us. When I was summoned within five minutes of his departure I became intrigued.

The colonel and the major were waiting. "You know that, further south, the Germans have attacked the French at Verdun?"

"Yes sir, we heard the rumours."

"Apparently their reconnaissance aeroplanes are being knocked out of the sky with alarming regularity and the French gunners are blind. It seems they want you and your flight for a couple of weeks until they can get their new aeroplanes delivered to the front. You will be based at Thierville."

"But I don't speak French sir!"

He smiled, "Then let us say that you are continuing your education. You will learn. Captain Marshall will arrange for a sergeant and two mechanics to accompany you in a lorry with spares. They will be leaving within the hour. I would suggest that you do the same."

The major handed me a map. "It is about two hundred miles from here and you will be close to the German border. Do not get lost." He was grinning.

Chapter 20

Freddy and Johnny were happy about what they considered to be an adventure. They were still little more than schoolboys. One good piece of news was that they both spoke French. Lieutenant Holt had rudimentary French but Lieutenant Carrick could speak it well.

Ted was in the officers' mess. "I'll be away for a couple of weeks. I have been ordered to take the flight down to Verdun."

He looked disappointed, "It will be quiet around here without you."

"Look after my letters for me will you. I am not sure how easy it will be to send them from the French sector."

"Will do."

I found Charlie by the FE 2. "Sergeant Sharp, we will have to wait a while for the pilot test. We are off to fight with the French down at Verdun."

"Righto sir. If you bring me your bag I will stow it here."

"There is a lorry going down with spares."

"Aye I know sir but that doesn't mean it will get there before you need a change of clothes. I'll pack them on the bus it will be safer that way."

We were ready to leave just ten minutes after the lorry left. "You two keep on my tail." I showed them the map. "We have to take a couple of detours because of German activity so make sure your observer keeps his eye on me."

We took off, the aeroplane slightly heavier than usual. Sharp had packed a can of fuel in case we needed it. We had a range of two hundred and fifty miles but that did not account for headwinds and problems along the way.

The first hundred or so miles took us over unspoilt countryside. Spring was just around the corner but there was still a chill in the air. When we neared the French sector we saw more evidence of fighting. There were scars on the landscape showing where fighting had taken place.

Our new home was just twenty miles from the front and I saw balloons along the front and adjacent to the airfield. This was a little too close to the Germans for my liking. As we circled I noticed that the aeroplanes were biplanes with tractor engines. There looked to be the old Caudron G3 and the slightly newer Nieuport 12. Some of our squadrons flew them. I could see why they needed us. The Caudron was unarmed and the Nieuport had one machine gun in the rear cockpit. They were like the BE 2; they were Fokker fodder.

Old habits die hard and I parked on the opposite side of the field from the parked French aeroplanes. I did not expect to see the lorry. It would take at least twice as long as we had to reach Thierville. Sharp took out our bags and we slung them across our shoulders. The others had sent their bags on the lorry.

We strode across the field to the buildings. I was pleased to see that we would not be in tents. I saw a flag fluttering from a large hut and I headed for that. It seemed logical that they would identify the headquarters thus. I knocked on the door. I recognised, "Entrez!" It was a good start.

"You sergeants wait outside. Have a smoke. Sharp, watch my bag and you two come in with me."

The three of us stepped into an office which reeked of the powerful Gitanes cigarette. It was a sergeant and he recognised our rank. He leapt to his feet and saluted.

"Un moment."

He stuck his head through the door of the inner office and fired off a barrage of French. I understood not a word. A captain came out and immediately began to chatter away in French. I did not get one word.

I held up my hand, "Sorry. I don't speak French." I could order moules and frites, I could ask for a beer, I could even enquire about a room but beyond that and please and thank you I had not the first clue.

He looked confused. I nodded to Carrick who spoke as rapidly as the French Captain. I was relieved when a smile appeared on his face.

"This is Captain Mandeville, he is the adjutant of the squadron. He welcomes us to his field."

He spoke again and Holt went towards the door. "He said he will take us to our quarters and introduce us to the commander."

As we stepped outside I said to the sergeants. "You had best follow us."

"Sir."

Suddenly the French Captain stopped and pointed at our aeroplanes. "Captain Mandeville asked me if those antiquated machines are ours."

I could answer this one, "Oui!"

The captain spoke again and I saw Carrick colour. He pointed at me and began rattling words off. The Captain looked at me and said, "Vraiment?"

Carrick said, "Oui."

"What did you say Carrick?"

"He said it was a shame to bring us all the way down here. When we were shot down and killed our families would have a long way to come to visit our graves."

"And?"

"And I told him how many Fokkers you had destroyed."

More French resulted and Carrick said, "He apologises and looks forward to hearing how they cope with the fearsome Fokker."

We walked to a barracks and Carrick said, "This is the Sergeants' mess, Sergeant Sharp."

"Righto sir," he saw my frown, "don't you worry, Captain Harsker. We can manage."

I picked up my bag and slung it over my shoulder. Captain Mandeville gave me a look which suggested I had committed an indiscretion. I did not care. We had been asked for and they would take us, warts and all.

"This is our barracks sir. The captain apologises but we have to share a room."

"Tell him that is not a problem." I dumped my bag in the small room with four beds, a small table and two chairs. It would do.

Colonel Berthier was not what I expected. For some reason, I expected a French version of Lord Burscough but he was more like a French version of Ted. He did, fortunately, speak English and he spoke it well with a slight American accent. After Captain Mandeville had spoken briefly to him he shook my hand, "Welcome Captain Harsker.

We are grateful that you have come. I understand that you have had some success against this Fokker menace?"

"I have shot down a couple."

He smiled, "Do not be modest, Captain. You have shot down ten and just been awarded a medal for your courage. I look forward to flying with you tomorrow."

That was a shock. I had expected a day or so to become used to the area. "Right sir. I will go and see my crews and we will make sure that our aeroplanes are ready."

He looked surprised. "We have mechanics."

"I know sir but it is just my way. I prefer to help my sergeant work on the aeroplane. That way I know it will not let me down."

He nodded, "That is sensible and I wish that some of my officers would take such an interest."

"Can I say sir, that your English is excellent? Where did you learn it?"

"America. I was sent there as a young officer to see how they operated their aeroplanes. It was most illuminating. I will see you at dinner."

As we left I said, "Johnny, go and fetch the sergeants. We have a great deal of work to do." Walking across the field I said, "Thank you for translating Freddy. I don't know what I would have done without you but don't build me up too much eh? It is a long way to fall."

"Sorry sir, it's just when he had a go at you and the bus I got a bit upset."

"Don't worry, I have thick skin and I can look after myself, but I do appreciate your sentiment."

When the sergeants joined us, I explained that we would be flying the next day. "Good job I packed a couple of extra magazines sir."

"Well done Laithwaite. Now, have you any idea where the fuel bowser is to be found?"

Charlie pointed to the far side of the field. "When we have serviced them, I'll go and get Alain he said he would fill them up for us."

"He speaks English?"

"Not exactly sir but it is amazing how far you can get with sign language and a couple of words in the other's language." He leaned in. "Don't tell the colonel but we have been saving our rum ration and Alain is partial to a drop of rum! That bit of barter helped too."

The resourcefulness of the British soldier never ceased to amaze me. We worked until we heard the bell which signified the evening meal. We had only to fuel the aeroplanes and we would be ready.

"Right chaps better wash up and keep your eyes and ears open. I have no idea what customs they have here. You are all bright lads. I am sure you'll manage."

"Yes sir."

As Freddy, Johnny and I washed up I said, "We are damned lucky with our sergeants. They are, all three, worth their weight in gold."

"I must say sir, I was quite worried about them before I joined. "I must have given him a quizzical look for he shrugged. "We were a little bit protected and cosseted at boarding schools. The local lads frightened me. They seemed so big and tough. They used to spit, swear and fight a lot. I expected that from the enlisted men."

That had been me growing up. It was just the way we were. You learned how to spit and you learned how to defend yourself. It was as simple as that. "I am pleased that your eyes have been opened."

The mess was a little more formal than ours but I was pleased that they did not expect our dress uniforms; we had not brought them. A French Captain sat on one side of me and a young Lieutenant on the other. I was dreading the conversation. In the end, it proved fairly simple. I was able to point at things and either Guy, the Captain, or Pierre, the Lieutenant, would say the French word. I was more comfortable around food and drink rather than around tactics and flying. Any difficult words were translated by either Holt, or more usually, Carrick.

They were both fascinated by our Gunbuses. They used tractor aeroplanes and thought that our pusher engine aeroplanes looked ungainly.

"Wait and see."

They discovered how many Fokkers I had destroyed from a slip of the tongue from Carrick who looked abashed. They asked me if that was all me or my gunner and me. When I told them, it was all me they were even more impressed.

When they opened up about their experiences I could tell it had been a nightmare. Their pilots lasted hours not days and they could not get replacements fast enough. It seemed that the only hope was the new fighter which was almost ready to be shipped to them. Now I understood our presence. We were the boy with the finger in the dyke. We were the stopgap. If we could buy them a few days then it might make all the difference. The Germans, it appeared, were close to breaking through at Verdun and unless this squadron could spot for the artillery they would break through very quickly. Our three aeroplanes were all that stood between survival and disaster.

I made sure we had little to drink, even though there was plenty on offer, and that we had an early night. The next day promised to be lively.

As we completed our last-minute checks Sergeant Sharp said, "They are rum buggers these French sir. They can't half drink. The food is a bit good though. We had something called cock oh van. Tasty, mind."

"The language wasn't a problem?"

"No, sir and I am learning a little. If we are here any length of time it might be handy."

I took Holt and Carrick to one side. "God knows what we can expect today. We may have to be adaptable but I couldn't be happier with you two as my wingmen. I have the best in the squadron." They smiled at the praise. "We will use our arrow formation. They don't know us and will not be expecting that. If there are large numbers then we might have to split up. Watch for my signal. If things get hairy do not be afraid to get back to the field. It is our first day and I would like us to be here for a second."

"What about the French sir?"

"Don't worry about the French, Freddy. If they want to have a go at someone then my shoulders are broad enough. One more thing; the Germans in this sector may not know about the pilot's Lewis. Let your gunner fire and when he reloads then you can fire. It might give them a surprise. You both have good gunners and Sergeant Sharp is the best. I am not worried." And, as we taxied, I realised that I was not.

There were three Nieuports flying that day. I discovered they were the last three. The colonel himself was flying. He had confided to me the night before that he could not, in all conscience, send young pilots to be slaughtered by these Fokkers. We let them take off first. I then took my flight and climbed to five hundred feet above them. The French artillery was silent. They were waiting for the signal lamps of the spotters. Below I saw the blue uniforms of the French in the trenches and, ahead, the grey of the Germans. The German battalions were advancing already. They still had to run the gauntlet of the machine guns but there were no French 75s hurling shrapnel at them.

The three aeroplanes began to flash their lamps and I took us a little higher. The first of the shells began to explode in the air. They were firing short. I had no further opportunity to observe the battle for Sharp shouted, "Three Fokkers sir!

I saw him cock his gun and, in the distance, the three Germans in line astern. "Right, Sharp, let's go."

We had the advantage of height and speed. I used both. I cocked my Lewis as we swooped down towards the first Fokker. Sharp fired at the same time as the Fokker. Neither did much damage. I suddenly realised that this pilot was going to do the turn, I had learned the previous night was called, the Immelmann Turn.

"Charlie, he is going to try that turn. Get on the rear Lewis."

Sharp was more agile than Lumpy and he spun around and cocked the gun. The Eindecker was barely ten feet above us when Charlie began to fire. He emptied the magazine and I saw flames from the German's engine as he spiralled to the ground. Even as he had been firing the second Fokker had been closing. He opened fire. The gunners of my two wingmen opened fire too and he was caught in crossfire. I felt a sharp kick on my leg. It was the sort of sensation you got as a kid playing football when you were kicked in the shin. It stung but I carried on. The last Fokker was hurtling towards us.

"Sharp, duck!"

As Sharp ducked I pulled my trigger and I kept firing until I heard the click of an empty chamber. I actually saw the bullets as they tore through his propeller and turned his face into a piece of raw meat. He too spiralled down to the ground.

"Any more out there?"

"Not that I can see sir."

"Right, reload both Lewis guns." I waved to the other two to take line astern. That way we were ready to protect each other. I saw that the French guns were now cutting the Germans down as though they were using a scythe. Even as we watched the attack stalled and we saw the Germans begin to pull back.

"Sir, the French are leaving."

I looked down and saw the three spotter aeroplanes heading west. I began a lazy turn to fetch up on the stern of the last aeroplane. We would shepherd them to safety.

Chapter 21

From our reception, when we landed, you would have thought that the war had just ended. Two of the pilots and the three observers mobbed us and pumped our hands. Whatever they said it was far too fast for me. Colonel Berthier lit a cigar and waited until they had left me to congratulate my bemused lieutenants.

He shook my hand and nodded, "I now see why you have such success. You and your gunner are fearless. How does a man stand on a cockpit like that and fire?" I laughed and he said, seriously, "No, I mean it, how does he do it? It looks impossible to me."

"It is not easy."

"You have done this?"

"I was a Sergeant Gunner before I became a pilot. You need to have trust between a pilot and the man standing on the cockpit. Sergeant Sharp knew that I would keep flying straight and level."

"Even with them firing at you?" He walked to the front of the Gunbus. The others were examining it too. There were at least fifty bullet holes in it. They must have hit when Sharp was standing and shooting down his Fokker. He had been lucky.

Suddenly Freddy shouted, "Sir, your leg! It is bleeding. You have been hit!"

I looked down and there was blood seeping from my leg. I remembered the hit on my shin. It must have been a spent round. "It isn't serious. When the lorry gets here see if they can repair the front of the bus."

The colonel shook his head. "And you my friend will get to the hospital. Such courage. Now I see why they gave you a medal. I begin to believe that we will beat these Boche!"

The bullet, although spent, had hit my shin and made a small tear in my skin. If my youthful days of football were anything to go by it would be stiff in the morning. Holt and Carrick were like my shadows and they waited for me.

"The lorry is here sir with the spares."

"Good." I was relieved. We had been lucky and the worst damage had been to the cockpit but I knew that worse awaited us on the morrow. I limped back to my new quarters.

"Tomorrow, we will not have it so easy."

They both looked at me in surprise. "But sir, we shot down three Fokkers."

"They only sent three aeroplanes because they knew they had the beating of the French. Why waste fuel, ammunition and wear and tear on precious aeroplanes if you do not need to?" The looks on their faces told me that they had not thought it through. "I expect at least nine aeroplanes tomorrow, maybe more. You will be on your own I think. We can use our arrow formation to blast through their line but if we are to protect their spotters then we will have to split up."

"You make it sound as though we might lose, sir."

I laughed; we had just reached the barrack's door. "That is precisely what I am saying. We can fire at two aeroplanes at once. We did that today but we cannot fire at three. Think on that. You will both have to use everything you have learned and more just to survive." They looked depressed. "We have already done what was asked of us. They stopped the German advance today and their new fighters are one-day closer. If we buy them more time tomorrow then they halt the attack again and the fighters are another day closer. We are fighting in inches gentlemen. Do not get carried away."

My words might as well have been spoken in Urdu for the welcome we received in the mess would have turned anyone's head. We were feted, we were honoured and we were cheered. We had question after question hurled at us. The colonel even sat next to me so that he could translate the questions for me. They had found Champagne from somewhere and it was all I could do to prevent them bathing me in the stuff. When most of the officers became too inebriated to pester me any more I sat, with the colonel smoking; he, his cigar and me my pipe.

"You are a most interesting character, Englishman. You rise from a gunner and a sergeant to an officer and a pilot. You have such coolness under fire and yet you are so young. How did you learn what to do when you fight in the air?"

I scraped out the burnt ash and relit my pipe. "I began as a horseman. I was in the cavalry. I loved horses and I found that I could ride without thinking. I learned to just react. I watched what was happening around me and I just did what I felt was right. It was the same when I learned how to fly. When I was a gunner the pilot tried to loop."

The colonel's cigar almost dropped from his mouth. "In that aeroplane?" I nodded. "Why are you not dead?"

I laughed, "I hung on. The point is when I became a pilot I approached it as I had when I was a horseman. What would happen if I did one thing as opposed to another? I also learned to have as many weapons as I could." I laughed, "One of my sergeants destroyed a Fokker with a hand grenade."

The colonel laughed so loudly that some of the drunks turned around briefly to stare at him. "Really?"

"Really. I have a rifle and a Luger in the cockpit. If I run out of bullets I shoot those. If they fail I will throw the damned things at the Germans."

"You do not give in." I nodded. "A hundred years ago we had an Emperor called Napoleon who seems to me to be much like this German Emperor. He came up against men like you; the Redcoats, your famous Foot Guards. They should have known they were beaten but no one told them and they won. You are just such a man but…"

"But tomorrow they will send more Fokkers and we will be outnumbered. In all likelihood, we will be shot down and die."

He laughed and threw away the stub of his cigar. "Good, you are a thinker too and you do not believe you are immortal. I do not think that you will die tomorrow but I agree. They will, as you English say, throw the kitchen sink at you."

"And you too. However, colonel, we will buy you time to get your guns on target. That I promise you."

"And I believe you. Thank you, my friend."

When I awoke the next day, my leg was indeed stiff. Although bandaged I could see the bruising higher up the shin. The leg, however, appeared to function satisfactorily. It was just painful and I limped towards the airfield after a breakfast of bread, butter, jam and coffee.

Sergeant Sharp and the mechanics led by Sergeant Johnson had worked wonders. The nose was repaired with more canvas and the bullet proofing cans and cardboard were back in place. "I'll tell you what sir. These Froggies know how to party. They helped us fix up the bus and then they opened bottle after bottle of all sorts of stuff."

I gave him a sharp look, "Are you fit to fly?"

"Of course, sir, me and the lads took it steady. We know we are going to get a pasting today. There's no point in giving the Hun a helping hand is there?"

"Good man. Right, have we plenty of magazines?"

"Yes sir and I even have a couple of Mills bombs. We call it the Lumpy Secret Weapon."

I noticed the colonel loading a rifle into his cockpit. He saw me looking and shrugged. I waved. He was a fine officer and I hoped he would survive the firestorm we were about to endure. We took off and I climbed higher than I had the previous day. I assumed that they had spotters who would have reported our height and our position. I needed the Fokkers to waste fuel climbing to reach us. I had told my wingmen of my new plan. When we had attacked them, we would climb and go into line astern. By spiralling up we would be able to allow our gunners to fire at the climbing Fokkers; there would always be one gunner with a shot. It would be like a climbing version of the Gay Gordons. With luck, they would all try to get us and leave the spotters alone. It wasn't much of a plan but it was the best I could come up with.

The next day the colonel had four spotter aeroplanes ready to take off. He was as realistic about the morning as I was. The Germans knew the time we would come. The artillery was predictable. They would need to fire as soon as the German infantry moved. This time the Fokkers would be waiting.

I was wrong; there were just eight aeroplanes waiting for us. Perhaps the others had some mechanical trouble. It happened. There were three pairs of eyes watching over my bus and that was why we had been lucky with mercifully few mechanical defects.

I had taken us even higher for I was gambling. I thought that the Germans would want to knock us out of the sky and pay for the destruction of their comrades. They would be able to deal with the spotters at their leisure. I wanted to tempt them high into the sky.

The gamble almost paid off. Six of them came in two lines of three, eager to battle us. The other two went after the spotters. The colonel, however, had listened to our description of the turn we had developed and used his own. As soon as he saw the Germans his aeroplanes began to circle. They could still spot but there would be a machine gun facing the enemy at all times. They were still sitting ducks but at least they could bite back.

"Here we go Charlie! I'll hold off firing my Lewis until you need to reload."

"Righto sir."

The two lines looked similar to the way we had flown up near Loos and I knew the efficacy of the formation. As soon as the first wave had passed I would be subject to attack from the second wave. Holt and Carrick were further away from me this time as we all needed space to manoeuvre. Importantly our guns could still cover each other for the initial attack.

The first flight opened fire at the same time as we did. The aim was slightly off from the German and they struck the side of the cockpit. Remembering the spent bullet, I winced as each 9mm hit home. Sergeant Sharp also managed to damage the wing of the first Fokker. I realised he was not going over me. He dived below. In an instant, I worked out that he intended to do the Immelmann Turn but come up behind me on my blind spot. They had thought this through.

"Charlie, hang on, I am going to loop."

The Gunbus was not the best aeroplane to perform the loop but I had to avoid being the meat in the sandwich. A Fokker from below and one from head on would mean certain death. The loop appeared to be my only option. I gave it all the power we had and pulled back hard on the stick. I had to avoid stalling and it was nerve wracking not seeing the other aeroplanes.

Bullets struck our tail as we began to return to earth; the second Fokker had adjusted to our new position. As I came around I saw that our slower turn had brought us on to the tail of the first Fokker. There was a danger we might collide. Although that would rid the air of one Fokker we would lose a third of our firepower. I just reacted and fired a full magazine. The tail of the Fokker fell off as my bullets cut the fuselage in two. It plunged vertically to the ground. The second Fokker was almost on us and Sharp opened fire, using the last of his magazine. He hit the engine and the aeroplane peeled off and limped east. Had we had a bullet between us we could have killed him there and then. I scanned the skies for the others. Below us I heard the chatter of machine guns. The four Frenchmen were still battling away. I saw, in the distance, my two companions battling it out with the remaining three Fokkers. The colonel was closer.

I saw that Sharp had reloaded and I knew that when I levelled out I might have the chance to do the same. "Just make them shift Charlie!"

We were spinning down to the two Germans and he would only have a split second to fire. I cocked my Lewis in case I had the chance. The two Germans were darting towards the circling spotters in tandem. They were firing short bursts and then diving beneath them to try to get to their blind spot. It was brave flying. They had damaged one of the spotters but the pilot gamely carried on supporting his companions. I dived outside the circle. Sharp's first burst took them by surprise and he caught the rear fuselage of one of them. It would take an extremely lucky shot to sever the cables operating the rudder but it served to make the Fokkers climb to engage us. As they flew up the French gunners emptied their magazines into the two of them. I banked after my dive and brought the Gunbus up to fire once more. As my nose came around I caught a glimpse of a black cross and I fired a short burst. A large hole appeared in the fuselage. The combination of Sharp, the French gunners and me had damaged the Fokker. They headed east.

"Charlie, I am going after them."

It was not foolhardy nor was it brave; it was logical. If these two could be further damaged then they would not be able to fly the following day and I would have bought us another day.

"Righto sir. I have put the last magazine in."

"I have one left." I reached down and grabbed it. I dropped it into Sharp's cockpit. I heard it clatter to the floor.

"Thank you, sir. I thought I was going to have to use the grenade."

"You still might. Keep it handy."

We now attracted ground fire but we were slowly gaining on the Fokkers. Sharp emptied one magazine at the undamaged Fokker. While he reloaded I fired a short burst too. He began waggling his wings to throw me off. It did not. I fired another burst and saw that I had struck his undercarriage. Sharp reloaded and when he fired and the German tried to climb Charlie's bullets struck his undercarriage and I watched it tumble to the ground. There were two more aeroplanes that would not fly tomorrow.

"Let's go home Charlie."

As I banked I heard him say, "A good job too I am out of ammo."

I saw the gunners below firing up at us. "Fancy laying your two eggs on those Germans below?"

"What a good idea sir."

I watched him pull the pin on one and drop it to the right of the bus and repeat to the left with the other. I counted to five and then looked over the side. The two bombs exploded in the air. There was a little turbulence but the bombs threw their shrapnel over a large area. The gunfire stopped and I continued my climb.

When I reached the colonel, there were just two of the Frenchmen left. I could see no wreckage and I assumed that they had flown home. I looked at the gauge. I could manage another fifteen minutes; no more. I circled but there were no enemy birds. I had chance to look at the effect of the artillery. The French guns had totally pockmarked No-Man's Land. I could see grey uniformed figures sheltering in the pot holes whilst those who could were crawling back. Another attack had failed.

The colonel stayed a mere five minutes and then he too headed back. As we passed the French trenches I saw the other two Gunbuses. They had both landed in a field. One looked to have had a fire in the engine while the other lay at an ungainly angle. Neither would fly the next day. All four crew waved as I passed and I waggled my wings to show them that they had been seen.

Sergeant Johnson was looking anxiously as we landed. He and the airmen with him raced to the Gunbus. "Where are the young officers, Captain Harsker?"

"They crash landed in a field over there."

The colonel wandered over. "I saw your comrades. Would you like some help recover them?"

"Yes sir, Sergeant Johnson knows what to do but it will need more than one vehicle."

"Quite." The colonel barked out an order and a French sergeant saluted. "The Sergeant will follow you."

Johnson sped off. "Charlie, just check the damage eh?"

He grinned, "Yes sir."

I took out my pipe and filled it. The colonel took out one of his cigars and we strolled slowly to the mess. "We showed them today, my English friend. Even with these obsolete machines we held them off. They hit us but they did not destroy us. We were able to do our job despite their efforts."

"I saw, sir, it was a marvellous effort."

"But we could not have done it without you. You and your sergeant are fearless. That loop was…" he raised his eyes to the heavens. Then he laughed, "I did enjoy the hand grenades. We might try that too!"

"The main thing is that your guns were able to fire."

"True but I am sad that you have two damaged aeroplanes."

"We are good at repairing them. It will be just me in the air tomorrow but they will fly again; believe me. The most important thing is that none of my men were hurt."

He paused and looked at me. "That is important to you, is it not?"

"It is. I like the Gunbus but it is a machine and can be repaired or replaced but a man, that is different. We should value our men more than we do, sorry, more than our generals do."

"You do not have a high opinion of generals then?"

"I do not and that includes the German ones. Those German infantry today stood no chance. Yet they were ordered forwards to face your guns, the barbed wire and machine guns. They are measuring gains in men's blood."

"And yet you still fight."

"I am a soldier and I believe in my country and my way of life. But I also have a mind and I use that too."

"Good! Get some rest this afternoon. Tomorrow it will just be the three of us in the air."

Chapter 22

I disobeyed the colonel's order. I washed and changed; ate a little lunch and then joined Sharp with the bus. The holes were soon repaired but Charlie had found an oil pipe which had been nicked. It had not made a hole but it might have broken in the air and that would have been a disaster. We changed it.

"Sir, you have been limping since we got back. Let me finish off here."

My leg had ached all the way through the flight and was aching now. "You are right, Charlie, but get some rest yourself too." I noticed my shin, when I changed my uniform, a tendril of blood dripping down; the leg itself was black and blue. It would do no good for me to collapse while flying and so I lay down on the bed to get some rest. I must have been more tired than I had thought for I fell asleep instantly.

It was late afternoon when the three lorries arrived back with the aeroplanes and their crew. The noise of their arrival woke me up. I felt much better although my leg was still stiff. I quickly dressed. Sergeant Sharp was sitting outside the barracks waiting for me. "Have a good sleep sir?"

"I certainly did."

We wandered over to Sergeant Johnson. "Mr Holt's aeroplane will take the most work, sir. The engine is pretty badly damaged. I am not even sure we can repair it. We can use Mr Holt's undercarriage to repair Lieutenant Carrick's."

"Good; when will that be ready?"

"The day after tomorrow?"

"I know you will do your best. They will be mended when they are mended. Carry on."

Freddy and Johnny were waiting for me. "We managed to get half a Fokker each sir!"

"Well done Johnny."

Freddy shook his head, "Then one of the damned Fokkers got in Johnny's blind spot and hit him before I could do anything."

"You have nothing to reproach yourself about. You both did well. We live to fight another day and the French did not lose any aeroplanes."

"That was a lovely manoeuvre sir. Did you plan it?"

"You mean before I took off? No. I just knew that the Hun was going to fly under me, do a turn and hit my blind spot."

Lieutenant Holt nodded, "That's how he did me."

"I think, and this is a new bit of advice, that you do not fly straight for more than five seconds when in combat. Otherwise you are a sitting duck."

"That makes firing more of a lottery."

"Use short bursts and get close. The last one I got was pure luck. His black cross flashed in front of me and I just fired. I couldn't miss really."

We had reached the mess. "You two get changed and we'll go into dinner."

"What about our gunners?"

"They can't do too much work, it is getting dark and Sergeant Johnson has already told me that neither of you will be flying tomorrow. So you see there is nothing for you to do today but tomorrow I want you to get Lieutenant Carrick's aeroplane ready to fly. Understand?"

"Yes sir."

There was still much excitement at dinner but slightly less alcohol was consumed. I had just one glass of wine. I would need all of my wits the next day.

Johnny and Freddy were up with the larks to see us take off. The Colonel just had one spotter with him. The other two were like ours, too damaged to risk flying. The sky seemed huge as we took off. I kept our height to just four hundred feet above the colonel. I needed their guns almost as much as they needed mine. We reached No-Man's Land and we armed our weapons. I suddenly remembered that I had planned to put some bully beef cans between Sharp and myself. Of course, the French did not have them but I was sure that Sergeant Johnson would have brought some. Quartermaster Doyle was nothing if not efficient.

We were slightly ahead of the French aeroplanes and I saw that the Germans were still in their trenches. Could it be that they were not going to attack? When the colonel arrived he and the other spotter flew the length of the lines. I followed, with Sharp keeping a weather eye on the sky to the east. We flew for an hour and then the colonel headed west.

"Is that it sir? Did we stop them?"

"I doubt it Sergeant. More than likely they have lost too many men and will be bringing up fresh regiments who haven't failed but I do think that we have hurt their ability to attack with impunity." I patted the cockpit. "This is as good as any Fokker and I think that we have proved it."

When we landed the colonel concurred with my opinion. "We have bought another day and this was the cheapest one yet. He pointed to the mechanics beavering away repairing the whole squadron. "Soon we will be able to field eight aeroplanes and with what we have learned from you we should be able to give a better account of ourselves."

I laughed, "Oh, so you want rid of us now?"

He smiled sadly, "No but a message came from your colonel asking how much longer we would need you. It seems your squadron also requires your presence." He patted my shoulder. But we will keep you for another week eh? Your aeroplanes need repairs."

Sergeant Johnson gave me the bad news. "Sorry sir, we can't repair Mr Holt's bus. Not here anyway. It'll need to go back to the field where we have a workshop and more spares. The engine needs a complete overhaul. I could cobble it together but I wouldn't trust it in the air."

I knew that he was a good mechanic. I believed him. "Right, get the bits on the back of the lorry. Lieutenant Holt and his gunner can drive it back. We will still need you lads. He can get someone else to bring back the lorry for you."

He smiled, "Righto sir."

"You're happy to be staying?"

"They're all right these Frenchies. And they treat us with real respect and know that's down to you and the other pilots sir but we normally get ignored. Here they drink a toast to us at every meal. It makes you feel special, sir."

"Carry on Sarn't."

It did not take much to give a soldier some respect and I wondered if we did not take them for granted. Certainly, we could not fly without them and yet when had we said 'thank you'. I was learning as much as the colonel was.

Lieutenant Holt was unhappy about being sent back but he understood why. "I have enjoyed this sir. It was like being our own squadron. It will be hard to go back to flying with the other boys."

"I know but we are soldiers and we follow orders. Are you confident about driving the lorry?"

"We have a tractor on the estate and I have had a go with that. This should be fun!"

We flew each day but the German attack had stalled. Even when we directed the French guns to shell the support trenches it took forever for the Fokkers to appear and we were able to beat a hasty retreat. They had come to respect the ugly Gunbus. At the end of the week the first of the new aeroplanes arrived. Three of the brand new Nieuport 11s arrived. These were to do the job we had done. They had one machine gun. They were as fast and, more important had ailerons. The Fokker used wing warping. The fact that it was smaller and had a tighter turn meant it would easily outclass the Fokkers despite the fact that its machine gun was still mounted on the top of the wing.

While Sergeant Johnson packed up the lorry the colonel and his officers came to say goodbye. We were given a great number of gifts. They were the kind of gift a soldier gave another soldier; they were either useful or enjoyable. The colonel gave a case of Champagne and a box of his favourite cigars. The Sergeants' Mess donated a fine ham. The officers' mess gave us a case of French Brandy.

We were all touched. "You should know, William, that I have put you in for the award of the Legion of Honour. The way you fought over our skies was inspiring."

"Thank you, colonel, but you had no need to do so. I did my duty."

He shook my hand and then kissed me on both cheeks. "None the less you deserve the honour. Take care Englishman and we will get together when this madness is finally over."

As Carrick and I travelled north I could see that spring had finally sprung and there was green everywhere. Everywhere, that is, that the war had not touched. The angry black scars marked where man's hands had been. In places, it looked as though a giant had grabbed the earth with his very fingers and torn it apart. The joy of spring was tinged with the sadness of the death which lay all around us.

We had learned, from the driver of the lorry, that our squadron had been taking casualties. The young pilots just arrived from England were too naïve and had little understanding of the concept of aerial combat. To many it was just a game. I had seen that with my two wingmen. I had changed them but four young pilots had not learned that lesson and died along with their unfortunate gunners. The field looked half empty as we landed. There were just five aeroplanes there. I knew now why the colonel had requested an early return.

Gordy and Ted greeted me when I landed. Lieutenant Holt diplomatically went to speak with Freddy to allow me to catch up with my old friends. "I hear you have been annoying Fokkers again."

I smiled at Gordy, "It would have been rude not to."

"Well we missed you and no mistake. These young lads need baby minders."

"Still as happy as ever, eh Ted?"

He shook his head. "I had two replacements. One lasted a day and the second just two longer. They don't know how to fight."

"How is the wound then Gordy?"

"Stiff but the pain helps me to realise that we have to be on our toes the whole time or we will be killed."

"I had better make my report."

As I turned, Gordy pointed to the two lieutenants. "How did they work out?"

"It was like having you two with me."

They knew that was the biggest compliment I could pay them and they nodded. Ted stubbed out his cigarette and said, "They are almost veterans now."

"I suppose that is the way it goes. If you survive more than a month here then you have a chance. It is that first month which is the killer. Oh, by the way, the French sent over a case of brandy and a case of Champagne for our mess." I couldn't resist a dig at Gordy. It would be a test of his character and if he had grown. "It's decent stuff, Gordy, not the firelighter you like to drink."

Ted and I watched for his reaction and he nodded. "I deserved that and I will try a glass… but no more than the one."

I clapped him on his back. "You'll do for me."

The Colonel and the Major were waiting in Captain Marshall's office. The both nodded when I entered. "Well done, Bill. That was a good job you did. Headquarters are delighted. The French are very pleased, deliriously so."

"They are good chaps, colonel and damned brave. The buses they were using were like the BE 2 but they have a lovely aeroplane now, the Nieuport 11. I think the day of the Fokker is coming to a close."

"That may be for them but they are still giving us some trouble. They keep getting behind our young pilots."

"How about using the arrow formation? It works for Holt and Carrick."

Archie shook his head, "We tried that but they tend to fire too soon and then the Fokker does that turn…"

"The Immelmann Turn?"

"Is that what they call it? Anyway, the German is right behind them and they get shot down. At least line astern means that one of them has a chance."

"One of them tried a variation on that turn with me. Instead of going over me he tried to go beneath me and then turn."

Archie took his pipe from his mouth and tapped it on the floor. "How did you get out of that?"

"I looped and came behind him." I chuckled, "Mind you, I almost crashed into him."

Archie began refilling his pipe. He used it to point while he spoke. "We have a new batch of pilots and gunners arriving today. The colonel and I would like you, Sharp and Hutton to give them a talk about how you fly and fight as a team."

"Me sir?"

"You are the nearest thing we have to a celebrity. With the M.C. and a dozen kills you have gravitas. The two gunners are also the best we have."

"Very well sir and may I ask if you will assess Sharp as a pilot? I think he is ready."

"Of course, Bill, but do you want to lose him?"

I gave a sly smile to Archie who had just started to get his pipe going, "Well I can always have Lumpy back can't I, sir?"

Archie began coughing and then he laughed, "Cheeky.... Aye, laddie. He's desperate to get back to you. But you know there is no aeroplane for Sharp yet?"

"I know but we know that we will need replacement pilots sooner rather than later and we all know that Charlie will last longer than a rookie."

"You are right. I'll test him tomorrow. Will you tell him?"

"Yes sir and I'll tell Lumpy about the little talk."

The colonel gave us the Sergeants' Mess for our talk. There was a real contrast between the almost juvenile pilots and the gunners who looked to be much older. Some could have passed for their fathers. There were five gunners and five pilots all told. The colonel sat at the back with a glass of the newly acquired brandy smoking one of Colonel Berthier's cigars. After I had introduced the three of us and explained why two gunners had flown with me I began. I kept it simple and as matter of fact as I could. The last thing I wanted was for them to think that they were some modern reincarnation of a medieval knight. When Lumpy and Charlie started the mood changed. They were like a couple of music hall comedians and the room was filled with laughter. I even spotted the colonel chortling. They had a way of making everything simple. I was delighted to see relief on the gunners' faces. This had been a good idea of the colonel's.

"Any questions?"

One young man who had had a snide look on his face throughout and had rarely laughed at the two sergeants' jokes raised his hand, "Yes er…"

"Second Lieutenant Garrington-Jones sir."

"What is your question?"

"Is it true sir that you began life as a gunner and trained to be a pilot on the job, so to speak?"

"Yes, Lieutenant. What of it?"

"Well it is just that I wondered about the value of what you just told us. Major Hamilton-Grant at the training school told us that only pilots who understood the theory of aerial warfare could hope to be good pilots."

I saw Lumpy and Charlie as their faces changed from a smile to a scowl and they bunched their fists. I put my hands on their shoulders and smiled at the Lieutenant. "Well Lieutenant, if I tell you that the three gunners who trained, 'on the job' as you put it, are the only three pilots left of the ones who served at the end of 1915 then you will see that is not something of which I am ashamed."

The other young pilots had all leaned away from Lieutenant Garrington-Jones, aware of the hole he was digging for himself. However, I saw in the young man the same look as Major Hamilton-Grant had had and he continued to burrow.

"Major Hamilton-Grant told us that sometimes a pilot who had trained on the job might be lucky but everyone's luck ran out sometime. Breeding and education do not."

I actually had no answer for such bigotry and I was lost for words. The colonel however was not. He angrily stubbed out his cigar, swallowed his brandy and strode forward.

"I think I have heard just about enough." He stood before the lieutenant who still had the same supercilious smile on his face. "Tell me Lieutenant, do you know how many German aeroplanes Major Hamilton-Grant shot down?" I saw the smile playing on the colonel's lips. He was laying a trap for the unwary lieutenant. "I ask because he served with this squadron. Did he tell you that?"

"Er no sir. How many aeroplanes? Er let me think. Well Captain Harsker has claimed twelve so I would assume that Major Hamilton-Grant destroyed thirteen or more."

I had noticed the word 'claim' and I began to wonder about this young lieutenant.

The colonel turned to face the others. "None! The Major has not shot down one German aeroplane." The lieutenant's face fell but the colonel had not finished. "And can I say, lieutenant that your attitude does you no credit." He pointed to Sergeant Sharp. "Tomorrow Sergeant Sharp will be taking his flying test and will, in all likelihood, become a pilot. That means I will have one more pilot than aeroplanes. Now lieutenant, you are educated." He managed to make the word sound like an insult. "You do the sums."

"But sir! I am a lieutenant and he is just a sergeant!"

"Then you had better be a damned better pilot than Sergeant Sharp or you will be transferred!"

He had not expected that answer and I saw his face fall.

The colonel said to the three of us, "Thank you gentlemen. I think we all learned something today. "Nine of the audience clapped loudly while Lieutenant Garrington-Jones sat almost shell-shocked.

The colonel took me to Archie and told the major what had occurred. He shook his head angrily, "That Hamilton-Grant is a snake! I'll take the young whelp into my flight."

"Sorry about that, Bill. I should have intervened earlier."

"Don't worry sir. I can fight my own battles." And I could but it had annoyed me that Hamilton-Grant was still oozing poison about me.

Chapter 23

Charlie did, of course, pass with flying colours. I was with the colonel when he spoke with him. "Of course, Sergeant Sharp, until we get another aeroplane and gunner you will continue to be Captain Harsker's gunner."

"That is fine by me sir."

Gordy and Ted had heard of the insults sent to us by Major Hamilton-Grant. All three of us were aware that the Lieutenant had just been the mouthpiece.

"I can't understand how he was appointed to run a training school."

Ted said, "Then you are as daft as a brush Gordy. It is obvious. He gets fewer pilots killed in England than he would over here running a squadron."

We had little time to dwell on the new batch of officers and the obnoxious Garrington-Jones in particular. The Germans launched a raid on Hulluch close to Loos. They used gas. Although the raid failed we were told to find the gas and destroy it.

"I want the four flights each to take one sector. Use cameras to photograph the ground but your eyes will tell you more."

Gordy asked, "Captain Marshall, what are we looking for?"

"Gas cylinders. They will want them kept away from other soldiers as they leak but there will be some sort of fence around them. They might even be in a tent but they will be within five miles of the German front lines. When you return, if you have not found anything, we will analyse the photographs and see if we can spot anything."

Charlie had used a camera before and was quite happy about it. "Might take a couple of snaps of the bus for after the war eh sir?"

He had grown in confidence since his flying test. "Just use the camera to find this damned gas." I growled

As soon as I said '*gas*' his face fell. He had suffered during the first gas attack the previous year and the memory was still a little raw. We only had one camera per flight and I took Freddy and Johnny to one side. "Use your observers to look for anything which looks out of place. I don't think that they will have hidden it from the air. We have not been behind their lines for some time."

"What about Fokkers?"

"I think that we will be safe today but when we return to destroy the gas, that will be a different matter."

We flew over the area where the gas had been used. It was not far from Loos and I began to worry about Albert again. Then I realised that there were thousands of men in the area and only a few hundred had been affected. We took photographs of every odd-looking structure and large tent but I saw nothing that resembled gas cylinders. We returned disappointed.

The photographs from all four flights had been developed by lunchtime. We were eating in the mess when an excited Randolph raced in. He proffered a photograph. "Here! Here is the gas!"

Archie and I joined him at a spare table. "You can see here, just four miles from the front there is this tent which is large enough to hold the gas and it is well away from their soldiers. There is a barbed wire fence around it too."

Archie said, doubtfully, "But it could be ammunition or anything."

It was on the tip of my tongue to say that if we could destroy ammunition then that would be as useful but I saw that Captain Marshall had not finished. "You are correct Major but," he took out a magnifying glass, "if you look here you will see four cylinders which have, somehow, become loose and rolled from the tent."

He was right. The cylinders were quite clear. Of course, they could contain anything but it was more than likely that it would be the gas.

Archie banged the table, "Right, get the bombs fitted. We'll go now!"

"Why not wait until the morning sir?"

"Because, Randolph, the buggers may well move it or the Fokkers might be waiting. This is our chance to catch them with their trousers down!"

The armourers and mechanics were well versed in fitting the four bomb racks and the bombs. "I'll go in first and drop my eggs. The two new lads can keep their bombs until we need them." I saw the disappointment on the faces of the young pilots. Then C Flight, D Flight and finally Captain Harsker with B Flight. If the four flight commanders can't destroy the tent then the others can have a go. We will start with B Flight, D, C and then the rest of A Flight."

"And if we do destroy it?"

"Then we drop our eggs on another target. So keep your eyes open for something suitable."

"Major, we have hit gas from the air last year. It might be as well for all the other aeroplanes to fly at higher altitude when the strike aeroplane goes in. And I think we need gas masks too."

"Right Captain, you have done this sort of thing before. I'll take your advice."

We took off after making sure that we had all taken a gas mask each. I did not want to use one for it made visibility poor but it might become necessary. We rarely flew in the afternoon and I hoped that would mean we could arrive unnoticed.

Archie led and as eleven of us circled above he dived in to attack. The bombs landed around the tent but did not destroy it. The Hun had placed some anti-aircraft guns there. They had not been there in the morning and they began to pepper the sky with shells. Gordy dropped down and his bombs went even closer. I suspect he might have hit it had it not been for the ferocious fire of the German flak. When Ted went in I was preparing Charlie to go next. Ted waited longer than the other two and all four bombs caused direct hits.

"Come on Ted, get out of there." We watched as Ted climbed desperately to out run the gas, smoke and flames which were rising. He was a canny flier and he flew towards the wind so that the smoke and gas was carried away from him.

We reformed our four flights and followed Major Leach north. He was looking for a target. I saw him point and his two young pilots dived to attack the road which had a line of vehicles on it. Their bombs fell fifty yards from the road. While A Flight circled above Gordy waved for his flight to attack. They dropped their bombs closer but they merely destroyed a field of new sown grain. Ted's flight was keen to emulate their commander and they hit the middle of the convoy.

Then it was our turn. We had three aeroplanes and I banked around to make a run down the road as opposed to across it as the others had tried. It meant that they could bring all their guns to fire but it also allowed us to have the best chance of hitting them.

"Keep your head down, Charlie, I am going to use my gun."

"Righto sir. I began to fire short burst and then Charlie dropped the bombs. He dropped his to the right and I knew that Laithwaite would drop his to the left. That would leave Johnny's gunner to choose which vehicles were the best target. We were low enough to see the faces of the Germans. My bullets had carved a line of dead Germans and when the bombs went off it was like flying through hell. I pulled the nose up and saw Sharp throw one last Mills bomb for good luck.

As I banked I looked over my left shoulder and saw that both my wingmen were safe and half of the convoy had been destroyed. I tucked in behind Ted's flight and we headed home.

The first we knew of the Fokkers was when they fired, prematurely, as they dived to attack us. "Charlie, rear gun!" The sound of the gun had alerted the others and I saw Archie's nose begin to turn to port. I prayed that the young pilots would not panic. Archie was trying our defensive circle. Head on we would have been able to fight them but they were coming from our most vulnerable position. I thought we were going to make it but one of the aeroplanes following the Major suddenly left formation and began to dive towards the west. Luckily Gordy was the next aeroplane and he retained the formation. When Archie tucked in behind Lieutenant Holt I breathed a sigh of relief.

The eleven gunners were able to pick their targets and, as the Fokkers tried to get underneath our formation, two or three Lewis guns would make it too hot for them. Gradually the major edged us further and further west. It was hardly rapid progress but, as we were just five miles behind the enemy lines we soon found ourselves over No-Man's Land. The Fokkers must have run out of ammunition or become frustrated. As we neared our lines they sped east, many of them with wings and fuselage riddled with bullet holes. It was a stalemate but our two bombing raids meant that we felt we were the victor.

When we landed we saw the single forlorn looking aeroplane of Lieutenant Garrington-Jones. I could see Senior Flight Sergeant Lowery inspecting the bus. The colonel would have wondered why one aeroplane arrived back alone. The lieutenant, if he did but know it, was in serious trouble.

As soon as we had landed I went to see Johnny. His Gunbus had been the last in line and I knew that he was more likely to have damage. I found him and his gunner inspecting the tail. He turned as I approached, "We were lucky sir, they just chipped a little from the propeller but they nicked one of the cables leading to the rudder." We could see that it was frayed where the bullets had struck it. Had it been severed then he would not have been able to stay in the circle.

"You were lucky but at least we know that the circle works."

Freddy had joined us, "Yes sir but that idiot over there nearly ruined the plan. If Harry Burrell, Major Leach's other new pilot, had followed him then the Fokkers would have been inside the circle."

I smiled at Freddy, he had grown immeasurably. "Criticising keen young pilots? Are you becoming a cynic Mr Carrick?"

"No sir, I just recognise stupidity. It is one of the many things I have learned from your sir."

"Then there is hope, young man!"

The colonel waited until Archie had made his report before he sent for the young lieutenant. It was a very red faced and angry officer who stamped down the stairs from the office. He glowered at everyone. I went in to speak with the Colonel and the Major.

Archie was lighting his pipe. He chuckled, "I take it yon lieutenant left in a tantrum?"

"Yes sir, his toys are well and truly out of the perambulator."

"Aye I thought he might. He took the dressing down and the warning the colonel here gave him but I could see that he was not happy."

"Warn Sharp that he may well be needed for flying duties soon. I warned the lieutenant that any more such acts of disobedience would lead to his suspension as a pilot."

"But sir, that would leave me without a gunner."

Archie laughed as he blew out a cloud of blue smoke, "No laddie, you can have Lumpy as promised and we will take a leaf out of your book. Mr Garrington-Jones can have a spell as a gunner. Let's see if that teaches him humility."

"You don't think he will learn his lesson do you sir?"

The colonel shook his head sadly, "No Captain Harsker. I am afraid I recognise the type. I went to school with them and he is cut from the same cloth as Major Hamilton-Grant. He is privileged and no one has ever said no to him. He probably played cricket and rugby for his school, rowed at Henley and was told that he was God's gift to the world. Had the war not come along he would have had rapid promotions and ended up an ambassador somewhere or perhaps a Member of Parliament. This war has little good to be said for it but it has, at least, levelled the playing field. Men like yourself and Archie have more chance of being rewarded than in the years before the war. Yes, I am afraid that our young lieutenant will think he can continue to disobey and his good looks and name will excuse him."

I kept the confidence of my commander's words. It would not help anyone to know what went on behind our closed doors.

Our little foray behind the lines had, however stirred the hornets' nest. We now had telephone communication with the front line and we were told, the next day that there was a formation of German aeroplanes heading west. It did not take a genius to work out they were coming to bomb us. The message had not specified the types of aeroplane but we knew that it was likely to be Fokkers and AEG G1 bombers.

We raced to our aeroplanes. Archie shouted, as we ran, "Four flights in arrow formation. Ted, you go after the bombers we'll take the Fokkers." We all waved our acknowledgement.

I decided to tell Charlie the good news when we landed. I did not want him distracted.

The disadvantage we had was that we were still climbing when we came across the enemy formation. The Fokkers would be able to dive and then turn to attack our rear. The advantage we had was that we would have to climb through their bombers and our bullets would aid Ted.

As we climbed Charlie sprayed the first bomber with a short burst. He hit it but I was unable to see the damage. I was too concerned with the twelve Fokkers which dived towards us. With D Flight busy with the bombers we would be outnumbered. I had taken the precaution of having a spare magazine between my knees. When I ran out I wanted a fast reload. Charlie emptied his first magazine at the Fokker who came directly towards us. As he reloaded I fired a burst. I was unlucky. The bullets struck his propeller and then pinged off the top of the engine. The noise did, however, distract him and he banked up and to the right. He would not do a turn and end up behind me.

I banked left and was pleased to see my wingmen had kept formation. The thought flickered through my head that they must be used to me by now and knew which way I would be likely to turn. It proved crucial for three of us with six guns suddenly had the sides of four aeroplanes before us. As we had discussed before we took off the three pilots all fired at the Fokker before us whilst the gunners were able to aim at vulnerable spots on the aircraft.

I aimed the Gunbus at the engine of the Fokker and fired. As it banked right to avoid me the bullets stitched a line along the fuselage and I hit the pilot. The aeroplane plunged to the ground. Two of the other three had been hit too and one was spiralling to its death whilst the third was limping east. As with all such aerial combats the sky had cleared as aeroplanes followed each other to battle it out in the blue skies over France. Our flight was the only one together. I saw three Fokkers to the east and they were pursuing Archie and one of his flight. I banked to lead my flight to his rescue.

I could see that the second of the aeroplanes was taking hits on the engine. The gunners of both aeroplanes were standing and firing at the Fokkers but they were below the two Gunbuses. It would only be a matter of time before they struck something vital.

The monoplanes were so engrossed on their victims that they did not see us as we screamed down to attack them. Six Lewis guns can cause massive destruction and the last aeroplane in their line was hit by at least three guns. It slowly spun to earth. Sharp sprayed the next aeroplane and I saw Sergeant Laithwaite targeting the first. With Holt and Carrick firing at the first Fokker I aimed our Gunbus at the other and fired. It too was hit and caught fire.

The Fokkers all destroyed, Archie turned around and headed west. I took station behind the damaged Gunbus. I saw that it was Lieutenant Reed. He waved as I circled him. He was telling me he could still fly. His rudder looked to have been damaged and there was a little smoke coming from his engine. Rolls Royce, however, built good engines. He would get back.

I saw one Gunbus lying in No-Man's Land and wondered if it was Garrington-Jones. I could see movement near it which meant that it was possible that the gunner and pilot had survived. There were the burning wrecks of a couple of bombers. Ted had done his job.

As I came in to land I saw Lieutenant Garrington-Jones' Gunbus on the ground. He had not been hit; I wondered whose was the aeroplane I had seen in No-Man's Land. When I saw Ted and a second Gunbus, I knew it had to be one of his flight. I was a little disappointed it had not been the arrogant Lieutenant and then immediately felt guilty. I was dong him a disservice. He might change and become a good pilot. It could happen.

Archie strode over. "Thanks Bill. I owe you and your laddies a glass of malt each."

"My pleasure."

His smile turned to a scowl as he scanned the field, "And I will have that young cockerel's balls for this." I cocked my head to one side. "When we climbed to engage the Fokkers he chased a bomber off to the north. That is why we were outnumbered. They did the turn and came up on Godfrey's rear."

When we reached the office Lieutenant Garrington-Jones was cheerfully telling Captain Marshall of his success. "And we got on his tail and the two of us filled him with lead. The pilot and observer both died and I saw it crash." He looked triumphantly in my direction. "One aeroplane on my second flight out, I think I will soon be in double figures!"

I thought Archie would explode, "Not as a pilot you won't. You are suspended from flying and, until further notice you will be my gunner!"

"But you can't do that! I am a pilot and I destroyed an enemy aeroplane."

"And you disobeyed orders and nearly got Lieutenant Reed killed." He turned to me, "Tell Sergeant Sharp he is now a pilot in A Flight."

The young lieutenant turned to the others crowded in the office to look for some support. There was none. Reed was popular and no one liked the arrogance of Lieutenant Garrington-Jones. Once again, he stormed, petulantly from the office. Captain Marshall said, "I think, so long as the lieutenant is based here I had better get the door strengthened."

Chapter 24

The only person who was unhappy about the decision was Garrington-Jones. Charlie was now a pilot and Lumpy was happy to be back with me and his best friend Sergeant Laithwaite. I wondered how the petulant schoolboy that was Garrington-Jones would take his punishment. Lieutenant Holt had appreciated the experience and was a better pilot because of it. I am not sure that the one kill wonder would do so.

The colonel decided to increase our patrols. The Germans had shown that they were, once again, active. Perhaps the stalemate at Verdun had released more Fokkers for our sector but the Colonel was a clever man and he would not allow the Hun to steal the initiative.

Lieutenant Holmes and Flight Sergeant Arkwright arrived with their broken aeroplane. It was wrecked beyond repair but Senior Sergeant Lowery could use the parts for spares. Both pilot and gunner were shaken up and a day or two off flying duties would be welcome. Landing in No-Man's Land was like playing Russian Roulette with three rounds in the chamber. They had both been lucky and their state of mind would not be conducive to efficient flying. We would fly with eleven aeroplanes and patrol three sectors. C Flight would fly with A Flight. They would have a new pilot in the shape of Sharp and a new gunner in the form of Garrington-Jones. It made sense to give them Gordy's two aeroplanes.

Ted and I celebrated in the mess that night. I had two kills to my credit as did Ted. He was as modest as ever. "Yours have more value, Bill, they were fighters. I could knock a bomber out of the sky with a catapult."

"I think you are exaggerating. They have a rear gunner and can do some damage." He shrugged, "By the way where is Gordy?"

"He had a letter waiting for him. It smelled of roses and so it must be from his lady love."

"Mary?" He nodded. I began to fill my pipe. I wondered what the letter would bring. I hoped, for Gordy's state of mind that it would be good news.

Just then Archie walked in with a bottle of malt. There was a large dinner gong on the table. I suspect someone had stolen it on a leave. He banged it loudly and the mess servants came rushing in. Archie waved them away.

"Gentlemen," I noticed Gordy come in, drawn by the noise, "come in Lieutenant Hewitt and join your friends." He came over and sat next to Ted and me. It was then I noticed the colonel in the corner smoking another of Colonel Berthier's cigars.

"Gentlemen as I was saying. Captain Harsker and his flight saved my bacon and that of Lieutenant Reed today. I promised him a glass of malt!"

Ted grumbled, loud enough for Archie to hear, "Miserable bloody Scotsmen. Tight as!"

Archie was in a good mood and he chuckled, "There is a reason why we are so thrifty with our malt, laddie. It is the life blood of Scotland we only share it with those who deserve it. We are honouring Captain Harsker."

I saw Lieutenant Garrington-Jones begin to rise. Archie roared like a Sergeant Major, "That officer sit down, sir, and learn some manners! I am the President of the Mess!"

A red-faced lieutenant sat, reluctantly, down.

"Now where was I before I was so rudely interrupted?" He gave a mock glare in Ted's direction. "Ah that is right, honouring Captain

Harsker. However, while I was getting the malt from the safe in my sporran," he was warming to the task and everyone laughed, "we received a message from the French." Johnny and Freddy must have exchanged a look because the major wagged the finger of the hand holding the glass. "No Lieutenant Holt, they do not need you again. They contacted us to tell us that Captain Harsker has been awarded their highest honour, the Legion d'Honneur, Chevalier." There was stunned silence. He walked over to me. "This is rarely awarded to someone who survives a heroic act." His voice became so sincere I thought his voice might crack. "You are a brave laddie and I am proud to serve with you."

He turned to the mess, "So I will give him the whole bottle and he can give me a glass in return!"

The mess, with one exception, erupted. I was patted on the back and showered with praises. My head swam. To win one medal was beyond my wildest dreams but to win two was unthinkable. The bottle of malt was soon emptied and we went on to the brandy. Garrington-Jones made an early exit and was the only one not to toast me. It was one of the best days of my life; not just winning the medal, although that was something to be proud of, it was the respect of my peers which meant more to me. The Colonel, the Major, Captain Marshall, Gordy, Ted and all the lieutenants, bar one held this estate worker from Lancashire in high esteem. The colonel was right. War was a great leveller.

Despite the drink we were all ready for our morning patrol. We did not make it a dawn patrol. The colonel thought we had more chance of catching the Germans if we flew later. Now that we had communication with the front we had a better idea of when they would be out and about. We were ordered to fly as far into German territory as we could manage. Our recent successes had made us more confident. The middle sector was taken by the Major and his two flights. Ted took the northern flank and I was given the southern flank.

Lumpy was delighted to be back with me and he was also happy about Sergeant Sharp's elevation. "And he'll be an officer too. He'll be a decent one. Not like some I know who are not a million miles away and sat in my former seat."

"Lumpy!"

"No names and no pack drill: I am just saying. I am glad to be back."

As we climbed to our patrol altitude I knew that I was lucky. I had had two gunners and both were dependable. Others could not say the same. I wondered how the arrogant young lieutenant would cope in the front cockpit. I had occupied it and knew the dangers therein. As we crossed the British lines I emptied my head of such thoughts. You had to concentrate in the air for one moment of distraction could cost you your life.

We were looking for movements behind the German lines. Since the German attack had stalled at Verdun the generals appeared, from what we could gather, to be looking for another place to attack. We headed south along the German trenches. We could see to the east as well as keeping an eye on the Germans below. Compared with the front around Loos it appeared to be almost peaceful below. The ground looked to have fewer craters in them and there were tendrils of smoke rising from the cooking fires of the soldiers.

I waved to the other two and we headed east to look at the roads and the railways. There were few vehicles on the road and we could see no build-up of forces there. We returned home safely and with a full complement of aeroplanes and men. We landed, partly relieved to have escaped unscathed and also disappointed to have had such an uneventful patrol.

The others had also had no encounters with the enemy. The difference was that we were the only ones who had discovered a weaker sector of the German lines. It was decided that all three flights would now investigate the area as far south as Amiens and the Somme River.

This was new territory for the squadron although my flight had skirted this area on our way to Verdun. We had not been looking for enemies on the ground then rather we were scanning the air for other birds of prey.

We reached the area some forty minutes after leaving our airfield. We left on our pre-arranged patrols to gather information. We headed for Cambrai. It looked, from the air, as though the war had never even touched it. I saw neither vehicles nor the grey of uniforms. I was about to return anyway when Lumpy shouted, "Sir, I can see an airfield!"

He had good eyes and I looked where he pointed. I could see the windsock and the unmistakeable shapes of aeroplanes on the ground. "Mark, it on the map and let's get out of here."

We found the others at the rendezvous and set off north. I was desperate to warn the major of the presence of German aeroplanes but, at that time of the war, we had no means of communicating whilst in the air. I had Lumpy man the rear Lewis to keep a weather eye out for the enemy. We were the last of the three flights and I saw that Freddy and Johnny saw what I had done and they ordered their gunners to do the same.

We were flying economically to conserve fuel. We were not at the limit of our range yet but we were close having tootled around the Cambrai skies for twenty minutes or so. Lumpy's face told me that he had spotted the Germans before he shouted the news. "Sir, Germans. They are climbing to get to us."

"Hang on we'll go down below the others."

If we remained at a higher altitude we were sitting ducks and we did not have the fuel to form a circle. By flying below the Major with the gunners on the rear Lewis it would tell the others of our danger.

I hoped that Freddy and Johnny would make it a gentle descent. Good gunners were hard to replace. We soon reached a position fifty feet below Major Leach. Lumpy pointed behind. I saw Lieutenant Garrington-Jones gingerly climb on to the rear Lewis. Soon all eleven aeroplanes had their rear guns manned. We were just in time as the Fokkers began firing.

I felt their bullets strike the rudder but most of the bullets must have gone through the fuselage which was largely fresh air. Lumpy had nothing to fire at and I could see the frustration on his face. Suddenly a look of pure joy spread and he put his right hand into his pocket and drew out a Mills bomb. I wondered how he would throw it for he was still clinging on to the Lewis. He used his teeth to remove the pin and then dropped it on our starboard side. He quickly gripped the Lewis and we both counted. The crump and crack of the grenade created a small wave of turbulence. The machine guns in our rear stopped.

"Did you get one?"

He shook his head, "No sir, but they are keeping a healthy distance now."

We were now approaching Lens and were close to our field. So far, the Fokkers had managed to avoid coming close enough to our guns but, after Lumpy's grenade, they risked attacking us from the side rather than from below. Lumpy's Lewis chattered away. He was no Sergeant Sharp and I could not fire my Lewis between his legs; he was shorter than Charlie. It was frustrating to see the black cross of a Fokker drift into my sights and I could do nothing about it.

And then they gave up the chase and headed east. The gunners all resumed their seats; you did not land with a gunner obscuring the ground. The first thing everyone did was to examine their craft for damage. Everyone, that is except for Lieutenant Garrington-Jones who vomited out of the side of the cockpit. He had had a rude welcome to the world of the gunner. The damage to our aeroplane was minimal and we would fly again on the morrow.

Archie wandered over. "That looks like a quiet sector; except for the Fokkers. Where did you find those monoplanes, Bill?"

"Not far from Cambrai. There was nothing else though."

"I'll write a report for headquarters. If you write one for your flight and give me your maps I will incorporate it into mine."

I finished my report and headed to Captain Marshall's office to hand it to him. As I entered I heard raised voices coming from the colonel's office. I say '*raised voices*' but, in truth it was just Lieutenant Garrington-Jones whose voice was raised. "Sir, I demand that I be returned to flying duties!"

Randolph looked at me and shook his head, he mouthed, "Demand?"

Archie barked, "You do not demand anything young man. You are an officer and you obey orders."

"It is a waste of my talents to be doing a job that any moron could do."

When the colonel spoke, his voice was so quiet it was hard to hear, "Until you learn to obey all orders without question then you will not be piloting a Gunbus."

There was silence so loud that you could have heard a pin drop. Then I heard a much quieter and calmer Lieutenant Garrington-Jones, "Then sir, I request a transfer."

I saw Captain Marshall smile and hold up a request for transfer form. He pointed to the name which was written on it. It was the lieutenant's. "I had a little bet with myself. I won." He placed it before him on the desk.

The major came out with the lieutenant. "Could we have a transfer form for…"

Like a magician Randolph suddenly flourished the form and handed it to Garrington-Jones who frowned and looked back at the captain. "Sorry, but I anticipated your request, Lieutenant. I thought this would save time. Better for everyone eh?"

He snatched it from Randolph's hand and stormed out. As the door slammed the captain shook his head. "I wonder if I ought to get that frame strengthened anyway."

He kept to his room for the week it took for his transfer to come through. He left on the lorry which had brought three replacements. Our replacement aeroplane and gunner had arrived the day before and so, by the first week of May we were back to full strength; our aeroplanes were in tip top shape and the morale was high because the bad apple had been removed.

Chapter 25

We were told to photograph the German lines around the Arras-Bapaume area. Ted's flight was fitted with cameras and the rest went as escorts. The German airfield was too close to allow just three aeroplanes to fly alone. Nine of us formed an umbrella above Ted and his cameramen. They had to be accurate. We had discovered in 1915 that good aerial reconnaissance could save lives and we were under no illusions, if we were taking photographs then the infantry were going to attack. If we made a mistake or were sloppy then thousands might die. We were all aware of our responsibility.

The Fokkers attacked us half way through the patrol. Once again, they climbed to attack us from underneath. The difference was that we could fly to face them. Our teeth would be bared! We flew as three arrows and they came at us in two lines. That was their first mistake. They assumed because they outnumbered us they would have the better of it. In gun terms, we outnumbered them. A Flight was in the centre. We were to the right and Gordy to the left. Once we had passed through I would bank to starboard, Gordy to port and the Major would turn and get on their tails. We had worked it all out and we hoped that they would be confused and not see a pattern to our actions. The major's plan was to cause as much damage with our attack and then surround them so that they could not fly beneath us.

"Ready Lumpy. When I bank right you should be able to get the Fokkers behind us."

"Right you are sir." I could hear him humming a tune. He was different in many ways from Charlie who was normally silent but behind the Lewis he was just as deadly.

The head on attack was always the one with the most unpredictable outcomes. Both sets of advancing aeroplanes had four options: right, left, up or down. I wondered if they had worked out their options. Approaching each other at a combined speed of a hundred and eighty miles an hour meant that decisions were measured in inches. Lumpy fired at the same time as the Fokker. Our speed was so great that they both missed. The German aeroplanes dived beneath us. I opened fire just as Lumpy let loose his second burst and we got lucky. We both hit the Fokker and its engine began smoking. Lumpy immediately changed his target to the aeroplane to our left. I sent another burst into the Fokker which peeled off from the others and headed east.

We banked. As we did so I heard an enormous explosion from our port side. The new pilot in A Flight, Lieutenant Lomas had misjudged his climb and he had crashed into the climbing Fokker. Both aeroplanes and the crews perished in a fiery inferno. Lumpy kept pumping bullets into the side of a Fokker. As I completed my turn he reloaded.

The Germans had had a plan. The first six had dived below us to turn and attack us from below while the other six had climbed above us to strike down on us. They were now three aeroplanes short for Lumpy had damaged a third aeroplane which glided down to land in an empty farmer's field.

Two Fokkers swooped to attack the Major's aeroplane but Sergeant Sharp was on hand and his Gunbus fired at almost point-blank range and a Fokker fell. Before he could celebrate I watched helplessly, as a third Fokker raked his front cockpit and I saw his gunner slump.

"Sir!"

I had been preoccupied and almost missed the two Fokkers flying almost wingtip to wingtip. They were aiming for us. I emptied my magazine, cursing my inattention. I saw and heard the fabric on the upper wing shred and the aeroplane began to yaw. I had to adjust my controls to bring her level again. Then one of the Fokkers disappeared in a smoking spin as Freddy finished him off. Lumpy and Sergeant

Laithwaite brought their Lewis guns to bear on the second Fokker which dived below us to avoid the wall of death which approached him.

As with most of our aerial battles the sky suddenly seemed empty. I saw Ted and his flight heading north. Gordy was flying towards Sergeant Sharp and his damaged bird and the remaining Germans were also heading home. Once again, the Gunbus had triumphed but the victory left a sour taste in the mouth. A fresh-faced pilot and a new gunner had lasted just one mission. As we headed home I realised that I too could have died. I had been too worried about Sharp and I should have concentrated on my own survival. I had learned a lesson.

The airfield looked even more welcoming as we approached our home. When the propeller stopped and we had descended, Lumpy asked, "Sir, what happened up there? That was not like you."

"I lost concentration, that's all. Sorry about that, Sergeant."

His smile returned, "Oh I wasn't worried." He patted his pocket. "I still had a hand grenade left."

Sergeant Sharp was upset. His gunner had been wounded. Doc Brennan thought that he would recover without going to the base hospital and there was a spare gunner. Sergeant Sharp, however, felt guilty.

"The thing is sir, I knew that you wouldn't have got me in that position when I was a gunner. I am not certain that I am cut out to be a pilot."

"Of course, you are. This is just part of the process of learning. You have survived in the air longer than most of the young pilots and you have a real kill to your name. Just believe in yourself."

When the photographs were developed they were sent by motor cycle to Headquarters. We, however, had examined them ourselves first. Captain Marshall had a good eye for photographs and maps.

"You see here, this is the road to that airfield. It crosses over a river just at this point." He ringed the bridge with a pencil, "If we destroyed that bridge then they would have a problem bringing fuel to the airfield. It might make their squadron less effective. I know that if Quartermaster Doyle didn't keep on top of things then we would be grounded quite quickly."

"What do you think sir?"

The colonel studied the map. "It seems likely that there will be some sort of attack in this area. Those Hun's aeroplanes will make an attack damned difficult. It seems to me that now is a good time to strike. We have knocked a couple of their aeroplanes out of the air. What do you think Major Leach?"

"We only have nine aeroplanes but it is worth trying just to eliminate the threat. If we use six to bomb and eagle eyed Harsker here to be our guardian angel then I think we can pull it off."

I could see that the plan might work but I also knew that the Germans would be waiting. "Yes sir, but we need to leave before dawn. If we have communication with the front line then you can bet the Germans will too. If we go well before dawn and fly high they might not report us."

"Good idea, Bill. Tell your pilots to get a good night's sleep. We leave at four o'clock in the morning."

I gathered my flight around my aeroplane. "Today we have to make sure that the rest of the squadron can bomb that bridge. They will outnumber us again. Johnny and Freddy, save your Lewis until your gunners run out of bullets. That way we may be able to drive them off."

"Don't you want us to try to destroy them sir?"

"Of course, Johnny but not if it means another aeroplane can get to the bombers. We will try to stay together but if we are separated, well, I know you will do your best." I paused, "I believe that you are both excellent pilots and we have been chosen because Major Leach and Colonel Pemberton-Smythe have the utmost faith in us." I was reassured by the confident smiles the comment brought.

I was more worried this time because we were going deeper into enemy territory than ever before. We would have to conserve fuel and that was always hard when you were pushing your aeroplane to its limits. As usual I checked my Luger as well as my Lewis. I had used it before and I had a feeling that I would need it again.

We had small fires running down the airfield. We knew it well but it seemed alien in the dark. I was the lead aeroplane as we needed to be at a higher altitude. We were also the pathfinder and that was nerve wracking in itself. We would be flying south east but it would take the dawn for us to discover if we were at the right place. The Somme River would be our signpost. Once we reached that marker we could follow it to the bridge. The others would be relying on me for protection and navigation. I felt the pressure on my shoulders. I was aching before we had even reached a thousand feet.

I watched the false dawn and then the true dawn in the east. Reassuringly we were still on course. When I saw the light glinting on the river I knew where we were and I changed direction to follow the silvery signpost.

"Lumpy, you had better arm your guns and keep your eyes peeled."

"Will do sir."

I waved to the other two pilots and saw their gunners arming their weapons. I began to circle the bridge, gradually increasing our altitude. It would give us better vision and help with our speed when we attacked. The rest of the squadron circled the bridge ready to begin their bombing run. The major would wait until he had good light before attacking and that meant we had more chance of the Fokkers finding us.

"Sir, Mr Carrick."

I looked to Freddy and saw him pointing to the east. Silhouetted against the rising sun were the little crosses that were the profile of the monoplanes. We had been heard when crossing the German lines and they were heading for us. I was mindful of my lack of concentration the other day and I totally ignored the bombers. They would have to do their own job themselves. I had to keep the monoplanes from wreaking havoc upon them. There looked to be ten of them and they were not in the usual formation. They appeared to be in three waves rising like a pyramid.

I had fought against them enough times to know what they would do. It would be a head on attack and then a turn to get on our tails and hit us where we were most vulnerable.

"Lumpy, when we have passed the last aeroplane get on the rear Lewis."

"Will do sir." I noticed that, now that it was almost June, he was wearing less layers and he had lost a little weight. He would be more mobile. We all learned at the front. It was adapt or die. I was also more confident about my wingmen. They were no longer the raw and naïve young pilots who had first joined me. They were as good as any pilots in the squadron. Soon they would be promoted to Second Lieutenant and, perhaps given flights of their own. They were more than capable.

I cocked my Lewis and kept my eye on the middle aeroplane. They outnumbered us but their formation gave us the edge. We would be facing three aeroplanes and have six machine guns at our disposal. I looked down the sight of the Lewis and saw the monoplane we would attack. I had been told of some Gunbuses which had twin Lewis guns for the pilot. With two machine guns, I would face odds of three to one. The one I had would have to suffice for the moment.

There was always a danger in these attacks of doing what you had always done. We expected the Germans to do the same as on previous occasions. This time they did not. Three of the Fokkers on their left peeled off and banked to attack Johnny from the flank.

Two others peeled off to do the same with Freddy. That left three Fokkers in line astern coming for me. They had effectively eliminated the chance for all three gunners to concentrate their fire on one aeroplane. Once again, I had to focus on my task; fight three German monoplanes. My two wingmen would have to learn how to do the same.

Lumpy held his fire, even though the first fighter opened fire as soon as we came in range. When he did fire he could not miss and the propeller and engine of the first Fokker were struck by half a magazine from the Lewis. It did not try to fly over or under us, it banked with smoke pouring from the engine. Lumpy fired another short burst and the pilot slumped dead in his cockpit.

There was no time for self-congratulation; the next monoplane was firing. Lumpy finished his magazine and held up his hand to tell me he was reloading. I felt the German's bullets striking our aeroplane and I gave him a short burst. As we closed I fired a second time and struck his wing. The Fokkers used wing warping and any damage to the wing made them less manoeuvrable. As the pilot struggled to control the aeroplane, which began to yaw, I fired a second burst and hit his propeller. He began to spin out of control.

Then the third Fokker fired. Perhaps he was aiming for me or perhaps my luck had run out. The bullets struck my Lewis gun and I felt a thump in my shoulder. I knew, without looking that I had been hit. The bullets continued to hit us. The Lewis gun stand before me was severed and the gun plummeted over the side to fall to earth. Lumpy emptied the whole magazine at this zealous young German. He had concentrated so hard on hitting me that he was almost within touching distance when Sergeant Hutton fired. He hit the engine and then the pilot. As he slumped forward the aeroplane dived vertically to earth.

"Three of them sir! That must be a record."

I could feel the blood dripping down from my wound. I glanced at the floor. There was a small puddle gathering. I had to get down or poor Lumpy would die with me. "I am hit, Sergeant Hutton, I will try to get you back. It has been an honour to serve with you."

I did not want to die without the Sergeant knowing how I felt about him. He looked around, his normally happy face ashen. When he saw the wound, he could not hide his shock. "You'll be all right, sir."

I shook my head. "I will try to get you back to the base but keep the Very pistol handy to warn them." I coughed and it hurt my chest. "This may be a bumpy landing."

I swung the aeroplane around and the sky was empty. I had no idea where the others were. I checked the compass and made sure that I was on course. As we flew over the river I saw that the bridge had been destroyed. The bombers had done their job and I could die happy. I had protected my comrades. I did a quick count in my head. I had destroyed a total of sixteen German aeroplanes. That was not a bad haul for a boy who had expected to grow up looking after horses. I had made Captain and won two medals. I hoped that my family would be proud.

Oddly the wound had stopped hurting but I began to feel a little lightheaded. I saw Lumpy looking around. Suddenly he stood and faced me. He was not a tall man but by putting his feet on the edge of the cockpit he could reach me.

He had removed his speaking tube. "Now you just fly her straight, Captain Harsker, and I will try to stop this bleeding." He had a field dressing and he jammed it beneath my flying jacket. He had a bandage and he sort of threw it around my back. "Lift your arm up sir. Your good one." I managed that and he tied and tightened the bandage to hold the dressing in place. It hurt and I winced. "Sorry sir. I am a clumsy bugger. There that might slow the bleeding down." He reached into his flying coat and pulled out a small hip flask. "Don't tell the colonel about this but I find a nip keeps the cold out. I reckon you need it more than me. Here sir. Have a swig."

He held the flask to my mouth and I swallowed a mouthful of the fiery rum. I coughed and Hutton dabbed at my mouth with his scarf. I saw it came away red. "Thanks, Lumpy, now you had better sit down so that I can see where we are going."

He did so and I saw the German trenches and No-Man's Land ahead. I could not risk climbing. I needed to be as close to the ground as I could. I expected to pass out at any time. The lower I was the more chance Lumpy would have of surviving. The crack and rattle from below us told us that they were firing at this foolish Englishman who was close enough to hit with their rifles. I heard pops and cracks and saw holes appearing in the lower wing. It could not be helped. And then the firing stopped as we crossed the British lines. I was finding it hard to use my right arm. Landing would be difficult with one arm. I was so low that if I passed out the Gunbus might not be totally wrecked when we hit the earth. The sergeant might survive. I saw the windsock in the distance and then heard the crack of the Very pistol.

The ground seemed to be coming at us really rapidly. I slowed down as much as I could. I did not want to stall and cartwheel. I had to do my Sunday best landing. It would be my last. As the nose wheel touched I prayed that I had the correct angle or we would tip. As soon as the main wheels hit the ground I cut the power. I heard Lumpy shouting,

"Hang on sir!" Through a red mist I saw Doc Brennan and his orderlies racing towards us and then it all went black.

Chapter 26

I have heard that, when you are dying, you see a long tunnel and there is a light at the other end. I didn't see any light. I was in the dark and I could hear voices all around. They were the voices of my comrades from the cavalry. There was a sudden flash of light and I saw Caesar, my horse. I heard machine guns and saw horses and riders tumbling to their deaths. I heard crying and realised it was a baby. It was my nephew William. Then Tom and John appeared. They seemed hazy but they were wearing uniforms. I head Tom say, "Come on our kid. You can make it."

They disappeared and mum was rocking in her rocking chair and knitting. She suddenly stopped and gave a small scream, I saw dad rush to her side. And then I was in the air. I was rising on a thermal. The Gunbus seemed to float. All was well again. Then the engine cut and I was spinning to earth. I tried to pull back on the stick but my arms would not work. I was heading for the ground. It was spinning closer and closer. I saw the trenches and the faces of the soldiers and then it all went black.

I wondered if this was death; this inky blackness in which I seemed to be floating. I felt no pain and so death seemed, to me, to be what I was experiencing. I had expected to see Tom and John. Then I remembered that I had seen them just before it all went black. Perhaps they would reappear. Were they to be my guides?

I heard voices. They seemed to be from far away. I was about to speak when I realised that the voices were not John and Tom. I recognised the Scottish tones of Major Leach. Was he dead too?

"Why has he not come to?"

"It is the anaesthetic. The bullet had gone through but I had a lot of stitching to do."

"He will live though."

"He should do. He is a strong young man with a hearty constitution."

"When will he be fit again?"

I heard a snort of derision. "You are not asking much are you?"

"Come on Doc, you know how they all feel about the laddie here. He is like a lucky charm. If he is in the air then they feel safer."

"He will need maybe three weeks to recuperate. That is in a hospital back in Blighty, mind. If he is here then I cannot promise anything. Then another week or so and he should be able to fly again."

"Well that is something."

I forced my eyes open. It was bright. I opened my mouth to speak and I found I couldn't. It was a sort of half cough. Archie's face lit up and Doc Brennan lifted my head and held a glass of water for me to drink.

"You had us worried, Bill. There was so much blood in the cockpit I wondered if you had any left."

"If it hadn't been for Lumpy I wouldn't have made it. He stopped the bleeding. He saved my life."

"Aye he is a good lad. He will be mentioned in despatches."

It struck me unfair that if it had been me then I would have had a medal but the enlisted men just received a mention in despatches.

"How long have I been out?"

"It was yesterday you were shot."

"What happened to the rest of my flight?"

His face clouded over, "Lieutenant Carrick and Sergeant Laithwaite were shot about a bit but they managed to escape without a wound. Johnny Holt's gunner, Sergeant White, bought it and Johnny was barely able to land his aeroplane. The three of you did a heroic service. We were able to bomb the bridge without any losses."

I closed my eyes. That was something at least. "They tried something different this time, sir. They didn't come head on they tried to attack from three sides. It nearly worked."

"I know, your two lieutenants told us. But I think the day of the Fokker Scourge is over. Your old friend Colonel Burscough has made mincemeat of them with his squadron of DH 2s. There are rumours we might get a couple."

"I think I would miss my gunner. I wouldn't be here today if it wasn't for Sergeant Hutton."

Doc Brennan shook his head, "That is enough. He needs rest. No more visitors until tomorrow. And then he is off to England!" He smiled as he said it, "You will have some convalescence and you need it Captain Harsker."

I did need the sleep. When I awoke it felt as though I had gone twelve rounds with a heavyweight. Perhaps the drugs had worn off, I don't know but I now knew I had a wound. Gordy, Ted and my two lieutenants were the first to visit me. I saw, through my half open eyes the look of worry on their faces. As I fully opened them they donned a mask of joy and relief.

"You had us worried there, Bill. You had a hole in you so big I could have put my fist in it."

Gordy shook his head and clipped Ted on the back of the head. "What a wonderful bedside manner you have! Never mind him, Bill. You look much better now and you will be off to a hospital in England. Do you know which one yet?"

I shook my head. "The Doc said I would find out later this morning. He reckoned it would be in London somewhere."

Gordy brightened. "You'll be there for a while. I'll write to Mary and ask her to visit you."

"I would like to meet her."

For some reason, the fact that I would be meeting the future Mrs Hewitt filled Gordy with pleasure. His grin stretched from ear to ear. I looked at Freddy and Johnny, "You two did very well the other day. I am proud of you."

Freddy nodded. "I think I had the easier task sir. I just had two to contend with. We shot one down and the other cleared off. They made a mess of the aeroplane but they didn't hit anything vital."

I looked at Holt. "Sorry about your sergeant."

He nodded, "We had been together since the start. Now I know how Freddy felt." He brightened a little. "The Major has given me Sergeant Hutton until you are fit to fly again."

"Then you are in safe hands. If it wasn't for him I would be pushing up daisies by now."

Doc Brennan came in to the room. "Now that is enough. Sergeant Hutton and Sharp have been waiting and I don't want to tire our patient out. He leaves this afternoon."

"Where to Doc?"

"Imperial Order of The Daughters of The Empire Hospital."

Gordy asked, "Where is that, sir? I was going to get my young lady to visit him."

"Hyde Park Place, London."

"I will write to her now, Bill just so long as you promise not to steal her from me."

I laughed, "That depends how pretty she is."

He waggled a warning finger at me. "Bloody heroes, all the same!"

Charlie and Lumpy looked fearful as they came in. "Don't look so worried. I have survived and it is thanks to you Lumpy."

He shook his head. "I was scared Mr Harsker. I saw all that blood and I just had to do something."

"Well you did the right thing. And now you have Mr Holt to watch over."

He laughed, "He's a nice lad but it is like having a school boy behind you." He suddenly realised what he had said and put his hands up, "No offence meant sir."

"I know what you mean. And you Charlie, how are things working out for you?"

"I am glad we have the bombing run over. I feel better now but when I saw those Fokkers coming after you I wished I was up there with you."

Doc Brennan came in, "Sorry boys, the ambulance is here to take Captain Harsker to Blighty."

They both shook my hand. "Glad you are in one piece sir."

"We'll have your aeroplane as right as rain by the time you get back."

The ride in the ambulance was not the most comfortable I had had. I shared it with a mechanic who had lost a hand to a propeller. His army career was over and the poor lad just stared at the ceiling for the whole journey. My attempts at conversation resulted in monosyllabic answers and I gave up. We reached the hospital after a boat, a train and another ambulance ride. It was late at night when we reached our new home. The last thing I thought about before I went to sleep was the smell. This smelled like England. I knew that I was home.

I was not in the same hospital as Airman Carmichael. He went to one for Other Ranks. As an officer, I had a room to myself. It was almost midnight when I was finally alone in my room. The orderly made me as comfortable as he could.

He grinned as he stood by the door, "Don't you worry Captain, blokes are only on night shift. You have pretty nurses tomorrow. They are much easier on the eye than the likes of me."

I smiled back but, before I could retort he had gone and closed the door. My head hit the pillow and I was out for the count. I had a troubled sleep. No-one had thought to give me anything for the pain. I had been handed from orderly to orderly and I assumed they all thought that the one before had seen to my needs. I am not the complaining type. I had been brought up to be polite and not pester people. It caused me pain and distress that night.

A particularly sharp pain jabbed me awake. I think I must have shouted. I smelled a subtle rose perfume and I found myself looking up at the face of the most beautiful girl I had ever seen. She had a look of concern on her face. "When did you last have anything for the pain Captain?"

I had to think. "Er yesterday before I left France. The Doctor gave me some morphine."

She shook her head. "That is simply not good enough! You have been in pain have you not?"

"A little but only in the last few hours."

"The night shift is manned by a bunch of layabouts." She must have been aware that she was sounding quite cross. "Sorry, Captain after what you have gone through the last thing you need is a harpy screeching in the room."

"Don't worry. I don't mind. You are the first pretty girt I have seen in a long time and the first woman I have spoken to since Christmas. Your voice sounds like an angel to me."

She actually blushed, "You flatterer. I'll get you something for the pain and then a little breakfast. How's that?"

"It sounds wonderful Nurse…?"

"Porter, Beatrice Porter. Now just lie back and I will be back in a jiffy."

The pain had already diminished before she returned. I was lying back with my eyes closed. Her perfume heralded her arrival. When you have smelled little else other than fuel fumes, engine oil and Lumpy Hutton's body odour, a perfume like Nurse Porter's was a welcome change. Once I had had my injection she scurried away and returned moments later with a breakfast tray. "Now you eat all of that up Captain Harsker, I want a clean plate."

"It's Bill and I will."

She had the most enchanting smile, "I am afraid we have to use rank here, Captain." She leaned in. "If Sister or Matron heard me being so informal I would be in serious trouble. But thank you for giving me your name. It suits you and I shall think of you as Bill in my head, Captain Harsker."

I ate my breakfast happily. I think I had just flirted with a nurse. I was not certain but Ted, the squadron's ladies' man, had said that flirting was the first stage to an assignation. I was getting ahead of myself. Goodness only knew how long I would be here.

That was the last time I saw the lovely Nurse Porter alone that day. The next time I saw her was with a hatchet-faced sister and a doctor who reeked of cigarette smoke. I was told that Doc Brennan had done a good job. That was superfluous information; I knew he had done a good job. I was told that I would be bed bound for a fortnight and after another week I might be fit to recuperate at home.

I wondered about that as I lay in the bed looking out at Hyde Park in the June sunshine. It was a long journey to Burscough and I would only be there for a mere four days before I would have to make the arduous return journey. I would cross that bridge when I had to.

I waited, eagerly, for Nurse Porter's appearance the next morning. I had wondered about getting up to shave. An orderly had completed that task the previous day but he had not arrived until ten o'clock. I decided it was not worth incurring the nurse's wrath. She was a little later than usual and she had a beaming smile on her face.

"I didn't know how important you were Captain Harsker."

I was nonplussed. "Me, important? I don't think so."

"Well we had a phone call this morning from a Lady Burscough who said she was on her way to town and could she come to see you this evening. She will be here at six o'clock." She seemed impressed. For me she was just Lord Burscough's wife; a nice lady but her presence would not make me an important man. "I'll get Cyril the barber to come a little later today so that you look smart for her ladyship."

The matron and the sister were of the same opinion as Nurse Porter, and my bed was completely remade, the room had a fresh bunch of flowers and, to my embarrassment, two nurses gave me a bed bath. Sadly, neither of them was Nurse Porter.

My evening meal was brought forward to five o'clock and the sister watched over me as I ate it. Had she been able to feed me she would have done so to get it over with quicker! Eventually I saw that it was nearly time for the visit. I knew that Lady Margaret Burscough would not have minded how the room looked but the matron obviously felt she had standards to maintain.

Nurse Porter flew into the room. "She's downstairs!" She was as giddy as a school girl. She smoothed my cowlick across my face and ran her hands down my pyjamas to straighten them. I enjoyed her touch and the fragrance of her perfume. She stepped back and gave me a critical look, "Well that will have to do." She heard footsteps and voices and she stepped to the side of the bed, almost at attention.

I heard the matron say, "This is the room, your ladyship."

Lady Burscough stood in the doorway. She cocked her head on one side, "You poor boy. What you have been through!"

She came towards me and planted a kiss on my cheek. I knew that her lipstick would leave a mark but it would have been rude to wipe it off. She stepped back and said, "I did not come alone. I have brought you a gift. Alice!"

And then my little sister stepped through the door. She had grown into a woman in the last six months. She was smartly dressed and she had a smile on her face. The smile belied the tears in her eyes. She flung her arms around me and began sobbing on my shoulder.

Fortunately, it was not my injured shoulder. "They told me you nearly died. I could not have borne that."

Nurse Porter said, diplomatically, "I am afraid his shoulder will be a little tender, miss."

Alice jumped off the bed as though bitten. I saw the glare from the matron but I admired the courage of Nurse Porter. "What are you doing here? You didn't come all the way for me did you, your ladyship?"

"You are worth it William but no, Alice here has shown a talent for design and I have a friend here in London who is a designer. He has agreed to take Alice on as an apprentice. We will be staying at the town house for a few days until we can get her accommodation sorted out."

"That is wonderful news sis but I bet mum is none too happy about it."

"No, she is not pleased but seeing as how it is her ladyship who has arranged it, she couldn't really say anything could she?"

"Nurse Porter, go and fetch two chairs for the visitors." While Nurse Porter trotted off the Matron came and smoothed down the bed covers again. She turned to Lady Burscough. "Would you like some tea your ladyship?"

Smiling sweetly Lady Burscough said, "If it is not too much trouble."

When they were seated the two of them gave me all the news from home and I heard that Bert was still at Loos but as the attacks had ceased he was safe. It turned out that his Lordship had sent the message about my wounds and that had initiated the visit. I was delighted. It meant I did not have to travel home. I had seen my family and I hoped to get to know Nurse Porter a little better.

When they left, an hour later, I felt happy. I had come close to losing my life but somehow it all looked a little rosier now. Alice looked to have a good job lined up and I found myself looking forward to Nurse Porter's attentions.

I found myself eagerly anticipating the times when she came to visit and tend to me. Each time she grew closer. I still do not know how. But every day was easier. I smiled more and we both seemed more relaxed. When it was another nurse I was disappointed. I felt guilty for enjoying my time in a hospital.

Two days later she stood in the doorway with her hands on her hips. "You must be a real Don Juan, Captain Harsker, you have another lady visitor!"

She was teasing, of course but I had no idea who it might be. A smartly dressed woman in her late twenties stood in the doorway and I had never seen her before. She said, "I'm Mary, Gordon's young lady."

Realisation dawned, "Of course, do come in." I looked at Nurse Porter. "Gordon is one of the pilots in my squadron." I think I detected relief on Nurse Porter's face, or perhaps it was my imagination.

"I'll go and get a cup of tea for you then."

"Don't trouble yourself on my account."

"It's no trouble believe me."

I had never seen Mary before but she came and planted a kiss on my cheek. "Thank you for what you did for Gordon. He wrote me a lovely letter saying how stupid he had been and how you had sorted him out." She touched my hand with hers. "He thinks the world of you."

I smiled, "And I know that you are everything to him."

She blushed, "That's nice."

Nurse Porter brought in a cup of tea, "You only have another half hour. Matron is very strict."

Unless, of course, you were Lady Burscough in which case you could stay as long as you liked.

"Thank you."

"Can I be honest with you Mary?"

"Of course. I always like to be straight with people." She smiled at me, "You and Gordon are both Northerners. I know you can be a little blunt at times."

"No, I wasn't going to be blunt I was just... well Gordy worries that we live such dangerous lives that any of us could die in an instant." I pointed to my bandage. "And I am living proof how dangerous it can be. Well Gordy doesn't want you hurt again. You have lost your husband and..."

"And he doesn't want to widow me twice." She looked relieved, "I knew there was something. Thank you, Captain."

"Bill."

"Thank you, Bill. Now I know that I can sort him out."

"He would be mortified if he knew I had told you."

She laughed; it was a musical tinkling laugh and it lit up her whole face, "I am not a Northerner Bill and I can pretend with the best of them. Don't worry. I will be discreet."

All too soon Nurse Porter came for Mary and led her out. She seemed to be away for an age. When she returned she had a strange look on her face. "Well aren't you the dark one?"

"What do you mean?"

"Your visitor told me about you Captain Harsker, how you have won medals and shot down sixteen Germans and yet you seem such a nice quiet gentlemen. You look as though butter wouldn't melt in your mouth."

I smiled, "It wouldn't."

"I think I know better. Well, my shift is nearly over so I will just sort out your bed." She padded my pillow and straightened the end of the bed. When she straightened the top sheet, her hand touched mine. I didn't move it and neither did she. Looking me in the eye she said, "Is there anything else you want, Captain?"

I squeezed her fingers gently and said, huskily, Yes ... you."

She squeezed my hand back and said, quietly, "We will have to wait until you are well then... Bill."

She drifted from the room and I was left alone with hope in my heart and a smile on my face.

Epilogue

It was at the end of my second week in the hospital. I had been up and about for almost a week and I wore my uniform each day. Nurse Porter was given permission to let me walk in Hyde Park, which I loved. The days were filled with sunshine, laughter and the nurse's pleasant company. One morning she suddenly burst into my room. "Matron is coming and you have a visitor!"

I had never seen her as excited. She fussed around me as she had never done before. "Who is it?"

She shook her head, "You will never believe me and it will be better as a surprise." That ruled out Mary and Alice who had both visited almost every other day and Lady Burscough had returned north.

And then Alice walked through the door looking beautiful in a brand-new outfit with her hair done nicely and make up on her face. This was a surprise. She stood on the opposite side of the bed. Matron and sister stood at the door and when they curtsied I wondered who was coming in. When King George V entered I think my mouth dropped open. I tried to get off the bed but he said, "No Captain Harsker, do not rise. You are one of our heroes."

There were two men in military uniform with him. One was a General I did not recognise but the other I did. It was the commanding General of the Royal Flying Corps, Brigadier General Sir David Henderson. There was also a foreign looking chap in a smart suit. Finally, there was a cameraman with his camera poised. It was a crowded room.

"I am here, Captain Harsker to present you with two medals." General Henderson took out a velvet covered box. "This is the Military Cross presented to you for your courageous actions in saving the lives of brother officers over Northern France earlier this year." He pinned it on my uniform. I nodded. "Allow me to shake you by the hand, Captain Harsker." I shook his hand. There was a flash as the cameraman took the photograph.

"The second medal will not be presented by me but rather the French Military Attaché Monsieur Jacques Lafitte."

The gentleman in the smart suit stepped forward. I noticed that the king stood a whole head taller than this diminutive Frenchman. "I have the honour to present you with the Legion D'Honneur. This award is for your bravery at Verdun where you slew many of our enemies and saved the lives of many of our pilots. This honour is rarely awarded to those who are neither French nor deceased but I know that you thoroughly deserve it. Colonel Berthier was fulsome in his praise of you and your actions. This is the true spirit of Entente Cordiale." He stepped up to me and pinned the medal next to the Military Cross. Then he kissed me on both cheeks. After the flash of the photographer he stepped back.

The King and the Generals applauded. General Henderson came over to me and shook me by the hand. He leaned in to speak quietly to me, "Thank you for all that you have done and I am just sorry that you had to endure that ridiculous court martial. I believe you are the future of the Royal Flying Corps. When you return to France you will find a new aeroplane waiting for you. We have created the best for the best." He nodded and stepped back.

"Well I think we will leave you with your family, Captain. Thank you on behalf of the Empire. We are grateful to you."

And then they were gone and the room emptied, almost. As Alice kissed my cheek there was a flash and the photographer said, "These will make nice little stories. Jutland upset a lot of people. This will make them a little happier." He closed the door as he left.

Nurse Porter said, "Well I will leave you two alone."

I reached out and grabbed her hand. "No Beatrice, I would like you to stay and meet my little sister, Alice."

Alice grinned and threw her arms around my neck. "And about time our Bill!"

My life was full and I was happy.

The End

Glossary

BEF- British Expeditionary Force

Beer Boys-inexperienced fliers (slang)

Blighty- Britain (slang)

Boche- German (slang)

Bowser- refuelling vehicle

Bus- aeroplane (slang)

Crossley- an early British motor car

Donkey Walloper- Horseman (slang)

Fizzer- a charge (slang)

Foot Slogger- Infantry (slang)

Google eyed booger with the tit- gas mask (slang)

Griffin (Griff)- confidential information (slang)

Hun- German (slang)

Jasta- a German Squadron

Jippo- the shout that food was ready from the cooks (slang)

Lanchester- a prestigious British car with the same status as a Rolls Royce

Loot- a second lieutenant (slang)

Lufbery Circle- A aerial defensive formation

M.C. - Military Cross (for officers only)

M.M. - Military Medal (introduced in 1915)

Nicked- stolen (slang)

Number ones- Best uniform (slang)

Outdoor- the place they sold beer in a pub to take away (slang)

Parkin or Perkin is a soft cake traditionally made of oatmeal and black treacle, which originated in northern England.

Pop your clogs- die (slang)

Posser- a three-legged stool attached to a long handle and used to agitate washing in the days before washing machines

Pickelhaube- German helmet with a spike on the top. Worn by German soldiers until 1916

Shufti- a quick look (slang)

Singer 10 - a British car developed by Lionel Martin who went on to make Aston Martins

The smoke- London (slang)

Toff- aristocrat (slang)

V.C. - Victoria Cross, the highest honour in the British Army

Maps

Courtesy of Wikipedia

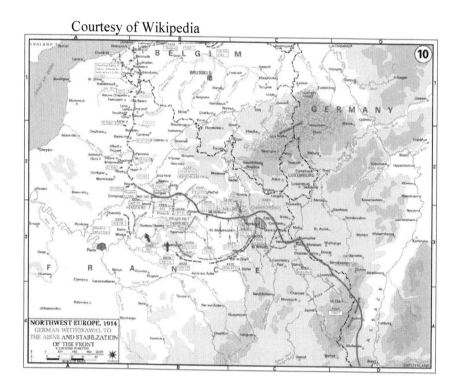

The Battle of Loos

Map courtesy of Wikipedia

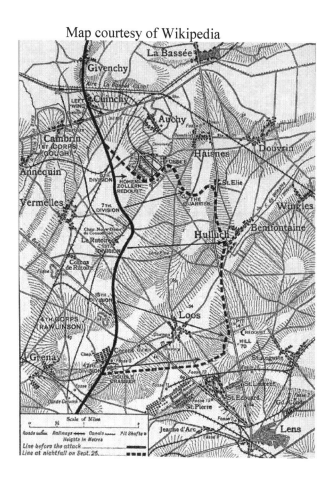

Battle of Verdun

Courtesy of Wikipedia

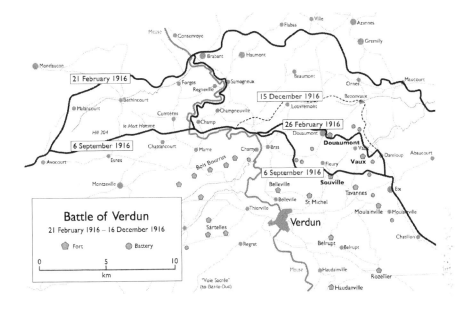

Battle of Verdun
21 February 1916 – 16 December 1916

⬠ Fort   ⬡ Battery

0   5   10
          km

21 February 1916

15 December 1916

26 February 1916

6 September 1916

6 September 1916

Montfaucon

Malancourt
Béthincourt
Hill 304   le Mort Homme
Chattancourt
Avocourt   Esnes
Montzeville

Meuse   Consenvoye
Brabant   Haumont
Forges   Samogneux
Regneville
Cumières
Champneuville
Champ
Marre   Chamy   Bras
Bois Bourrus

Flabas   Ville   Azannes
Gremilly
Beaumont
Ornes   Maucourt
Bezonvaux
Louvremont
Douaumont   Douaumont
Vaux   Vaux
Fleury   Damloup   Abaucourt

Belleville   Souville
Belleville   St. Michel   Tavannes   Eix
Thierville   Moulainville   Moulainville
Sartelles   Verdun
Regret   Belrupt   Chatillon
Belrupt
Meuse   Haudainville   Rozellier
"Voie Sacrée"   Haudanville
(to Bar-le-Duc)

Historical note

This is my second foray into what might be called modern history. The advantage of the Dark Ages is that there are few written records and the writer's imagination can run riot- and usually does! If I have introduced a technology slightly early or moved an action it is in the interest of the story and the character. I have tried to make this story more character based as I have used the template of some real people and characters who lived at the time.

As with all my books I have used fictitious regiments and actions. The organisation of the Lancashire Yeomanry and the Cumbrian Hussars is compatible with actual regiments. Their role is exactly that of the real Yeomanry. Compared with the regular regiments and especially compared with the foot soldiers, the Yeomanry casualties were very light. The total cavalry losses for the whole war were 5,674 dead and 14,630 wounded. Compare that to the Northumberland Fusiliers who had 16000 casualties alone. The Yeomanry losses were even fewer.

The Short Magazine Lee Enfield had a ten-shot magazine and enabled a rifleman to get off 20-30 shots in a minute. It was accurate at 300 yards. Both cavalry and infantry were issued with the weapon.

For those readers who do not come from England I have tried to write the way that people in that part of Lancashire speak. As with many northerners they say *'owt'* for anything and *'eeh'* is just a way of expressing surprise. As far as I know there is no Lord Burscough but I know that Lord Derby had a huge house not far away in Standish and I have based the fictitious Lord Burscough on him. The area around Burscough and Ormskirk is just north of the heavily industrialised belt which runs from Leeds, through Manchester, to Liverpool. It is a very rural area with many market gardens. It afforded me the chance to have rural and industrial England, cheek by jowl. The food they eat is also typical of that part of Lancashire. Harsker is a name from the area apparently resulting from a party of Vikings who settled in the area some centuries earlier. Bearing in mind my Saxon and Viking books I could not resist the link albeit tenuous with my earlier books.

The rear firing Lewis gun was not standard issue and was an improvised affair. Here is a photograph of one in action.

The photograph demonstrates the observer's firing positions in the Royal Aircraft Factory F.E.2d. The observer's cockpit was fitted with three guns, one fixed forward-firing for the pilot to aim, one moveable forward-firing and one moveable rear-firing mounted on a pole over the upper wing. The observer had to stand on his seat in order to use the rear-firing gun.

An F.E.2 this image (or other media file) is in the public domain because the copyright has expired.

The circle devised by Bill and Billy really existed. It was known as a Lufbery circle The gunner of each,F.E.2, could cover the blind spot under the tail of his neighbour and several gunners could fire on any enemy attacking the group. There were occasions when squadrons used this tactic to escape the Fokker monoplane and the later fighters which the Germans introduced to wrest air superiority from the Gunbus.

The Immelmann Turn was named after the German Ace Max Immelmann who flew the Fokker E1. He was apparently shot down by an FE 2 although one theory is that his interrupter gear malfunctioned and he shot his own propeller off. I prefer the first theory. This is the Immelmann Turn as a diagram.

I have no evidence for Sergeant Sharp's improvised bullet proofing. However, they were very inventive and modified their aeroplanes all the time. The materials he used were readily available and, in the days before recycling, would have just been thrown away. It would be interesting to test it with bullets.

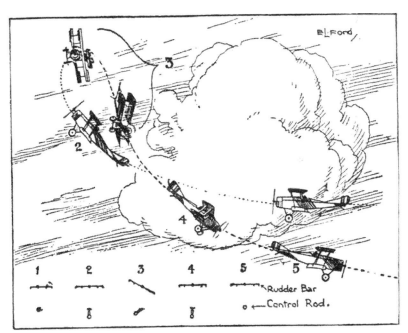

The Mills bomb was introduced in 1915. It had a seven second fuse. The shrapnel could spread up to twenty yards from the explosion.

Hulluch was the scene of a German attack with gas. The Bavarian regiment attacked the British near to Loos. They had some forewarning of the attack as a German deserter told them and rats were seen leaving the German trenches. (A sure sign of leaking gas bottles.) The Germans had nearly as many men incapacitated as the British but the inferior nature of the British gas mask meant more deaths amongst the British. The bombing raid is pure fiction.

General Henderson commanded the RFC for all but a couple of months of the war. The Fokker Scourge lasted from autumn 1915 until February 1916. It took the Gunbus and other new aircraft to defeat them. The BE 2 aeroplanes were known as Fokker fodder and vast numbers were shot down. There were few true bombers at this stage of the war and the Gunbus was one of the first multi-role aeroplanes. The addition of the third Lewis gun did take place at this stage of the war.

More aeroplanes were shot down by ground fire than aeroplanes and I have tried to be as realistic as I can but Bill Harsker is a hero and I portray him as such. The novel ends shortly before the start of the Battle of the Somme and book 3 in the series (1916) will begin with that monumental battle.

Selected Specifications for the aeroplanes mentioned in the novel

FE2b

2 crew

47 feet wingspan

12 feet 6 inches height

Rolls Royce Eagle engine 360hp

Maximum speed 91 mph (up to 98 at higher altitude)

Ceiling, 11000 feet

2 Lewis machine guns and up to 517lb of bombs

Aviatik B1/B11

Crew 2

Wingspan 40 feet

Height 10 feet 10 inches

Mercedes D11 Engine 99hp

Maximum speed 60 mph

Ceiling 16404 feet

1 machine gun

Fokker E1

1 crew

29 feet wingspan

9 feet 5 inches height

.7 Cylinder air cooled rotary engine 80 hp

Maximum speed 81 mph

Ceiling 9840 feet

1 machine gun (later variants had a machine gun firing through the propeller

Arco DH2

1 crew

28 feet wingspan

9 feet 6 inches height

Gnome Monosoupape 10 hp Rotary engine

Maximum speed 93 mph

Ceiling 14,000 feet

I machine gun either fixed or moveable

Book List

I used the following books to verify information:

World War 1- Peter Simkins

The Times Atlas of World History

The British Army in World War 1 (1)- Mike Chappell

The British Army in World War 1 (2)- Mike Chappell

The British Army 1914-18- Fosten and Marrion

British Air Forces 1914-1918- Cormack

British and Empire Aces of World War 1- Shores

A History of Aerial Warfare- John Taylor

Thanks to the following website for the slang definitions

- *www.ict.griffith.edu.au/~davidt/z_ww1_**slang**/index_bak.htm*

Griff Hosker July 2014

Other books

by

Griff Hosker

If you enjoyed reading this book, then why not read another one by the author?

Ancient History

The Sword of Cartimandua Series (Germania and Britannia 50A.D. – 128 A.D.)

Ulpius Felix- Roman Warrior (prequel)

Book 1 The Sword of Cartimandua

Book 2 The Horse Warriors

Book 3 Invasion Caledonia

Book 4 Roman Retreat

Book 5 Revolt of the Red Witch

Book 6 Druid's Gold

Book 7 Trajan's Hunters

Book 8 The Last Frontier

Book 9 Hero of Rome

Book 10 Roman Hawk

Book 11 Roman Treachery

Book 12 Roman Wall

The Aelfraed Series (Britain and Byzantium 1050 A.D. - 1085 A.D.

Book 1 Housecarl

Book 2 Outlaw

Book 3 Varangian

The Wolf Warrior series (Britain in the late 6th Century)

Book 1 Saxon Dawn

Book 2 Saxon Revenge

Book 3 Saxon England

Book 4 Saxon Blood

Book 5 Saxon Slayer

Book 6 Saxon Slaughter

Book 7 Saxon Bane

Book 8 Saxon Fall: Rise of the Warlord

Book 9 Saxon Throne

The Dragon Heart Series

Book 1 Viking Slave

Book 2 Viking Warrior

Book 3 Viking Jarl

Book 4 Viking Kingdom

Book 5 Viking Wolf

Book 6 Viking War

Book 7 Viking Sword

Book 8 Viking Wrath

Book 9 Viking Raid

Book 10 Viking Legend

Book 11 Viking Vengeance

Book 12 Viking Dragon

Book 13 Viking Treasure

Book 14 Viking Enemy

Book 15 Viking Witch

Bool 16 Viking Blood

Book 17 Viking Weregeld

Book 18 Viking Storm

The Norman Genesis Series

Rolf

Horseman

The Battle for a Home

Revenge of the Franks

The Land of the Northmen

Ragnvald Hrolfsson

The Anarchy Series England 1120-1180

English Knight

Knight of the Empress

Northern Knight

Baron of the North

Earl

King Henry's Champion

The King is Dead

Warlord of the North

Enemy at the Gate

Warlord's War

Kingmaker

Henry II

Crusader

The Welsh Marches

Border Knight 1190-1300

Sword for Hire

Modern History

The Napoleonic Horseman Series

Book 1 Chasseur a Cheval

Book 2 Napoleon's Guard

Book 3 British Light Dragoon

Book 4 Soldier Spy

Book 5 1808: The Road to Corunna

Waterloo

The Lucky Jack American Civil War series

Rebel Raiders

Confederate Rangers

The Road to Gettysburg

The British Ace Series

1914

1915 Fokker Scourge

1916 Angels over the Somme

1917 Eagles Fall

1918 We will remember them

From Arctic Snow to Desert Sand

Combined Operations series 1940-1945

Commando

Raider

Behind Enemy Lines

Dieppe

Toehold in Europe

Sword Beach

Breakout

The Battle for Antwerp

King Tiger

Beyond the Rhine

Other Books

Carnage at Cannes (a thriller)

Great Granny's Ghost (Aimed at 9-14-year-old young people)

Adventure at 63-Backpacking to Istanbul

For more information on all of the books then please visit the author's web site at http://www.griffhosker.com where there is a link to contact him.

29832310R00177

Made in the USA
Lexington, KY
04 February 2019